Acclaim for Plain Perfect

"Wiseman's Christian Romance Novel is just 'plain' good."

— *Fayette County Record*,
La Grange, Texas

"What makes life perfect? For many, the pursuit of a 'perfect life' can lead to disappointment. At the very heart of humans, the perfect life is one of peace and contentment. Beth Wiseman pens a tale of a woman's search for peace. The pursuit takes Lillian to an unlikely location—her mother's Amish birthplace. But the lifestyle of these Plain, honest people turns Lillian's heart upside-down. For a sweet journey toward faith, enjoy reading *Plain Perfect*."

— Kim Vogel Sawyer,
best-selling author of
Bygones and *My Heart
Remembers*

"*Plain Perfect* is a perfect read. Beth Wiseman's characters come to life on the pages."

— REVIEWYOURBOOK.COM

"Beth weaves a wonderful, sweet love story. Her characters are real, and the description and details put me right into the heart of Lancaster County. Once I started this book, I couldn't put it down. I highly recommend *Plain Perfect*."

— Amy Clipston,
author of
A Gift of Grace

"[*Plain Perfect* has] well-developed characters, honest emotions, strong spiritual growth, and [Beth's] writing style kept me turning pages."

— LENA NELSON DOOLEY,
award-winning author of
Wild Prairie Roses

"Beth Wiseman gives the reader a delightful glimpse into the life of [the] Amish. [Her] writing is truly inspired."

— *SCHULENBURG STICKER*,
Schulenburg, Texas

Plain Perfect

A Daughters of the Promise Novel

BETH WISEMAN

THOMAS NELSON
Since 1798

NASHVILLE   MEXICO CITY   RIO DE JANEIRO

Published in Nashville, Tennessee, by Thomas Nelson. Thomas Nelson is a registered trademark of HarperCollins Christian Publishing, Inc.

Thomas Nelson, Inc. books may be purchased in bulk for educational, business, fund-raising, or sales promotional use. For information, please e-mail SpecialMarkets@ThomasNelson.com.

Scriptures taken from the King James Version of the Bible.

Publisher's Note: This novel is a work of fiction. Names, characters, places, and incidents are either products of the author's imagination or used fictitiously. All characters are fictional, and any similarity to people living or dead is purely coincidental.

ISBN 978-0-7180-3096-4 (RPK)

Library of Congress Cataloging-in-Publication Data

Wiseman, Beth, 1962–
    Plain perfect : a Daughters of the promise novel / Beth Wiseman.
        p. cm.
    ISBN 978-1-59554-630-2 (softcover)
    I. Title.
PS3623.I83P57 2008
813'.6—dc22   2008028801

Printed in the United States of America

14 15 16 17 18 RRD 5 4 3 2 1

To Reneé Bissmeyer,
my best friend.

Glossary

ach—oh

Aemen—Amen

appeditlich—delicious

baremlich—terrible

boppli—baby or babies

daadi—grandfather

daed—dad

danki—thanks

Deitschi wege—Dutch ways

Die Botschaft—a weekly newspaper serving Old Order Amish communities everywhere

dippy eggs—eggs cooked over easy

eck—special place for bride and groom at the corner of the wedding table

Englisch or *Englischer*—a non-Amish person

fraa—wife

guder mariye—good morning

gut—good

haus—house

hochmut—pride

in lieb—in love

Kapp—prayer covering or cap

kinner—children or grandchildren

kinskind—grandchild

mamm—mom

mammi—grandmother

mei—my

naerfich—nervous

Ordnung—the written and unwritten rules of the Amish; the
   understood behavior by which the Amish are expected to
   live, passed down from generation to generation. Most
   Amish know the rules by heart.

Pennsylvania Deitsch—Pennsylvania German, the language most
   commonly used by the Amish

redd-up—clean up

riewe—red beets

roasht—traditional main dish at an Amish wedding, consisting
   of cut-up chicken and stuffing

rumschpringe—running-around period when a teenager turns
   sixteen years old

rutschich—squirming

schnitzboi—snitz pie

schnuppich—snoopy

verhuddelt—confused

wedding nothings—dessert reserved for weddings; fried pastries
   sprinkled with confectioner's sugar

wunderbaar—wonderful

ya—yes

yummasetti—a traditional Pennsylvania German casserole

1

LILLIAN PEELED BACK THE DRAPES AT THE FRONT WINDOW and squinted against the sun's glare. She'd called the taxi almost an hour ago. If her ride didn't show up soon, she would have to forego her plan and spend another night with Rickie. Biting her lip, she worried if she had enough cash to change her flight if she didn't make it to the airport on time.

She lowered the drape and paced the living room in Rickie's house, silently blasting herself for ever moving in with him in the first place. Her stomach writhed at the thought of one more day under the same roof with him. And yet her window of time for her departure was closing, she realized, glancing at her watch.

She tugged at the drapes again. Relief fell over her when she saw the yellow cab pull into the driveway. Snatching her red suitcase and purse, she bolted for the door, shuffling toward the driver as he opened the trunk.

"Please hurry," she said to the driver, handing him her suitcase.

The driver stowed her luggage without comment and was climbing into the driver's seat when she saw Rickie's black Lexus rounding the corner and heading up the street. Her heart sank.

"Where to?" the driver asked.

"Bush Intercontinental Airport," she answered. "Hurry, please."

As the driver made his way down Harper Avenue to make the long drive to the northwest side of Houston, Lillian watched out the rearview window. Rickie's car slowly neared the house.

The cab driver turned at the corner. She'd made it. A clean getaway.

Irma Rose Miller couldn't help but notice the bounce in her husband's steps. The cancer kept him down and out on most days, but not today. Today Lilly was coming, and his anticipation and joy were evident.

"*Danki*," Jonas said as Irma Rose poured him another cup of coffee.

"You're welcome."

Her tall husband, once muscular and strong as an ox, sat hunched over the wooden table between them. His healthy load of gray locks and full beard were now thinning and brittle. Dark circles under his eyes and sunken features revealed the many sleepless nights of pain he had endured over the past few months. God had given her husband of forty-eight years a challenging road to travel, and he was making the trip with dignity and grace.

"Our Lilly will be here this afternoon." Jonas smiled and raised the cup to his mouth. His hands trembled, but his eyes twinkled with a merriment Irma Rose hadn't seen since the first mention of their granddaughter coming to stay with them. She hoped he wouldn't be disappointed. They hadn't seen the girl in seventeen years, since she was ten years old.

Irma Rose stood to retrieve some doughnuts from a pan atop the wooden stove.

"It will be *wunderbaar gut* to have her here."

Irma Rose placed two doughnuts on her husband's plate. "*Ya*, that it will. But, Jonas, you must keep in mind how different our ways are. We will seem like foreigners to our *Englisch* granddaughter."

"These doughnuts are *appeditlich*," Jonas said.

"*Danki*. But, Jonas, you need to prepare yourself. Sarah Jane raised Lilly in the outside world. We don't know her. As a matter of fact, we don't know exactly how Sarah Jane raised her."

The thought twisted Irma Rose's stomach in familiar knots. It had been hard enough when her daughter chose to leave the Old Order Amish community at the age of eighteen, but even more difficult when she wrote to tell them she was in a family way soon thereafter . . . with no husband.

"She was a glorious child," Jonas said. "Remember how quickly Lilly learned to ice-skate? What a joy she was. What a *gut* Christmas holiday we all had."

Irma Rose shook her head at her husband's ignorance of the obvious. Lilly wasn't a child anymore. She was a grown woman. Jonas had talked about that last Christmas together until the next season came and went. When Sarah Jane and Lilly didn't show up the following year, he merely shrugged and said, "Maybe they will visit next year." And each Christmas thereafter Jonas anticipated a visit that never happened.

Jonas never uttered a negative word about Sarah Jane's choices. But she'd seen the sadness in his eyes when their daughter left home, and she knew the pain dwelled in his heart over the years. But he only said it was impossible to always understand God's direction for His children—their child. Their *only* child. The good Lord had only seen fit to bless them with one. A beautiful daughter who had chosen a life rife with hardship.

Irma Rose had prayed hard over the years to cleanse herself of any discontentment with her daughter. Sarah Jane's choice to leave the Amish faith was prior to her baptism and church membership. Therefore the community never shunned her daughter. She had chosen to avoid visits with her parents. From the little Irma Rose gathered over the years, Sarah Jane and Lilly had lived with friends and moved around a lot.

An occasional letter arrived from her daughter, to which Irma Rose always responded right away. More times than not, the letters were returned unopened. It was less painful to assume Sarah Jane had moved on and the postal service returned the letters. Although sometimes it cut Irma Rose to the bone when she recognized her daughter's penmanship: *Return to sender.*

She was thankful her last letter to Sarah Jane wasn't returned. She couldn't help but wonder if the news about Jonas's cancer had prompted her granddaughter's visit. When Lillian's letter arrived over a month ago, Irma Rose had followed her instructions not to return a letter but to call her on the telephone if at all possible. She wasted no time going to the nearby shanty to phone her granddaughter. The conversation was strained and the child seemed frantic to come for a visit.

"I'm a teacher and when school is out in May, I'd like to come for a visit," her granddaughter had said on the phone. "Maybe stay for the summer. Or maybe even longer?" There was a sense of urgency in the girl's tone.

Irma Rose feared her faith was not as strong as her husband's and that a tinge of resentment and hurt still loitered in her heart where Sarah Jane was concerned. She didn't want any of those feelings to spill over with her granddaughter. She would need to pray harder.

As if reading her mind, Jonas said, "Irma Rose, everything will be fine. You just wait and see."

It wasn't until the plane was high above the Houston skyline that the realization of what she'd done hit Lillian. After landing in Philadelphia, she caught a train to Lancaster City and hopped a bus to Paradise, which landed her only a few miles from her grandparents' farm. She was glad there was a bit of a walk to their property; she wanted to wind down and freshen up before she reacquainted herself with her relatives. Plus, she'd had enough time on the plane to wonder if this whole thing was a huge mistake. Her mom hadn't wanted to be here, so why think it would be any better for her?

Not that she had much choice at this point. She had no money, no home, no job, and she was more than a little irritated with her mother. When her mom had begged Lillian to loan her money, Lillian reluctantly agreed, with the stipulation she got her money back as soon as possible. But her mom had never repaid a loan before. Lillian didn't know why she thought it would be any different this time, and she was determined to move away from her "boyfriend" Rickie. So Lillian quit her job and made a decision to distance herself from her mother and Rickie by coming to a place where she knew neither of them would follow: Lancaster County.

Lillian shook her head, wondering if she was making a bigger mistake by coming here. She didn't know if she'd ever understand what ultimately drove her mother from the Plain lifestyle. From what she read, it rarely happened—Amish children fleeing from all they'd ever known. The circumstances must have been severe to drive her mother away.

Although . . . it didn't look so bad from Lillian's point of view, now that she was here. Aside from having a dreadful wardrobe, she thought the Amish men and women strolling by looked quite content. They seemed oblivious to the touristy stares. The women wore simple, dark-colored dresses with little white coverings on their heads. The men were in cotton shirts, dark pants with suspenders, and straw hats with a wide brim. Box-shaped, horse-drawn buggies were abundant.

Ironically, it all seemed quite normal.

She took a seat on a bench outside the Quik Mart at the corner of Lincoln Highway and Black Horse Road and watched the passersby. Clearly, Paradise was a tourist town, like most of Lancaster County, with everyone wanting to have a look at the Amish people. Watching them now, she wondered if the Amish were all as peaceful as they appeared. Despite her initial thoughts, she decided they couldn't be. Everyone had stress. Everyone had problems. Surely the Plain People of Lancaster County were not an exception.

But they could have fooled Lillian.

Samuel Stoltzfus gave hasty good-byes to Levina Esh and Sadie Fisher and flicked his horse into action, hiding a smile as his buggy inched forward. The competitiveness of those two widow women! First Levina had presented him with her prize-winning shoofly pie. Not to be outdone, Sadie quickly offered up her own prize-winning version. Stalemate. The two of them had stood there glaring at each other while he tried to think of ways to escape unhurt . . . and unattached.

He might have to rethink his shopping day. Both women knew he went to the farmer's market on Thursdays . . .

Once he cleared town, he picked up the pace. The road to his farm near the town of Paradise was less traveled, and he was particularly glad of that on this day. It was a glorious sunny afternoon, perfect for a buggy ride through the countryside. Pleased he had chosen his spring buggy instead of his covered one, he relished the warmth of the late afternoon sun. Rachel had loved this time of year, when spring gave way to summertime and all the world felt full of promise.

God's soil was tilled, and he had planted corn, alfalfa, and grain. Life would be busy as he awaited the bountiful rewards of spring's labor. There was the garden, with peas to pick. The strawberries would be ready. Lots of canning and freezing. Much time went into preparing a garden for harvest.

And Rachel's garden had always been lush and plentiful. Gardening was work for the womenfolk, but Samuel had done the best he could the past two years. He was thankful his sisters took care of most of the canning and freezing.

He closed his eyes, his shoulders lifting with his sigh. He missed Rachel the most this time of year.

Lillian felt like a fool. Didn't "down yonder a spell" mean right down the road? The friendly Amish boy had pointed down Black

Horse Road and uttered those exact words when she'd asked for directions to her grandparents' farm. She'd thought the walk would do her good—help her shed some of the calories she ingested while sitting at the Quik Mart with a large cinnamon roll and cola.

Evidently, she'd mistranslated "down yonder a spell." There wasn't a farmhouse in sight.

She really should have considered the strappy sandals she was wearing before opting to venture down the road to nowhere. Her capri blue jeans and short-sleeved, pink-cotton shirt were good choices, however. The clement sun mixing with a soft breeze made for a perfect day. An excellent day for a walk . . . if only she'd worn better shoes.

Setting her red suitcase on the grassy shoulder of the paved road, she plopped down on top of it and scanned the farmland surrounding her. It was so quiet. Peaceful. She could only hope that some of the peacefulness the Amish were known for would rub off on her during her stay. She needed it. Life had not been easy on her the past few years.

Her mom's idea of parenting had left much to be desired— jumping from one man to the next, looking for something she never seemed to find. All the while she'd toted Lillian along. Lillian had grown up changing schools, saying good-bye to friends, and continually hoping Mom's next boyfriend would be better than the last. At the first chance, Lillian had bailed on the situation, telling herself she could do better.

Despite her good intentions, she'd ended up close to follow- ing in her mother's footsteps. After putting herself through college while living with three other girls in a small apartment, she'd landed a teaching job. There were boyfriends, and she'd definitely made her own share of mistakes.

But always, something had whispered to her that there was another way to live. Sometimes she'd listened, sometimes not. But she never felt comfortable enough to ask herself just where that voice was coming from—she just didn't know enough to form an opinion. She didn't listen to the voice when it cautioned her not to move in with Rickie. But when the voice became too strong to ignore, she knew it was time to get out of that situation.

Despite the complete lack of religious upbringing, she always suspected there might be a God looking down on her. But in light of her mom's thoughts on church, she couldn't ask her about it. Her mother seemed angry at religion. While she heartily encouraged Lillian to attend various churches with her friends when she was a child, she herself would have no part of it. It was a huge contradiction in parenting, and Lillian didn't understand it to this day.

Now, knowing the Amish to be solid in their faith, Lillian decided it might be best to keep her suspicions about God to herself around her grandparents.

"Guess I better get moving and find out how far 'down yonder a spell' really is." She jumped off the suitcase, gave it a heave-ho, and started back down the paved road, gazing to either side where the acreage stretched as far as she could see. The sun pressing down on the horizon left her a tad worried about how much farther the farm was.

"Whoa, boy!" Samuel yelled to his horse. The animal slowed his pace to a gentle trot, bringing the buggy alongside an *Englisch* woman cumbersomely toting a bright-red suitcase. She was minus a shoe . . . if you called a flat-bottom sole with two small straps a shoe. Certainly not a good walking instrument.

"Can I offer you a ride?" He pulled back on the reins and came to a complete halt, as did the small-framed woman. When she turned, he was met by radiant green eyes in a delicate face. Delicate, that is, until she grimaced and blew a tendril of hair out of her face.

Then she smiled, and her face transformed, lighting up like the morning sun. He was momentarily struck dumb.

It didn't matter. The woman was focused on his horse. Deserting her suitcase on the side of the road, she stumbled over to Pete and reached out to stroke his nose without so much as a "May I?" Thankfully, Pete was a gentle giant.

"He's beautiful," she said, glancing briefly in Samuel's direction, eyes sparkling.

He cleared his throat. "*Ya.* And a fine work horse too."

What an interesting woman this was. Unafraid. And beautiful, he had to admit. He watched as her long brown hair danced in the wind, framing her face in layers. She wore no makeup and seemed lacking in the traditional *Englisch* look, although her brightly colored blouse and calf-length breeches certainly gave her away. A tourist, most likely. But a tourist walking alone down Blackhorse Road?

The woman's mouth curved upward in delight as she cooed over Pete. The horse gently snorted, nudged her, and she laughed heartily, her head thrown back. It was a thoroughly enchanting scene.

Suddenly uncomfortable at his thoughts, he straightened

and coughed. It was enough to bring the woman's attention back to him.

"I would love a ride!" With a final kiss on the old horse's muzzle, she went back for her suitcase. "Where should I put this?"

"*Ach*, my manners." Samuel jumped out of the buggy and made his way to the woman. "Let me." He took the suitcase from her, quite surprised at how heavy the small bundle was. After stowing it behind the double seat, he offered his hand to assist her into the buggy.

"Thank you." Now she was studying him . . . seemingly from head to toe. At her open glance, he felt a flush tint his cheeks.

"I'm Samuel Stoltzfus," he said, extending his hand but avoiding her questioning eyes.

"I'm Lillian Miller."

Her hands were certainly that of an *Englisch* woman, soft and void of a hard day's work. The Plain women in Lancaster County tilled gardens, shelled peas, kneaded bread, and a host of other necessary chores uncommon to *Englisch* women from the city. City women's hands were not only smooth and manicured, but pleasing to the touch.

Returning to his seat, he started up the buggy again. The woman was obviously tired and happy to be resting; with a slight groan she stretched her legs out. He found his eyes wandering her way and silently remonstrated himself.

"Where are you from, Lillian? Or, more important, where are you going?"

"I'm from Houston."

"*Ya*, Texas," he said, slightly surprised. They didn't usually get

Texans walking the roads out here. "Lots of farms in Texas. What brings you to Lancaster County, Pennsylvania?"

"I'm coming to stay with my grandparents for a while." She smiled. "They're Amish."

Amish? He was once more at a loss for words. Not to worry—the *Englisch* woman wasn't.

"Actually, I guess I'm Amish too," she added.

Discreetly glancing at her *Englisch* clothes, he wondered how that could be so.

"My grandparents are Irma Rose and Jonas Miller. I'll be staying with them for a while." She looked his way as if waiting for a response that never came. "I'd like to adapt myself to the Amish ways. I need a peaceful, calm lifestyle away from the city. Anyway, I've decided to be Amish for a while."

Samuel had been trying to connect this vivacious outsider with the staunch Irma Rose and Jonas he knew, but these words jostled him out of his musings. "You'd like to be Amish for a *while?*"

"Yes. Although I don't plan to wear one of those dark-colored dresses or white caps like the women I saw strolling by earlier."

In spite of himself, Samuel chuckled. "Do you even know what being Amish means?" He didn't mean the remark as harshly as it sounded.

Lillian slanted her eyes in his direction, as if slightly offended.

Unexpectedly, the buggy wheel hit a rut. With an *oomph*, his new friend bounced in her seat. She was a tiny little thing. Luckily, she didn't catapult right off the seat and onto the pavement.

"Yikes!" she said when her behind returned to the seat. And then she giggled. As Pete's ears swiveled back to catch the commotion, Samuel couldn't help but grin. The woman's enthusiasm was contagious.

He decided to drop the subject. He knew Irma Rose and Jonas well enough to figure they'd set her right about being Amish and what it really meant. Samuel reckoned they'd have their hands full with their granddaughter.

As Samuel righted the buggy, he asked, "When is the last time you saw your grandparents?" He hadn't even known Irma Rose and Jonas had a granddaughter.

"When I was ten. Seventeen years ago. It was the first time I saw snow. *Real* snow." Her eyes twinkled from the memory. "Anyway, I know things will be different from what I'm used to. But I can live without television. There's too much bad news on TV anyway. And I know Amish women cook a lot. I'm a great cook." She shrugged. "I'm a hard worker in general. I know Amish get up early and go to bed early. I know they work hard during the day. And if that's what it takes to feel peaceful and calm . . . I'm in!"

Samuel found her enthusiasm charming, no matter how misdirected it was. "Lillian, I'm sure Irma Rose and Jonas will appreciate you helping with household duties, but it will take more than chores and giving up worldly things to provide you with the peacefulness you're lookin' for."

"Well, it's a start," she said, sounding optimistic.

As for that . . . who was he to argue?

Lillian remembered the Christmas visit with her grandparents at their farm, especially the snow. Unlike the icy mix of sludge found rarely in her hometown state, snow in Lancaster County glistened with a tranquil purity. Almost two decades later, she could still recall the towering cedar trees blanketed in white and ice skating on the crystalline pond in her mother's old ice skates.

There were few presents. She remembered that. And while she recollected her grandparents as warm and loving, she also remembered the tension between them and her mother. Her grandfather had kept the mood festive, suggested the ice-skating, and seemed to make it his mission for Lillian to have a good time—even carting her to town and back in his gray, horse-drawn buggy. It had been the highlight of her trip.

"I remember liking the way my grandparents talked," she recalled to Samuel. "I didn't understand a lot of things they said. Things like 'Outen the lights until sunrise when we'll *redd-up* the house.' And 'It wonders me if it will make wet tomorrow.' Mom translated those to mean *'Turn out the lights until in the morning when we'll clean up the house'* and *'I wonder if it will rain tomorrow.'*"

"That would be right," Samuel said.

Grandma and Grandpa both spoke another language she'd later found out was *Pennsylvania Deitsch*. Lots of times they would comingle their language with English. "Danki, *Sarah Jane, for bringing our little* kinskind *for a visit*," her grandfather told her mother that Christmas. To which Sarah Jane Miller forced a smile and nodded.

"*Grandma, why are you and Grandpa wearing those costumes?*" Lillian recalled asking her grandparents.

Grandpa had just laughed and said, "*It is our faith, my* kinskind.

We wear these plain clothes to encourage humility and separation from the world."

At ten, Lillian had little understanding of what that signified. Except somewhere in the translation she knew it meant they couldn't have a television or a phone. Several times after their one and only trip, Lillian had asked her mother if she could call her grandparents. Mom reminded her that Grandpa and Grandma did not allow phones at their house.

"Evidently, my grandparents came to Houston a couple of times before our visit at Christmas, but I don't remember," she told Samuel. "That Christmas was my last trip to Lancaster County and the last time I saw my grandparents. Until now."

"I reckon Irma Rose and Jonas are really looking forward to seeing you."

"I hope so."

Lillian tried to keep her gaze focused on the road in front of her. But her eyes kept involuntarily trailing to her left. Samuel Stoltzfus was as handsome a man as she had ever seen in the city. His plain clothes did little to mask his solid build and appealing smile each time she glanced in his direction. But it was his piercing blue eyes Lillian couldn't seem to draw away from.

"So, how long have you been married?" *Nosy, nosy.* The astonished look on his face confirmed her worry. She was crossing the line. "I'm sorry. I just noticed that you have the customary beard following marriage." She'd done her research before arriving here. "And . . . I was just . . . curious." *And curious why? He's Amish, for heaven's sake.*

"I'm not married. I'm widowed."

"Oh," she said softly, thinking how young his wife must have been when she died. " I'm so sorry. When did your wife die?"

"*Mei fraa*, Rachel, passed almost two years ago," he answered without looking her way.

"Again, I'm so sorry."

Samuel continued to stare at the road ahead. "It was God's will."

There was no sadness or regret in his tone. Just fact. Lillian knew she should leave it alone, but . . . "I'm sure you miss her very much."

He didn't glance her way. "There's Irma Rose and Jonas's farm," he said, pointing to their right. "I better take you right up to the house." He coaxed Pete down a long dirt drive leading from the road to the white farmhouse.

"Oh, you don't have to do that. I can walk." She wondered if Samuel Stoltzfus was ready to be rid of her.

His eyebrows edged upward beneath his dark bangs and he glanced at her shoeless foot.

Point taken. "A ride to the house would be great."

As Pete trotted down the dirt driveway toward the farmhouse, reality sank in. This would be her new home for the summer—or however long it took to accomplish her goal. At first glance, everything seemed lovely. Neatly mowed, prodigious fields were on either side of the lane, and the white fencing in good repair. But unlike the farms she passed on the way, there were no signs of new life planted. It wasn't until they drew closer to the farmhouse that she spotted a small garden off to her left enclosed by a wire-mesh fence. Parallel rows of greenery indicated vegetables would be forthcoming.

There was a large barn off to her left, the paint weathered and chipping. Another smaller barn to her right also was in need of a fresh paint job. She recalled the barns they had passed on her journey down Black Horse Road. Most were a bright crimson color.

The white farmhouse appeared freshly painted, but with flowerbeds absent of flowers or shrubs. They must have been beautiful at one time. But now they—and the rest of the yard—lent an air of neglect to the farm.

A wraparound porch with two rockers looked inviting. But while the idea of curling up with a good book in one of the rockers was appealing, Lillian knew it was the inside of the house and its inhabitants she feared most. Her grandma had seemed pleasant enough on the phone, but what if she and her grandfather were too set in their ways to make room for her? And what if she couldn't adjust to their ways? No electricity meant no hair dryer, curling iron, or other modern conveniences she considered necessities. How would she charge her cell phone? And she couldn't imagine a summer without air conditioning.

Grimacing as the thoughts rattled around her head, she reminded herself why she'd come. She'd had a month to consider all of these factors. She thought she had. But as her fantasy of leaving everything behind for *this* became absolute, her tummy twirled with uncertainty.

She was still attempting to envision her new way of life when Samuel brought Pete up next to a gray buggy parked on one side of the house. Samuel moved quickly to get her suitcase from behind the seat and extended his hand to help her out of the buggy. Towering over her, he promptly released her fingers.

"Thank you for the ride. Maybe I will see you again." She

could only hope. But his lack of response as he quickly jumped back in the carriage left her wondering.

Lillian waved good-bye and watched until horse, buggy, and man were back on the paved road. She knew she was stalling. Her grandparents would be strangers to her, and she would be a stranger to them. Yet they had encouraged her to come and stay with them. *"For as long as you like,"* her grandmother had said.

Striving to cast her worries aside, she turned around, picked up her suitcase, and headed up the walk toward what would be her new home . . . for a while.

2

"THE BOPPLI IS HERE!" JONAS EXCLAIMED. HE CLOSED THE window blinds and staggered to the door to welcome their granddaughter.

"She's hardly a *baby*, Jonas. She's a grown woman." Despite her confident tone, Irma Rose fiddled with her apron strings as she followed her husband.

"Irma Rose, there's no need to look so *naerfich*. I reckon things will be just fine. The Good Lord will see to it." Jonas winked at her as he reached for the doorknob.

"I can't help but be nervous, Jonas. We don't know this girl," she whispered.

Jonas flung the door open and walked onto the front porch. Irma Rose followed her husband and noticed immediately that the young woman before them looked nervous as well. But, as was his way, Jonas plowed through the tension by making a joke.

"Irma Rose, this poor girl must have walked here all the way from Houston, Texas," he teased, his eyes narrowing in on his granddaughter's shoeless foot. "First thing to do is get her some proper walking shoes."

Irma Rose shook her head at Jonas as she scooted past him and toward the stranger in her front yard. Jonas didn't move. Hunched over, he kept his hands on his hips and continued studying the girl's feet with a wide smile.

"Welcome, Lilly," Irma Rose said. She embraced her grand-daughter for the first time in seventeen years.

"Lillian," the young woman said as she awkwardly returned the hug. "I go by *Lillian* now."

"Oh, I'm sorry. We called you Lilly when you were young and assumed . . ."

"It's okay. I just grew out of 'Lilly.'"

"Well, Lillian—" Irma Rose began. Jonas interrupted her.

"I like *Lilly*. I am going to call you Lilly," he said firmly, with a boyish grin still plastered from ear to ear.

"Now, Jonas, if she prefers to be called *Lillian* . . ."

"No. I like *Lilly* better," her husband insisted. "Now, Lilly, let's get you into the house. We've got warm brownies and lemonade ready for you."

"Jonas!" Irma Rose tried to intercede. She often wondered if her husband's various medications had caused his already strong personality to escalate over the past few months. Sometimes he seemed to swing whatever way the wind was blowing and other days . . . Well, it was either his way or nobody's way. Today was clearly the latter.

"Brownies and lemonade sound great," Lillian said. She shot Irma Rose a soft look, assuring her Jonas's persistent ways didn't offend her.

Irma Rose watched Jonas struggle to tote the bright-red suit-case up the porch steps. She knew better than to assist him. His determined look left no question that he wanted to appear as much a man as he had ever been to his granddaughter. Irma Rose knew he'd pay for it later.

"Whatcha got in this thing . . . bricks?" he asked as he maneuvered through the front door ahead of the women.

Irma Rose studied the suitcase with curiosity.

"Mostly books," Lillian said, grabbing the suitcase from Jonas. "I like to read. I was an English teacher for several years . . . until recently."

Irma Rose considered asking Lillian what *"until recently"* meant, but stopped short, sensing regret in her granddaughter's tone. Perhaps Lillian had been fired from her job and had nowhere else to go. Or some other such embarrassing situation.

Lillian took in her surroundings and was pleasantly surprised. Not remembering much from her last visit, she'd built up an image in her mind. But the room was not as sparse as she'd envisioned. Dark-green blinds that were drawn halfway up covered the windows, and the whitewash walls were bare. But lovely furniture was placed throughout the room, including two high-back rockers with blue cushions, an oak sideboard and matching hutch, and a shelf that held four lanterns. Intertwined between the lanterns was a leafy ivy plant that was draped across the length of the shelf. There was even a worn brown recliner in the corner. No television, of course. The aroma of freshly baked goods lent even more warmth to the room.

Following her grandparents into the kitchen, she noticed the same dark-green blinds covering the windows. Unlike the den, there was definitely a focal point in this room: the wood-burning stove nestled against the far wall, the keeper of the fabulous smells permeating throughout the house. This room was more of a step back in time.

"Welcome to our home, Lilly," her grandfather said, beaming. She couldn't help but smile at his gleeful energy. Her grandmother was another story. Irma Rose seemed guarded and hesitant. Even her hug felt strained. Lillian knew she herself was partly to blame for the tension.

"Thank you for having me." She glanced at the pan of brownies atop the stove. Normally, she would shy away from such caloric luxuries, especially since she'd already blown it for the day with the big cinnamon roll she wolfed down earlier. But her grandmother offered her the biggest brownie in the pan. She accepted, deciding the walk had evened out the caloric playing field again.

"Lillian, Jonas and I already ate supper. We eat at four-thirty. But I saved you some chicken and mashed potatoes."

As her grandmother headed toward the refrigerator, Lillian shook her head while trying to quickly swallow the above-average bite of brownie. "No, no," she said, gulping the last of the warm dessert down. "This brownie is fine for me."

"I should have offered you some supper, I suppose, before brownies," her grandmother said, sounding regretful. She returned to one of the long wooden benches facing Lillian.

"Propane gas, Lilly," her grandfather belted out, seeing her eyes go to the gas bottle next to the refrigerator. "We use propane. No electricity. No connection of wires to the outside world."

"Oh." Lillian glanced upward at the gas lantern hanging above the table.

"We have an indoor bathroom," her grandmother added. "In case you were wondering."

"Yes, I remember that." The old outhouse was still outside, but she remembered indoor plumbing from her last visit.

"How did you get here, after your plane flight and train ride?"

Lillian recalled her journey with fondness. "I took a bus to Paradise and then Samuel Stoltzfus brought me in his buggy."

It was hard to miss the look of bewilderment on both their faces.

"Really?" her grandmother asked, her eyes lighting up with interest.

Lillian shrugged. "I guess he took pity on me when he saw me walking down the road with only one shoe on. I must have looked a mess. But the Amish boy in town said this farm was 'down yonder a spell.' Uh, it was considerably farther than I thought."

"Samuel Stoltzfus is a *gut* man," her grandma said. "He was a fine husband. His son works here in the afternoon on most days. Now that school is out, he's able to put in a few more hours. He chops wood, mows . . . the things Jonas and I can't get to anymore."

"That's a shame about his wife." Lillian took a sip of her lemonade.

"You talked about Rachel?" Grandma seemed surprised.

"Not much."

"It was God's will," her grandfather said softly.

"I guess." Lillian said and got questioning looks from both her grandparents. It didn't seem like God's will to take a man's wife at such a young age. "She must have been young. How'd she die?"

"The cancer got her, just like it's gonna get me," Grandpa said matter-of-factly and seemingly with no bitterness.

"Maybe not," Lillian said, not looking at him. She knew her grandfather had bone cancer and that it was a painful way to go. Grandma had mentioned the cancer in her last letter to Mom. The thought of anyone going through that kind of agony bothered her immensely.

"God has blessed me with a *gut* woman in Irma Rose. It's God's will that she will have to bury me first."

"Now, Jonas, you don't know that."

"She's right, Grandpa. They come out with new treatments all the time for cancer patients." Surely her grandpa would be open to every available option.

It felt strange to call her grandfather "Grandpa," but what else should she call him? That's what she'd called him when she was ten. The look on his face told her that he picked up on it and was pleased.

It seemed even stranger to call her grandmother "Grandma." Lillian felt sure Grandma had some strong reservations about her being here. And that was fair. Lillian had her own strong reservations about being here. Her worldly ways were as foreign to them as the lantern dangling above the table was to her.

It was a tiny bedroom, and Lillian slept like a rock. She probably would have kept sleeping if her cell phone hadn't started ringing. She peeled back the quilt on her bed and reached for the phone atop the nightstand.

"Hello."

"Are you okay? I didn't hear from you." The connection was a bit crackly, but adequate.

"Hi, Mom. I didn't know I was supposed to check in."

"How is your grandpa?" Mom went on, ignoring Lillian's irritated tone.

"He seems okay. He looks a lot older than Grandma, who by the way seems okay too."

"Well, I still can't imagine why you would want to go and live there, Lillian. You will never make it in their world. I'm staying with Paul, and he said you're welcome to come stay here."

"Mom! Why would you do that? Paul treated you like dirt when you were dating him before!" Lillian sat up and pushed back tangled strands of hair. "Why do you keep choosing the wrong men?" Wondering if this wasn't the pot calling the kettle black, she was determined to learn from her mistake with Rickie.

"Lillian, things are different now."

"They're always *different*, Mom."

"Just come home."

"I don't have a home, Mom."

"I will get you back all the money I borrowed, Lillian. I promise. Then you can start fresh somewhere. Although I think it was a mistake leaving Rickie. He took such good care of you."

Lillian threw herself across the bed in disgust. *If you only knew.* "Why don't you just come here, Mom? Spend some time with your parents and find some peace." She knew it was a safe request. Her mother would never come, nor did she want her to.

"Is that what you're doing, Lillian? Looking for *peace*?"

Lillian bristled. "I don't know what I'm looking for, Mom. I just needed to get away, and I'm broke."

"Well, I hope you find what you're looking for."

"I wish you meant that."

"You're my daughter. Of course I mean that. But just remember that you have options. You can always come and stay with Paul and me and—"

"Good-bye, Mother. I'll talk to you later." Hanging up on her was better than enduring a full-blown fight. It was too early in the morning. She pulled the quilt over her head and buried her face in the pillow.

"Shame on you, Irma Rose," Jonas whispered with a chuckle as he passed her in the hallway outside Lillian's room. "That looks like eavesdropping to me."

"I was just wondering if the child was still alive. It's nearly seven o'clock. She missed breakfast hours ago. And she's either talkin' to herself or she's on a portable telephone." She continued to press her ear against the door.

"I'm going to hope it's a mobile telephone," Jonas said jokingly, then paused. "Give her some time, Irma Rose. I think our Lilly has had a hard life. God sent her to us for a reason. You can't expect her to give up all her worldly possessions overnight."

"*Ya*, I know. I really do, Jonas. But she said in her letter that she wanted to find peace in her life. If she meant that, I'd think she might try to live our ways while she's here. You're probably right, though. It's going to take her some time."

As Jonah kissed her on the cheek and headed down the hallway toward the bathroom, Irma Rose stood there trying to shift doubt to hope. Just because Sarah Jane wasn't happy here didn't mean Lillian couldn't be.

"Is that Samuel's son outside?" Lillian asked her grandma as she sat at the kitchen table eating a bowl of oatmeal. The blinds were open, and she could see the boy chopping wood off to the side of the barn. She wished her grandfather would join them. Felt like less tension when he was around.

"*Ya.* He's been a huge help ever since Jonas got down." Her grandma walked to the window and watched the boy. "He's a fine lad."

"His father seems like a nice man too."

"*Ya.* He's been a good father to the boy since his *mamm* died."

Lillian saw her grandma taking note of her attire. Blue jeans and a white T-shirt. She'd purposely not packed any of her flashier clothes and had thought her attire plain enough, but Grandma seemed to have her nose turned up a tad.

"I hung some dresses on the peg in your room. I thought they might be more appropriate for our community."

Lillian had seen the dresses the night before. She couldn't help but cringe at the thought of having to wear them and wondered if Grandma intended her to do so. Evidently. Plain dark-colored dresses that would hit her about mid-calf. *Ugh.* She was more comfortable in her own traditional attire. Plus, blue jeans seemed much more practical for farm life. Although maybe Grandma would be embarrassed to introduce her to the community dressed in blue jeans? Might bring forth questions Grandma didn't want to field. She'd think about it, but for now she decided it best to change the subject.

"I'm sorry I slept so late this morning. I know you get up early and we have lots of chores to do. I don't want you to think I'll do this every morning—sleep late. I was just really tired from the trip. But I'm a pretty good cook if you'd like for me to cook supper tonight."

Grandma straightened the black apron atop her dark-brown dress and turned to face Lillian. Her sheer exhaustion was apparent, along with doubt Lillian could do the job. "Well, I wouldn't know how to act if I was given a break in the kitchen." She paused and considered the idea. Then shook her head. "It's a mite challenging to cook on a wood-burning stove. And Jonas likes to have things a certain way. I don't know . . ."

"I'll be glad to give it a shot, Grandma. Cooking is the one thing Mom did really well, and I learned early on how to prepare a meal. You said you and Grandpa eat at four thirty. I can have it ready."

"Your *mamm* is a *gut* cook?"

Lillian sensed her need for a *yes*. "She is. She said she learned from you."

Grandma's face flooded with emotion. "And she taught you to cook . . . like *we* do?"

"I suppose I didn't know it at the time, but yes. I made my first shoofly pie when I was nine. And I know how to make apple butter." Lillian was about to tell her grandma those types of delicacies were few and far between, but when she saw the elated look on her grandmother's face, she held her tongue.

"There are a few meats in the freezer above the refrigerator. We keep the bulk of our meats in a freezer at Kauffman's Market in town. And there's plenty of canned goods in the basement. You'll see them long 'bout the far side on some shelves. If you need anything extra, I—"

"I'm sure I can find everything. I just might need you to show me a little bit about cooking on this woodstove." Lillian studied the ancient piece of equipment. "Take a break, Grandma. Let me help you some while I'm here."

Lillian washed her cereal bowl, thinking how worn out her grandma looked. Twice she'd heard her up during the night with her grandpa. It sounded like he was vomiting. She'd thought about going to see if she could help, but her grandpa seemed like such a proud man, and she didn't want to embarrass him.

"I think I'll go introduce myself to David," Lillian said as she dried her hands on the dish towel. She headed toward the door, then impulsively turned around. "Grandma, is Grandpa okay this morning?"

"Your *daadi* had a bad night. He ate a little breakfast and went back to bed."

"What about chemotherapy? Would that help him?"

"He's chosen not to have any such thing."

"If it's an option, did he consider it?"

"He's on medications for the pain. Jonas says it's God's will and that he will ride it out at home, as best he can."

"Oh," Lillian said. She wanted to argue that God—if there was a God—would want him to fight. But it seemed she and her grandmother might be moving in a positive direction amid very different worlds. Offering to prepare supper earned her some points. She hated to rock the boat, especially about God.

"You start work early," Lillian said when she walked up behind the boy busily chopping wood. The sun was still working its way upward, and dewy droplets speckled Lillian's tennis shoes as she walked across the freshly cut yard. "I'm Lillian."

David removed the oversized glove on his right hand and extended it. "Nice to meet you. I'm David."

As he removed his straw hat with his other hand in a polite gesture, David's traditional bangs fell forward and his bobbed haircut came into view, a lighter shade of brown than his father's. He had inherited Samuel's handsome square jaw and natural good looks.

"I'm Jonas and Irma Rose's granddaughter." Lillian moved toward the boy and shook his hand.

"*Ya*, I know," he said, smiling. He put his glove back on and motioned for her to step aside as he drew the axe back and swung at the log centered before him.

"Oh, they told you about me?"

"No, my *daed* did." He placed another log on the pile and prepared for another split.

Lillian waited for him to swing the axe before she spoke. "Really? So, your dad mentioned me?"

"*Ya.*"

David looked about eleven or twelve years old. Old enough to interpret any interest she might have in his father. She'd have to be careful. "Did he tell you I came here all the way from Texas?"

His expression shifted to contemplative, and his tone took on a hint of mischief. "He said you were real pretty, like my *mamm*." Grinning, he heaved another log on the pile.

The compliment made her stomach flip. "I'm sorry about your mother," she said softly.

"It was God's will."

She grimaced, thankful the boy's back was to her. How could they all accept tragedy as simply being *anyone's* will? His mother must have been in her twenties when she died of cancer. How horrible to be taken from your husband and child at such a young age, whatever the motivation of a suspected Higher Being.

Knowing it was best to leave it alone, she said, "Well, I just wanted to come and introduce myself. I'm sure I'll be seeing you around."

David nodded and tipped his hat in her direction.

Samuel finished plowing for the day and headed to the house to clean up before picking up David. He wondered if his son had met Irma Rose and Jonas's granddaughter. He wondered how her first day had gone without the modern conveniences she was used to.

As he bathed, thoughts of the *Englisch* woman filled his mind. Reaching for the bar of soap, he pondered what would bring an outsider into their world. To be *Amish for a while*, she'd said. Interesting. Maybe trouble had found her. The *Englisch* Samuel knew always seemed to seek out Amish ways when they were in trouble. Although her spirited laugh led him to believe the woman didn't have nearly a care in the world.

It had been a long time since he'd laughed.

Samuel knew it was always best to keep a comfortable distance from the *Englischers*. And practicing separation from the rest of the world came easy to him . . . most of the time.

Lillian was glad she'd offered to prepare supper that evening, but she was exhausted from the daily chores that Grandma evidently struggled with every day. Normally a night owl, Lillian felt sure she'd hit the bed by sunset. Otherwise, she'd never make it up by four-thirty to start all over again. Her face twisted in disbelief that she hadn't thought out more carefully her choice to come here. And this was only day one.

But given the day's events, preparing supper was the right thing to do. She had watched her grandma take numerous trips up and down the stairs to take care of her grandfather, patiently instructing Lillian as to the daily chores in between. The dark circles under her grandmother's eyes were testimonial to her exhaustion, but she never complained.

Grandma obviously enjoyed the hard work, taking pride as she instructed Lillian on how to use the treadle machine for sewing, how to fire up the gas-powered washing machine, the proper procedure for hanging clothes on the line, and which strawberries were ripe for picking in the garden. Grandma had also managed to knock out three loaves of homemade bread and bake a rhubarb pie while Lillian watched.

She'd said she didn't want to overwhelm Lillian with too much work on her first day. Surely she was kidding.

"I'm on a light load," her grandma had said earlier that afternoon. "I thank the Good Lord for sending us David to help with the outside chores. And we gave up our milk cows when Jonas got too sick for us to milk twice a day. And goes without sayin' that we don't harvest the fields anymore. We have a small garden and plenty of meat in the freezer. And the *gut* people in our district never let us go without."

Lillian was worrying what the next day would bring when Grandma offered up the information. "Tomorrow, we'll add some canning to the other chores, and we'll see 'bout picking some peas," she'd said merrily. "We'll start out slowly."

Forcing an enthusiastic smile to match her grandma's eagerness, Lillian wondered if she'd even make it to sunset this evening.

After locating a rump roast in the freezer, along with some potatoes and carrots, Lillian was now topping off the meal by preparing a salad, along with laying out some applesauce and jellies, which Grandma said was a necessary part of every meal. In between one of her many trips upstairs, Grandma had laid out one of the loaves of homemade bread on the table.

As the roast and vegetables simmered atop the wooden stove, Lillian wondered if coming here had been a bad idea—for several reasons. Evidently her grandfather was sicker than she suspected. Sickness made her uncomfortable. Cancer made her even more uncomfortable. People with cancer died. And death . . . well, death was something she hadn't come to terms with.

"Lillian, it sure does smell *gut* in here." Grandma had returned from another trip upstairs. Her hair was in the traditional bun beneath her white prayer *Kapp*, and several strands of gray had fallen forward.

"I hope you like it." She took a break from chopping the tomatoes for the salad and checked on the roast. "Grandpa's having a bad day, isn't he?"

Her grandma took a seat on the wooden bench and rested her

head in her hands. As if sensing Lillian's fears, she said, "*Ya,* he is. But they're not all bad days. Some days he does real *gut.* Then he gets down for a spell. Maybe tomorrow he'll be better."

Lillian didn't say anything. She was at a loss for words.

"Ah, there is Samuel to pick up the boy." Grandma nodded toward the window. The blind was open, and Lillian looked past the blooming begonias along the windowsill above the sink. She heard the clippity-clop of hooves and then Samuel directing Pete with a "Whoa, boy."

Foregoing her preparation of the salad, Lillian bolted toward the screen door, then turned back to face her grandma. "I thought maybe I'd invite Samuel and David for supper. Is that okay?"

Grandma's face scrolled into a questionable expression and Lillian feared she might be going to nix the idea, so she added, "Or, maybe, since Grandpa isn't feeling well today, it might not be a good day for . . ."

"I think that's a nice idea," her grandma interrupted. "I'll finish the salad. You go talk to Samuel and the boy."

"Great!" She flew out the door to catch Samuel before he carted David away.

———

Irma Rose dragged her tired body off the bench and started slicing the tomatoes. She peered out the window as Lillian jetted off toward Samuel and David. The glow in the girl's eyes had been unmistakable at the mention of Samuel's name. Now, her brow furrowing, Irma Rose watched her granddaughter near Samuel. Widowers Samuel's age were rare in their Old Order district. Choosing not to remarry by now was even rarer. It had been almost two years since Rachel's passing. Samuel should have already found a good Amish woman and remarried. That's the way it was done—to move on as quickly as possible. She'd hate to see a good man like Samuel get distracted.

Tending to a farm and raising a child was more than a full-time job. Samuel needed a good woman. An *Amish* woman. But as she watched her *Englisch* granddaughter through the window, laughing with Samuel and David, pangs of worry gnawed at her insides.

Samuel looked distracted indeed.

3

Samuel heard the screen door of the farmhouse slam and looked up to see Lillian darting across the yard toward them. He helped David stack the last of the chopped firewood, but his eyes remained on the *Englisch* woman.

"She's real pretty, Pop. Just like you said."

Samuel glanced over at his son, who was also watching the approaching woman. "And *she's* very different from us, David."

"And *we're* different from her," David said shrugging. "So?"

Samuel didn't say anything but waved at Lillian as she drew nearer.

"Hello!" she called out, catching her breath as she came to a stop before them. "I thought you both might like to stay for supper. I cooked a roast."

The woman was clearly proud of her work in the kitchen, and her bubbly spirit made the offer tempting. He and the boy hadn't eaten roast in a long time.

"Roast sounds real *gut*," he said. He put a hand on David's shoulder. "Are Jonas and Irma Rose up for it?"

"Grandma said you are both welcome."

"What do you think, David?" Samuel asked.

"Are you kidding me? That'd be a real treat. *Danki,* Ms. Lillian!"

"Go get cleaned up, David." Samuel motioned David toward the watering pump near the barn.

"How old is David?" she asked.

"He'll be twelve come August." Samuel started toward the farmhouse.

Lillian's face registered a variety of questioning expressions, and he assumed she must be curious about the Amish ways.

"I suppose he has a few years, then, before his *rumschpringe*," she said confidently, as if to impress him with her Pennsylvania Deitsch. Although . . . she was looking a bit too smug . . .

"What's a *rumschpringe*?" he asked.

Her face went blank. "Oh, I'm sorry. Maybe I pronounced it wrong or got it confused with something else. I thought it was when an Amish person turned sixteen and ventured out to explore the world, leading up to courtship."

She looked so confused, but he was having fun. He nodded thoughtfully. "Hmm, never heard of it."

As they neared the front porch, she turned toward him and planted her hands firmly on her hips. "Well, I could have sworn that's what *rumschpringe* was and—"

She caught sight of his face. "Are you messing with me, Samuel Stoltzfus?"

At her expression, he couldn't help but laugh.

"Shame on you," she fussed. But her eyes twinkled.

"I might be Plain, Lillian, but I do have a sense of humor, no?" He opened the door and motioned her inside ahead of him, grinning all the while.

Lillian placed the platter of roast surrounded by potatoes and carrots on the table. Grandma brought the salad and some chowchow. Once they were all seated—all but Grandpa—Lillian enthusiastically motioned toward the food, "Dig in!" She was anxious to see how everyone liked the meal.

All three of them stared blankly at her.

"Did I forget something?" She didn't think so.

With a significant look, her grandmother bowed her head, followed by Samuel and David. *Ouch.* Chagrined, she lowered her own head as Grandma blessed the food.

Following the prayer, Samuel seemed to sense her embarrassment and gallantly began a conversation. "David, it's been a while since we've had such a fine meal laid before us." He winked at Lillian. *Or did he?* It was quick, but she sure thought it was a wink. Her stomach flipped again. She could feel a blush building in her cheeks.

"*Ya*, Ms. Lillian, this is a fine meal," David said, stuffing a bite of potatoes in his mouth.

"Thank you, David. I wish my grandpa was well enough to join us, but he—"

They all heard a loud, gruff voice at the bottom of the stairs. "The smell of *gut* food and the promise of *gut* company ain't gonna keep me away."

"Jonas, I declare," Grandma reprimanded. "You should have let me help you down those stairs."

Giving her an incredulous look, he asked, "What for?" When he reached the kitchen, he rubbed his forehead and looked hard at Lillian and then at Samuel. "What have we here?"

Feeling the need to defend her invitation, Lillian began rambling like a crazy person. "I, uh, invited Samuel and David for supper. David has been working so hard, and I figured Samuel probably worked hard all day too. And . . . and . . . maybe a good meal would be good for both of them. And I haven't had anyone to cook for in such a long time. And, uh, Grandma looked tired. And, by gosh . . . I don't know much about sewing, working in a garden, or much of the Amish ways . . . but I can cook!"

Lillian drew in a breath and held it. She wanted to crawl in a hole. Forks halted midway to mouths. No one was moving or talking. They were all just staring at her as if she was nuts. Maybe she was.

Grandpa's tired face rolled into the biggest smile Lillian had ever seen. "I *meant* . . . what have we *here*? What's for supper?"

Samuel and David sat motionless. Lillian glanced at her grandma, pleading for assistance.

"Lillian prepared supper, Jonas. She cooked a roast with potatoes and carrots."

"Our Lilly can cook?" Grandpa took a seat at the chair on the other end of the oblong table, across from Grandma.

"She's a *gut* cook too," Samuel said.

"*Danki*," Lillian said sheepishly.

"*Gut!* You're learning the *Deitsch wege*," Grandpa said. He helped himself to a slice of roast. "I told you, Irma Rose. The girl will come around to our ways in no time."

Lillian suspected her grandma doubted any type of transformation was in the works.

A distant trill sounded. *Oh, crud!* There couldn't have been a worse time for her cell phone to start ringing. Maybe no one had noticed.

"Is that a telephone I hear?" David asked, glancing toward the stairway.

"It's probably Mom." Lillian said sheepishly as the phone continued to ring. She hoped it was Mom and not Rickie. Mom being the lesser of the two evils. "I'll get it later."

Her grandmother looked up at her and started to say something, then hesitated. Lillian assumed Grandma was about to reprimand her for having the phone in the house, but evidently that wasn't what was on Grandma's mind.

"How is . . . um . . . how is your *mamm*?" Grandma looked back at her plate and shuffled her food around a bit.

"Same as always," Lillian said, knowing it was an undignified response. "I mean, she's fine."

Grandma nodded. An awkward silence followed. Everyone ate.

It wasn't long, though, before Grandpa spoke up. "So how was your first day, Lilly?"

"Well, I slept too late. But otherwise I tried to help out the best I could."

"Lillian had a *gut* first day. Cooking supper was a mighty big help too." Grandma smiled in her direction as she took a bite of carrots. "And the meal is delicious."

"*Appeditlich* it is!" Grandpa said. "But tomorrow maybe you should go to the neighboring town of Intercourse. There is lots to see in town, and you can pick me up some of that special root beer I like."

"Sure, that'd be great."

Lillian looked up to catch Samuel gazing in her direction. Then felt another set of eyes on both of them. She shot a look in Grandpa's direction. He was grinning like a fat cat.

"Maybe Samuel can show you around? It's a far piece to town and I don't think you'd better be headin' off in the buggy so soon." He lifted his chin slightly, putting the question to Samuel.

It was hard to miss the look Grandma fired in her husband's direction. But before she could say anything, Samuel stepped up to the plate.

"I'd be happy to show Lillian around."

Irma Rose began clearing the dishes, watching Samuel and David thank Lillian for the meal and say their good-byes. She feared trouble was brewing—a concern that intensified as she watched Lillian head out the door with them toward Samuel's buggy.

While the thought of Samuel and their granddaughter developing a courtship was a farfetched notion, stranger things had happened in their district over the years. And now, thanks to her husband, a date was set for the following afternoon. She couldn't help but think of what the Good Book said: "Be ye not unequally yoked together with unbelievers: for what fellowship hath righteousness with unrighteousness? and what communion hath light with darkness?"

Someone would have to be pretty thick to miss the looks going on between Lillian and Samuel. They'd taken a bit of a fancy to each other. She would like nothing better than to see Samuel settle down with a good woman and for Lillian to settle down with a good Amish man and become part of their community. But such things just didn't happen. As much as she'd like the chance to make up for her failures with Sarah Jane, she knew anything more than a friendship between Samuel and Lillian was wrong. They

were just too different. She'd need to keep a close eye on this and
pray about it.

Lillian watched Samuel and David climb into the box-shaped
gray buggy, which was unlike the topless two-seater she'd ridden
in with Samuel the day before. What was it about Samuel that
piqued her interest so? The fact that he was Amish and myste-
rious to her way of life, or the fact that she was wildly attracted
to him?

Not that it mattered much either way. She planned to be
Amish to some extent—to avoid the use of modern conveniences,
work hard, and find some sort of peace in her mixed-up mind. A
quiet lifestyle far away from Rickie and her mother, void of the
complications of the city, would bring her peace. She'd just wait
for it to come. In the meantime, having a new Amish friend would
be nice. But nothing more than that.

"See you at four-thirty tomorrow?" Lillian asked, reaffirming
their plans for Samuel to pick her up the following day.

"What about me?"

"You can come too," Lillian said quickly, thinking it would
seem less like a *date* with David along. She glanced at Samuel.

"David, you have evening chores to do." Samuel settled into
his seat and prepared to give Pete a flick of the reins.

"I promise I'll get them all done." The boy glanced at Lillian,
his eyes coaxing her to come to his defense.

"We don't have to stay too long, Samuel, if David needs to get
home to do his chores."

Looking defeated by the two of them, Samuel nodded.

"Then I will pick you and David up at four-thirty when he finishes his chores here. Since it's suppertime 'bout then, we can eat at the Family Cupboard Restaurant between Bird-In-Hand and Intercourse, if you want. Me and David treat ourselves every couple of weeks anyway. They sell the homemade root beer Jonas talked about near there. "

"Sounds great."

"*Danki* again for supper!" David yelled as Samuel turned the buggy around and headed down the dirt drive.

"I like Lillian, Pop," David told his father as they both walked up the stairs to bed.

Samuel started to tell his son he was sure Lillian was a fine woman but not to get any ideas.

David caught his hesitation. He nudged his father in the arm and snickered. "You like her, too, no?"

Samuel knew where his son was heading. "Of course I like her. She seems like a fine woman."

"No. I mean you *like* her," David said as he reached the door to his bedroom.

Might as well nip this right now, Samuel thought. "David, listen to me. The *Englisch* woman seems nice enough, but don't be gettin' any ideas. It's not like that. We're just gonna show her around town. She's Jonas and Irma Rose's *kinskind*, and it's a favor to them."

He could tell by the grin on David's face that he wasn't buying it. "She's funny. She's got lots of energy. And she sure is pretty."

"David, I already told you . . . Lillian is not like us. So get any crazy notions out of your head, boy." He tried to keep his tone firm. Last thing he needed was for his son to take a fancy to an *Englisch* woman. No question, the boy needed a mother. But while Levina and Sadie might not fit the bill, Lillian was certainly no better for him and his son. Maybe agreeing to show Lillian around town tomorrow was a mistake.

In an attempt to practice the Amish lifestyle and help Grandma more, Lillian got up and headed downstairs for breakfast at four-thirty. She cheated, though, setting the alarm on her cell phone. That was the one modern convenience she wasn't ready to give up—it was her only connection to the outside world. But the phone was slowly losing the charge.

She didn't hear Grandma get up with her grandpa during the night, and she was glad to see him joining them for breakfast.

"*Guder mariye*, Lilly," he belted. His jolliness so early in the morning warmed her heart. But then she saw Grandma's disappointment at her choice of attire. What was the problem with blue jeans and a T-shirt? *Scowl away*, she thought. *I'm not wearing one of those frumpy dresses on the peg upstairs.*

"Why doesn't my bread look as pretty as yours?" Lillian asked that afternoon. She and her grandma stood in the kitchen making bread.

"Maybe you didn't knead it enough."

"I sure *thought* I did. I pounded on that dough till my elbows couldn't take it anymore."

Grandma smiled. "I've had years of experience, Lillian. You'll get it with time. It's only your second day here and the first time to make bread, no?"

"Yeah, but I've always thought of myself as a pretty good cook." She glared down at the lopsided mound before her and frowned. "I'm sure disappointed in this bread. Might have to feed mine to the birds or something."

Grandma laughed. "The bread is fine, Lillian. I'm sure it tastes mighty *gut*." She patted Lillian on the arm.

"Where's Grandpa?"

"He's resting."

"Did he have a better night last night?"

"*Ya*, he did." Grandma popped another loaf into the wooden stove. "As I said, he has *gut* days and bad days."

"Grandpa's funny. He makes me laugh."

Her grandma closed the door on the stove and turned to face her. "You're a lot like him, Lillian. You have the fire in your belly, a zest for life."

Hmm. A compliment from the woman who seemed more than a little apprehensive she was there . . . with her blue jeans and cell phone in tow.

"Why did my mom leave, Grandma?"

Lillian wished immediately that she hadn't brought up the subject. The pain registered instantly on her grandma's face.

"Your mother was of age to choose whether or not to seek baptism into church membership. She chose to seek out the world." The tone in her voice indicated she'd rather not elaborate.

"But isn't that pretty rare?"

"'Train up a child in the way he should go: and when he is

old, he will not depart from it,'" her grandma said softly. "I suppose we failed."

"It was her choice, Grandma. That doesn't mean you failed." Lillian took a seat at the kitchen bench, hoping her grandma would take a break and do the same. But she stayed occupied at the kitchen counter, rinsing dishes and avoiding Lillian's gaze.

"Your mother wasn't shunned, Lillian. She could have come to visit any time." She paused. "But we saw very little of her over the years. I wrote letters to her, but . . ."

"Mom made a lot of bad choices over the years, Grandma. It's just hard for me to understand how she grew up in such a faithful home and then turned from it. She never even took me to church."

Her grandma bent slightly over the sink, shook her head, and reached for her chest as if Lillian had stabbed her in the heart.

"I mean, I went to church with friends when I was growing up. I just didn't have any formal religious education."

This wasn't going well. The woman remained hunched over the sink, and Lillian was afraid she might be crying. "Grandma?" she said softly. "I didn't mean to upset you. I just have a lot of questions where my mother is concerned."

Her grandma slowly turned to face her. "As do I," she said softly, forcing a half smile before changing the subject. "Now, let's get this next loaf of bread into the oven."

Lillian headed to the woodpile where David was diligently splitting wood.

"Your dad should be here soon." She walked up behind David, who was stacking the chopped logs.

The boy spun around. "Hi, Lillian." Breaking from the chore at hand, his eyes were dancing with curiosity.

"What is it?" she asked as he stared a hole through her.

The boy hesitated, tilting his head to one side, pushing back his straw hat. "What's it like out there?"

Oh, boy. This was probably an area she shouldn't be delving into. How much had his father told him? She didn't want to speak out of place.

She said the first thing that came to mind. "Complicated."

"Huh?"

"It's complicated *out there*." Lillian said, letting out an absent-minded sigh, briefly reflecting on her own life. "And people just aren't always nice to each other."

"Why?"

"That's a good question."

She could tell David's young mind was awhirl. But his next question caught her completely off guard. "Do you have a boy-friend?"

"No," she answered, thinking about Rickie and surprised he hadn't called her by now. Knowing her brief good-bye letter had probably left him reeling, it was a welcome relief he hadn't contacted her.

"Why aren't you married? You seem kinda old."

"I'm twenty-seven. Is that *old*?"

David chuckled. "I guess not too much. Do you want to get married?"

"I don't know." Lillian frowned. She had watched her mother

survive two bitter divorces, and the whole marriage thing had left a bad taste in her mouth. "Maybe."

David cocked his head to one side. His amazing blue eyes—just like his father's—squinted thoughtfully as he pondered a question he quite obviously wanted to ask her.

"What?" she asked, while wondering where Samuel was. It was after four-thirty by now.

"If Irma Rose and Jonas are Amish, why aren't you?"

"I'm *kinda* Amish," she said sheepishly. "I mean, my mother was raised Amish, and my grandparents are Amish." What a dumb answer, even in response to an eleven-year-old boy.

"I don't think you can be *kinda* Amish."

"I'm living on an Amish farm with my Amish grandparents. I gave up modern conveniences, and I even made bread today." No response from her young friend, who clearly needed more. "And I want to feel peace in my mind and in my heart."

He stared blankly at her. "Oh."

As he continued to study her, Lillian could tell there was more coming. "Why do you wear those boy breeches?"

Lillian glanced down at her blue jeans. "Well," she began, "I guess that's why I said I'm *kinda* Amish. I'm working on it . . . slowly."

"Oh."

Hoping that had satisfied him, she glanced down the dirt drive toward the road and looked at her watch. "Wonder where your dad is? It's almost five o'clock."

"I better get cleaned up." She watched while David stowed the axe near the woodpile and headed toward the water pump by the barn. As he splashed water on his face, she thought about what his life must be like. So Plain. So uncomplicated. How she wanted that for herself.

"My *daed* is never late," David said, drying his hands against his trousers as he met her near the farmhouse.

"He's late today." She smiled and took a seat in one of the wooden rockers on the porch. David sat down on the porch step.

"Hum," he said after a while. "Hope nothin's wrong."

"Probably just running late."

The sound of a running horse carried across the field. Lillian and David moved toward the yard. As Samuel's buggy peeled around the corner and onto the driveway, she figured he was rushing because he was late. But as clods of dirt flew from the speed of the horse's hooves and Samuel's face came into focus, Lillian knew this was more than trying to make up for lost time. Something was wrong.

4

SAMUEL SLOWED PETE TO A STOP. "WE HAVE TO HURRY, David," he yelled without addressing Lillian. "Ivan said Lilly's birthin's gone breech."

"Huh?" Lillian asked David. Instinctively she followed him to the buggy.

"Lilly's our cow!" The boy picked up his pace. Lillian continued right behind him.

"I'm sorry, Lillian," Samuel said as she reached his side of the buggy. "We'll have to schedule our trip to town for another day."

"Your cow is delivering breech?" She leaned in toward him, scoping out how she was going to crawl into the backseat. "I've never seen a cow giving birth. Can I come? And who is Ivan?" She paused. "And your cow's name is *Lilly*?"

Samuel's mouth twitched to one side and his brows drew inward. He was either irritated or amused. She wasn't sure. When he finally did open his mouth to speak, she was fairly certain he was going to deny her request to go see Lilly the Cow have her baby. But luckily, David had other plans.

Hurriedly, he jumped out of the passenger seat of the buggy and motioned for Lillian to crawl into the backseat, requiring Samuel to exit the buggy in order to fold the front seat forward.

Samuel moved with hesitancy, so she wasted no time crawling in the back. She didn't want him to change his mind.

David was barely back in the front seat when Samuel motioned Pete to make a U-turn and head down the dirt drive. Once they reached the road, it was full-speed ahead.

"Wow," she said, more to herself than anything. She had no idea the buggy could move so fast.

Samuel wondered what Ivan would say when he showed up at his farm with an *Englisch* woman. A chatty *Englisch* woman, at that.

"Where are we going? To your farm? Is Lilly your cow or Ivan's cow? Now, who's Ivan? She'll be okay, right?" Lillian paused and drew in a breath as she grabbed on to the back of the seat to steady herself from the increasing speed. "*Lilly.* Lilly will be okay, right? And her calf too?"

"I don't know about Lilly yet," Samuel responded.

David started giggling before Samuel could attempt to answer the rest of her questions. Samuel feared what the boy might say. Rightfully so.

"You have the same name as our *cow.* Jonas calls you *Lilly.*" His son turned around to face her, snorting with delight, and Samuel wondered if the boy was offending her. But then Lillian laughed.

"Yep! I certainly do," she said. "And the first time you make a *mooing* sound toward me, we're gonna have a problem." She playfully poked David's arm, and he grinned. "Now, who is Ivan?"

"Ivan is my older brother, and we're going to his place," Samuel answered, pleased to see his son enjoying her company but a little worried just the same. "Some of our cattle graze on his land." He glanced briefly over his shoulder. Her face was aglow with anticipation.

"I've never seen a cow give birth before," she said. "I hope everything goes okay for Lilly. Thank you for letting me tag along."

Letting you? Samuel didn't know he had a say-so. He hadn't had the time to waste arguing with either of them. He had a cow in distress.

"There's Ivan's place." He pointed to his brother's farm toward the left.

"This will be a first for me," she repeated.

Samuel didn't see what all the fuss was about.

Lillian wondered why she rambled on like a silly teenager every time she was with Samuel. She made a mental note not to do that any more, then concentrated on her surroundings.

Ivan's farmhouse looked a lot like her grandparents' farmhouse—white with a large porch. Although amongst the greenery were flowering blooms, unlike at her grandparents' place. She'd assumed Grandma had given up gardening when Grandpa got so sick. Maybe planting some flowers would be a good project for her to undertake at their own farm—to brighten the place up. She'd heard that gardening brought peacefulness.

As they pulled up the dirt driveway, Lillian honed in on a man in a straw hat hovering over a cow out in the pasture. Standing beside him was a woman dressed in a brown dress and black apron. The traditional white *Kapp* held her dark hair in a bun underneath. They waved as Samuel's buggy drew near.

"Poor Lilly," David said, suddenly realizing the gravity of the situation. "Bet she's in a bad way 'bout now."

"She's hurtin' for sure." Samuel hopped out of the buggy and folded the seat up. He extended his arm to help Lillian step down. She noticed his strong hands.

She must have misgauged how far down the ground was because falling into his arms was an unplanned action that caught them both off guard. His arms around her waist . . . her head burrowed against his firm chest . . .

However, Samuel moved fast, freeing himself of any contact with her like she had a contagious disease he didn't want to contract.

"I'm sorry," she sheepishly said. "I guess I lost my footing."

"No harm done," he replied nonchalantly. But Lillian caught his eyes veering in his brother's direction. He cleared his throat. "Better go tend to Lilly."

She followed him to the pasture, where David was already leaning down beside the ailing animal. The cow made an agonizing sound. Maybe witnessing the birth of a calf was a bad idea—especially one that was having this much trouble entering the world.

"Calf is backwards, hind end first with both hind legs bent," Ivan said as he leaned down beside David. "Gonna have to turn it around and pull it out. I got some baling twine right here that we can tie around the limbs once we get it where it needs to be. It's gonna take both of us, Samuel, to pull."

Ivan looked up as if just noticing Lillian.

She smiled. "Hi. I'm Lillian." She offered him her hand. He rose slightly to reciprocate but didn't follow through. Instead he eyed his hands, which were clearly not fit for shaking, and shrugged. He glanced at Samuel and then at the woman standing nearby.

"I'm Ivan. This is *mei fraa*, Katie Ann." The woman nodded politely but didn't move from her spot a few feet away.

"This is Jonas and Irma Rose's *kinskind*," Samuel said, looking slightly uncomfortable.

Both Ivan and Katie Ann looked surprised. "I didn't know Jonas and Irma Rose had a granddaughter," Katie Ann said. "How long will you be visitin'?"

"I'm not sure. I'd like to find out more about the Amish lifestyle since I am Amish," Lillian answered. "Amish by birth," she added, noticing the confused looks on their faces.

Ivan and Katie Ann turned to Samuel, apparently waiting for further clarification from him.

David spoke up before anyone could gather their thoughts. "She wants to feel peace in her mind and heart." He nodded his head up and down as if to tell the others that it was a fact and didn't warrant further discussion. But when they all looked like they might have a thing or two to throw into the conversation just the same, poor Lilly let out a wail of a *moo*.

"You goin' in or me?" Ivan asked his brother. "This ol' girl ain't gonna be able to take much more."

"I'll go in, turn the calf, and get it right," Samuel said. "Then we'll tie on with the twine and pull. Lilly won't have the strength."

Go in . . . ? Lillian watched as Samuel rolled up his sleeve and soaped up. *No way.*

She cringed as she watched him go to work. Poor Lilly had been in distress before, but this new sound escaping from her was indicative that his arm was in a place it didn't need to be. It was a gut-wrenching, agonizing, horrible, mooing sound. And she could swear the cow's eyes were rolling back in her head.

"Stop!" she finally said. "Stop! She can't take any more."

They all looked at her with sympathy, but it was Katie Ann who walked to her side and spoke up. "They gotta do this, Lillian. Otherwise, the calf will die."

Death. She was suddenly very uncomfortable. This was a bad idea. "No, no . . . of course," she said. "I know they have to do this. But can't you give her something for the pain?"

Ivan and Katie Ann looked at each other.

"I mean, don't they have drugs for this type of thing?" she asked, when no one commented.

Samuel continued working. Now he called out. "Ready. Give me the twine."

Lillian looked at Katie Ann. This couldn't be right.

"They gotta hurry and get that calf out, and it would take poor Lilly too long at this point," Katie Ann said. "It's the only way to try to save them both."

Lillian watched as David stroked the cow's head. "It's okay, girl. Everything is gonna be just fine."

"Ivan, I'm ready," Samuel said, standing up with a double strand of twine in his hand.

Ivan grabbed the twine with his brother. Lillian couldn't believe she'd opted for this type of adventure.

It seemed like an eternity of pulling and tugging. And all the while poor Lilly voiced her objections. But when two front legs emerged, followed by a tiny little calf's head, it was a sight to see. And Lillian was thrilled.

Ivan brushed past her and briefly inspected the calf. After he nodded to Samuel that all was well, Lillian dropped to the ground to welcome the new baby.

"Hello," she said softly as she stroked the slithery, wet skin. "Look at you." What an amazing event. She had just arrived in Lancaster County and already she had witnessed the miracle of birth. Fabulous. Just fabulous. "You are so beautiful," she said, leaning in closer to the new baby. "Welcome!" Ah. It was a good feeling. A peaceful feeling.

"Look, guys!" When no one responded, she looked toward them all, huddled near Lilly's head. She knew immediately what was wrong. "No," she said softly. "No."

"Poor girl just couldn't take it," Ivan said, patting David on the shoulder.

"No," Lillian repeated softly. "What about her calf?"

Samuel sat down beside her. "The baby is *gut*," he said with a tenderness in his tone she hadn't expected.

She looked at the mother cow. Someone should close her gaping eyes. She'd never gotten to see her calf.

"Some things are just His way and not meant to be," Samuel said, still in a soothing tone.

"*Whose* way?" Lillian blurted, tired of them writing off everything as God's will around here. *Don't say it*, she thought.

"God's," Samuel said as he gave her a questioning look.

That was enough. She'd had enough about God's will. First it was God's will that Samuel's wife died so young. Next it was Grandpa's cancer. She would tell them exactly what she thought about God's *will*.

She was prepared to do just that when she glanced at David.

His face registered a pain far greater than her own. He was struggling to fight back tears, and his eyes were pleading with her. Pleading for what, she wasn't sure. She walked to where he was sitting near Lilly's head and sat down beside him.

"Where there's life, there's death," he said softly with a maturity beyond his years. He tried to choke back any sign he might possibly cry.

"Yes," Lillian replied as she looked into his young eyes, unhardened by worldly ways.

It was a quiet ride back to Irma Rose and Jonas's farm. Samuel's heart hurt for David and their friend. Understandably, David was taking it pretty hard. He'd had Lilly for four years. He'd been there when she was born. When she'd grown, Samuel had wanted to take her to auction, but David wouldn't hear of it. He was attached to the old girl, so Samuel didn't push it.

His new *Englisch* friend, on the other hand, didn't even know Lilly. But she was taking it hard too.

"Here we are," he said as he pulled in front of Jonas and Irma Rose's farmhouse.

"I'm so sorry," she said, shaking her head.

"Sorry for what?" Her voice was the saddest thing Samuel had ever heard.

"About Lilly." She shook her head again. "I know it was just a cow. And I didn't *know* the cow. But it made me incredibly sad just the same."

"There's no need to be apologizin', Lillian," he said, finding it a bit odd she'd react this strongly. "With so many farms in

Texas, I'm surprised you've never seen a calf birthed. And this happens sometimes. The momma dying."

"I live in the *city*," she said with a hint of irritation.

Samuel shrugged.

As he stepped out of the buggy, their eyes met before she hopped down. How beautiful she looked, he thought, even with her sad eyes. She looked lost on a whole bunch of levels.

"I promise I won't fall this time," she said, forcing a smile as she stepped out of the buggy with ease. "Thank you for allowing me to come with you."

Samuel nodded and watched her walk to David's side of the buggy.

"I'm sorry about your cow, David."

David nodded his head. *"Danki,* Lillian." Then to Samuel's surprise, David hugged his new *Englisch* friend. Alarms began going off in Samuel's head.

Lillian avoided David and Samuel for the next two days. She was embarrassed about her reaction to Lilly's death. It was understandable for David to be so upset. It was *his* cow, and he was a child. But she was unsure what Samuel must think of her at this point. He definitely gave her funny looks sometimes. Still, after busying herself in the kitchen with Grandma for two days, she was ready to venture out. She needed a break.

As Grandma had warned, they had incorporated more activities into their daily routine. Lillian felt like a professional canner at this point. They'd made red-beet jelly, rhubarb jam, apple-cider jelly, and apricot preserves. It was somewhat tedious at first and she had to learn which recipes required hot packing and which ones required cold packing, but she had to admit, she was enjoying it. And to her surprise, she enjoyed the lengthy conversations with Grandma.

She especially enjoyed hearing how her grandparents met and about their wedding—an all-day affair that sounded incredible.

"Your *daadi* Jonas was a handsome man," Grandma said proudly. "And he still is in my eyes." Her eyes twinkled when she spoke of their younger years. Although Lillian noticed her grandma avoided any conversations having to do with her mother, even when Lillian tried to nudge the conversation in that direction.

The canning came easy. And she was getting the hang of the bread making. The sewing was another story. Getting the treadle machine to function at the right speed while trying to sew a straight line—or worse, a curved line—was a challenge. She felt relieved when Grandma said that might be a chore she'd keep for herself.

"Grandma, I think I'll go to town today." She held up a loaf of bread ready for the stove. "Hey! This one looks much better."

"*Ya*, much better. I told you that you'd get the feel of it." Grandma accepted the bread and headed for the stove. "It's a long walk to Intercourse and Bird-In-Hand. It would take you half a day on foot. You and Samuel didn't plan another trip?"

"Uh, I haven't actually talked to them since Lilly died."

Grandma closed the door of the wooden stove and turned to face her. "I would take you myself, but it wonders me if Jonas would be doin' well unattended."

"How far is it?"

"It's a good piece. You go up Black Horse Road, cross over Lincoln Highway into Beiler's Bed and Breakfast drive. Use it as a throughway to get to Leacock Road. Just keep goin'. When Jonas is havin' one of his better days, we'll saddle up Jessie and you can practice driving the buggy."

"Really? That would be great! Jessie is a beautiful animal." Lillian went to the barn every afternoon and lavished attention on the horse. And how fun it would be to drive the buggy to town.

Grandma's face twisted. Lillian knew exactly what was causing her displeasure.

"Maybe you ought not ride the buggy dressed that way, Lillian."

She watched as her grandma scanned her attire from head to toe. It was the same as it was every day—blue jeans and a T-shirt. Today, a red T-shirt. And Lillian still didn't see a problem.

Oh, I see. You'll let me drive the buggy if I wear one of the frumpy dresses on the peg upstairs. No deal.

"Well, I'll be walking today, anyway," she said, turning away from the woman before she told her exactly what she thought of those dresses. All the Amish women wore them. There was no sense of style, little choice of color. And they hung halfway to the floor! It was the one Amish custom she was not going to partake in. Wasn't the fact that she didn't wear makeup or jewelry enough? *The blue jeans stay.*

"Glad to see you have some better walking shoes." She pointed to Lillian's tennis shoes. "We can talk about learnin' you how to handle Jessie on another day when Jonas is feeling better." Her brows jutted upward as if wanting a commitment that Lillian would indeed wear the dress at some point in the future.

Time for a change of subject. "I thought maybe I might plant some flowers in the flowerbeds and around the trees in the yard," she said. "Is that okay with you?"

Grandma lit up. "I think that would be *gut.* I've been telling myself to make time for tending to the yard. But with Jonas and all . . ." She shrugged and glanced upstairs. "We have accounts in town. You can charge the flowers, and there's a scooter in the barn you better use. It was your *mamm's.* The towns of Paradise, Bird-In-Hand, and Intercourse are close enough together to use a scooter. Lots of Amish use them. It's much too far for walkin' on foot." Her tone indicated she was willing to forget the blue jeans for now.

"That'll be fun. I'll use the scooter and get some flowery plants in town."

"You won't be able to tote much back. There's a basket on the front of the scooter, though, that you can use for carryin' your buys."

"Maybe I'll get a ride back from some nice Amish person, like I did on my way here." She thought of Samuel, starting to regret avoiding him for the past couple of days.

Grandma rubbed her hands on her apron, her mouth pursing in obvious indecision.

"What, Grandma?"

"Samuel came callin' for you yesterday."

"Came calling? When?" *And why didn't you tell me?*

"He came to the door yesterday. Him and David both," she said, sounding fearful she'd made a mistake by not telling Lillian. "You were resting upstairs."

"I was reading a book." Her tone was indicative of her frustration at not being told she had a visitor.

Grandma began to pace across the wooden slatted kitchen floor. "I was worried that you might have taken a fancy to him." She shrugged. "I don't want to see you get hurt."

Lillian chuckled. "Grandma, I can take care of myself. And, I assure you, if Samuel 'came callin', he was only being friendly. Maybe he wanted to apologize for not being able to take me to town," she speculated. "Did you think he might have taken a fancy—so to speak—to *me*?"

"Oh, *ya!*" Grandma belted. "Yes, I did. And it worried me too. The both of you are very different." She shook her head.

"It's okay, Grandma," she said smugly, feeling a newfound sense of pleasure that Samuel had come looking for her. "It will be fine."

"*Ach*, I know that *now*. Katie Ann came by earlier to bring me some vegetables from her and Ivan's garden. She explained to me that Samuel was courting Levina Esh. She saw them having lunch today." She waved her hand. "It just feared me for a minute that he might be thinking of courting you. I saw you both laughing together the other day and my mind ran amuck about it. But now I know it was just silly thinkin' on my part."

"Oh," Lillian said softly. "That's wonderful for him . . . and *Levina*." She whipped around and headed toward the screen door. "I'm off to town."

As the door slammed, she bolted down the porch steps, feeling anything but wonderful.

5

Samuel was admiring the craftsmanship on a fine Amish table he hoped to purchase someday. Someday when he had a wife and more children. The shop was his favorite in Bird-In-Hand, and his friend Big Jake was a mighty fine woodworker. But the table was too big for just him and David. Maybe someday he would see fit to make the purchase.

"Why don't you just buy that table, Samuel?" Sadie Fisher asked as she approached Samuel. "You've been eyeing that thing for months."

"Hello, Sadie," he said, not feeling up to making small talk. He'd done enough of that with Levina earlier in the day when she pinned him down for lunch. No more going shopping on Thursdays for him.

"How've you been, Samuel?"

"*Gut*, Sadie. And you?"

"*Gut, gut*," she said, taking a step backward and eyeing him up and down. "Samuel Stoltzfus! You are thinning up. Do I need to come over and fix you and David some of my special meatloaf? And maybe a lemon meringue pie for dessert?"

"No need, Sadie," he said, forcing a smile. "Me and the boy do just fine."

Looking only a tad defeated, she said, "Oh, I think my cookin'
would plump you right up. It's just what you and David need." She
leaned closer to him and grinned.

There couldn't have been a better time for Lillian Miller to
pull up on a scooter.

"Hello, Samuel," Lillian said, out of breath as she approached
him and Sadie. He was glad to see her happy. Last time he'd seen
her, she was a mess. "I don't know what Grandma was thinking.
It was a long way to get here, even on a scooter." She curled her
bottom lip, blew upward, and cleared a strand of wayward hair
dangling across her face.

He glanced at Sadie and then back at Lillian. The two women
seemed to be waiting for an introduction. There was a tension in
the air he couldn't quite put his finger on. He should have never
hesitated. He should have introduced them right off. Lillian beat
him to the punch, though.

"And you must be Levina?" Lillian asked. "I'm Lillian Miller."
She extended her hand to Sadie.

Samuel cringed when he saw the fire blazing in Sadie's eyes.
He opened his mouth to make the correction, but Lillian
wasn't through. "My grandma told me how the two of you were
a couple—or 'courting' I believe is what she said. And she also
said—"

"This is Sadie!" he quickly interrupted when he saw Sadie's
mouth draw up and her hands land on her hips.

Lillian dropped her extended hand. "Oh . . ."

What she was smiling about, Samuel would never know.

"My grandma said you came to see me yesterday. I'm sorry I missed you. I was upstairs reading." Lillian's smile broadened. "Maybe you could come by later?"

Sadie ripped him to shreds with her piercing eyes. And yet, for the first time since he'd known her, Sadie Fisher was speechless.

Once again, his *Englisch* friend was not. "I just want to apologize again about the other night, the way I carried on when the cow died. How's the little calf, though?" Her eyes lit up, and Samuel couldn't help but smile.

But venom was spewing from Sadie's direction. Ignoring Lillian, she turned to Samuel. "Samuel Stoltzfus, exactly who *are* you courting these days?"

"I'm not courting *anyone*," he said cautiously, glancing back and forth between the two women. Although he kept his focus pretty much on Sadie. She was mad as fire and a mite scary looking.

Lillian spoke up first. "Uh, I'm sorry if I caused a problem. I just—"

"I best be gettin' on," Sadie interrupted, making sure her voice drowned out Lillian. She straightened her apron and held her chin high as she allowed herself a long hard look at Lillian. "Nice to meet you, Lillian," she finally said and walked off. No, *stomped* off was more like it.

"Sorry," Lillian mumbled when Sadie was out of earshot.

"For what?"

"Uh, for messing things up with your lady friend."

"Sadie and Levina are both widows in our district. And I am a widower. Need I say more?"

Of course he needed to say more.

"So, which one is it? Sadie or Levina?"

"Neither," he answered. "Why does it interest you so much?"

He reached up and stroked his beard, sporting a curious smile. He was dallying with her. Her insides flipped, and her cheeks took on a tingly sensation, which she knew meant they were red as her T-shirt. "It doesn't," she snapped in a much too defensive tone.

"Coulda fooled me."

"Well, aren't you a little full of yourself, Samuel! I believe you are the one who came to see me yesterday." She shot him a catty smile.

"David wanted to make sure you were doin' okay. You were so upset when Lilly died." His expression shifted to a look of concern, and he leaned down toward her as if to see if she really was all right.

"I'm fine. And, as I said, I'm sorry for my emotional display."

"No apology necessary." He tipped his hat. "Well, we're in town. Want me to show you around?"

"I guess," she said, unsure what she wanted from the handsome Samuel Stoltzfus. "I actually want to buy some flowers. Grandma said she didn't have time to do much gardening with Grandpa so sick. I thought it might be nice to brighten the place up."

"Do you know anything about planting flowers?"

"How hard can it be? Dig a hole and put them in."

He shook his head. "It's May. Do you know what *kind* of flowers to plant this time of year?"

"Uh . . . I guess not."

"Come on. I'll help you."

Two hours later, Samuel helped Lillian load flats of colorful foliage into his buggy.

"How exactly were you going to get all this home, since you scooted all the way here?" He lifted the scooter up and placed it in the backseat.

"I knew you'd come around and give me a ride," she said in a playful tone. Her eyes flashed alongside her smile.

Something twisted in Samuel's gut. He shook his head as she handed him a flat of flowers to store in the back of the buggy.

"What?" she asked.

"Nothing," he mumbled, suddenly reticent.

"Oh, come on," she said, poking him lightly on the arm. "Must be *something* on your mind."

He shook his head. "No, nothing." After loading the last of the flowers, he walked around and opened the buggy door on her side.

"*Danki!*" she said as she hopped in. There was that childlike enthusiasm again—a quality he found mighty attractive.

Which was the whole problem. Lillian Miller stirred things in him better left alone. She was beautiful. She was interesting. And she was off limits.

It was almost four-thirty. He better pick up the pace to get her home and pick up David.

"Jonas, the three of them are *still* sittin' out by the barn," Irma Rose said as she peeped out the window. "They've been out there almost three hours. Since right after supper. For goodness sakes, what could they have to talk about for so long?"

"Irma Rose, you might be gettin' thick around the midsection, but I didn't think you were gettin' thick in your head too." He chuckled. "Our young *kinskind* is being courted by Samuel. Now quit your spying."

She was glad Jonas was having a good day, but his sharp tongue was about to get him in a mess of trouble.

"Ouch, Irma Rose." Jonas snickered. "You're hurtin' me with that look you be givin' me."

"This is serious, Jonas. Samuel is courting Levina Esh. Katie Ann saw them having lunch today. It isn't proper for him to be spending so much time with Lillian." Their *Englisch* granddaughter didn't even go to church. And she couldn't see fit to wear a more appropriate outfit either. Lillian was a high-spirited, lovely child. Irma Rose wanted nothing more than for her to be happy. But she had seen Samuel and the boy suffer. This just had trouble written all over it.

"Are you sure Samuel is courting Levina? Both those widows—Levina and Sadie— have been chasin' that Samuel for a long time." Jonas chuckled. "He don't seem to want to be caught by neither of 'em."

"Katie Ann sure saw fit to tell me about their lunch today."

"That don't mean they're courtin'." Jonas shook his head.

"It just scares me, Jonas. I don't want to see our Lillian or Samuel and the boy get hurt." She took another peek out the window.

"Irma Rose," Jonas said in a softer tone. "It ain't up to you."

"I know." She walked away from the window. "But I'm still going to worry."

Lillian was impressed with how little it seemed to take for Samuel and David to be happy. Their Plain, uncomplicated lifestyle provided them with everything they needed. Despite her worldly ways, she'd never been able to achieve the one thing they seemed to possess in abundance: peace.

The one thing both father and son talked about with pride was their love of the land and sense of stewardship to care for God's creation.

"Tilling God's earth and providing plentiful crops is an important part of our lives," Samuel said now. "With more of our farmers having to venture out into the *Englisch* workplace, some of us are still blessed to harvest our land and enjoy the fruits of our labor."

Lillian thought hard about what he was saying. "Tomorrow, I'm going to plant all those flowers I got in town today," she said.

"It'll be nice to see some flowers here again."

"What are we going to do tomorrow, Pop?" David enthusiastically asked, as if assuming the three of them would spend time together.

Evidently, that was *not* Samuel's plan. "David, you've already missed today's chores. I think it'd be best if we headed home tomorrow after your work is finished here." Samuel lifted himself from the tree stump he was sitting on. "As a matter of fact, maybe we can salvage some chores tonight."

"But, Pop—" David protested, only to have Samuel interrupt him.

"Lillian, please thank Irma Rose again for that fine meal."

She stood up from the wooden chair she had placed in the

front yard earlier. "I will," she said softly, trying to mask her disappointment.

Hot and cold. One minute Samuel was warm and kind and seemed pleased by her presence. The next minute, he was formal and withdrawn. Just like earlier today, in town. Yet despite his quiet demeanor on the ride home, they'd had a good evening, laughing and talking about all sorts of things. She felt like after tonight she knew him and David much better.

And yet . . . hot and cold. Samuel could turn on a dime.

"*Ya*, we best be on our way, David," he said as he extended his hand to Lillian. "Bye, Lillian."

His tone was curt, as if forcing distance between them. But as she latched onto his hand, she thought she felt him hold it longer than normal. Maybe she was just imagining that.

Samuel could sense that something was on David's mind. He hadn't said a word since they left Lillian. He pulled back on the reins and slowed Pete to a trot. "It was a mighty fine meal, *ya*?" he asked.

The boy nodded but kept staring ahead.

"Something on your mind?" He slowed Pete even more, to allow a chance for the two of them to talk. Once at home, they'd need to work on the chores they had let go to spend time at the Millers' farm.

David shrugged. "Nothing, I guess."

Samuel wasn't convinced. "You like Lillian, don't you?" He suspected whatever was on David's mind had to do with her.

"You like her too!" The boy's tone was defensive and bordering on angry.

"Of course I like her. She's a very nice person, and—"

"No, I mean you *like* her, and you don't want to admit it!"

"Whoa, boy," Samuel instructed Pete as they pulled into the yard. He turned to David, surprised at his son's tone of voice. "Boy, what is goin' on in that head of yours?"

Children start getting rebellious at this age—he remembered his own temperament at that period. But David had never taken such a sharp tone with him before.

"I think you should court Lillian." He turned and faced Samuel with a look that almost demanded he consider the notion.

Samuel opened his mouth to reprimand the boy for thinking *he* could choose a courting partner for his pop. But seeing the look in David's glassy eyes stopped him short. Clearly the boy had taken a hard fancy to Lillian.

Another reason they should stop spending time with the woman.

"David," he began slowly, "it wouldn't be proper. She's from a worldly place, and it just wouldn't be right." He shook his head.

The boy instantly cheered up, obviously sensing Samuel's defenses were down. "She's gonna come around, Pop. You'll see. It's just gonna take her some time to learn about our ways. She wants to make a change. Maybe we can help her."

"It's not that easy, David."

David crawled out of the buggy and turned to face Samuel, who was still sitting and pondering his son's words. He seemed to be waiting for his dad to go on, to give him a better reason not to pursue a courtship with this woman who was so different from them.

His son knew to reject pride, arrogance, and haughtiness. The boy had been studying the *Ordnung*. How could he explain to the boy that submitting to the will of God does not come easily to an outsider? It wasn't always easy for an insider.

"'Come out from among them, and be ye separate, saith the Lord,'" Samuel said, hoping to remind the boy of their need to resist influences from the outside world.

David smiled. "'And be not conformed to this world: but be ye transformed by the renewing of your mind, that ye may prove what is that good, and acceptable, and perfect, will of God,'" he responded proudly. "Lillian just needs our help to find her way. That's all. We're not conforming to *her* world, we're just giving her a hand to renew her spirit and find that peace of heart and mind she wants."

Samuel stared at his son with a combination of admiration and fear. Where had the boy learned of such things at such a young age? It was a maturity way past his years. But leave it to a boy his age to find a loophole in the Scriptures. "It's not that easy." Samuel repeated softly. But David was already on his way into the farmhouse.

It was nearing eight o'clock when Lillian headed upstairs. She knew Grandma and Grandpa were already in bed. As she plopped down across her quilted counterpane, she looked around her small room. "Sure would be nice to watch some TV," she whispered. Glancing at the dark-colored dresses on the peg, she frowned. Sadie had sported one of the Plain dresses—a dark green one—while she was goggling all over Samuel earlier.

Lillian realized she'd certainly messed things up for any potential courtship between Samuel and Sadie. She wasn't having much regret about it. The more time she spent around Samuel, the more time she wanted to spend with him. She just wasn't sure if the feeling was mutual.

A familiar trill. She grabbed her cell phone on the first ring, hoping she hadn't wakened her grandparents. She was glad she'd thought to borrow a shopkeeper's electricity to charge up the phone while she browsed in the market today—awkward, to be sure, but he hadn't seemed to mind. And she just wasn't ready to part with this last modern convenience.

"Hi, Mom."

"Lillian, how are you?"

Something was wrong. Lillian could tell by her mother's tone. She'd heard it before, way too many times. "What's wrong, Mom?"

"What makes you think something is *wrong*? I just called to check on you . . . and your grandpa."

"I'm fine, and Grandpa had a pretty good day today." She waited for her mother to get to the point.

"Good, good."

When her mother didn't offer up the reason for the call, Lillian decided to step up to the plate. "Mom, I want to know why you left the Amish faith and chose to go out on your own." She knew her tone was demanding, but she needed an answer.

"Lillian, I have too much going on to get into this with you right now." Mom's tone was equally as sharp.

"You've *always* had too much going on to talk to me about it, Mom. And Grandma doesn't seem to want to talk about it either."

"You asked your grandma about it? Don't do that, Lillian," Mom exclaimed.

Realizing she struck a nerve with her mother, she went on. "I will ask her again if you don't tell me what happened. Because I know *something* happened, Mom."

"I chose to leave, Lillian. That's all. It was my choice to choose baptism into the church or to leave the Old Order district."

"Then why do I get the impression there's more to it than either you or Grandma are telling me?"

"I have no idea." Her tone was still sharp, and once again Lillian could tell they were heading down a bad road. "Now, tell me about your grandfather. Is he in a lot of pain?"

"Why don't you come see for yourself, Mom? He's *your* father." It was a mean thing to say, especially since she knew her mother wouldn't come. And even more so, if she was honest with herself, because she didn't want her mom there.

"Did I raise such a hateful child?"

"*Raise?* Is that what you're calling it these days?"

"Lillian, let's don't do this. Why does everything have to be a fight with you?" She could hear her mother's voice crack, but she wasn't sure if it was for effect. There was another reason for her mom's call. She just hadn't gotten to the point yet.

"I don't want to fight with you, Mom."

"Sweetie, I don't want to fight with you either. The reason for my call was to check on you and your grandparents, and also to tell you that I'm mailing you a thousand dollars. I know I owe you much more, but I have sent you what I could for now, to help you while you're there."

Lillian silently hung her head.

"It might be a couple more weeks before I can send you some more," her mother went on when Lillian didn't respond. "My new job at the employment agency pays commission for every placement. It turns out I match up employees with employers quite well."

"Thanks, Mom," Lillian said. Guilt rose to the surface. Why couldn't she just once give her mom the benefit of the doubt? Probably because history had a way of repeating itself. Sarah Jane Miller had filled her life with promises and disappointments. She was certain the phone call was because her mom needed something from her.

"Now, I have to go get ready for dinner. Paul is taking me to the new Italian restaurant in town. Things are going fabulously well with us." Her mother paused. Lillian closed her eyes, shook her head, and sighed. "Anyway, the offer still stands for you to come and stay with us, sweetie."

"I like it here, Mom."

"What about all the things you've had to do without? Television, for starters."

"I miss TV sometimes, but I stay busy. I've learned how to make homemade bread and jellies, and I even sew a little. There's tons to do around here. Tomorrow I'm going to plant some flowers. And Grandpa is a hoot." She laughed, thinking about some of the things her grandfather said sometimes.

"You're a lot like your grandfather," her mother said lovingly.

"That's what Grandma says." *Odd.* Was this turning into a

normal conversation? Maybe this would be the new norm. That would be a welcome change.

"Your grandma? She's well?" Her mother's tone resonated with the same sense of hesitation Lillian heard when her grand-mother asked about her daughter.

"She's tired a lot from taking care of Grandpa."

"Are you wearing the Amish dresses?" Her mother chuckled, which hit Lillian the wrong way. She might not want to wear the frumpy dresses, but she didn't want her mother making fun of them either.

"No. But Grandma sure wants me to." She glanced at the three dresses on the pegs—dark blue, dark green, and a deep purple. "It's hard to picture *you* wearing them."

"I didn't know any different. They are a far cry from the black pants outfit I will be wearing to dinner. Which reminds me, I need to go get ready."

The conversation was going so well. It felt good to have a normal one with her mother. Maybe she would go out on a limb. "Mom, I met a man here."

"Really? So soon?" Lillian could hear shower water turn on in the background. She knew her time was limited.

"His name is Samuel. Samuel Stoltzfus."

Lillian heard the shower water shut off. "Lillian, listen to me," her mother said, pausing. "That is an Amish name. Please tell me you don't have a crush on an Amish man."

Oh, how quickly her mother's tone changed. "Yes, he's Amish," she said firmly.

"Oh, Lillian! That will *never* work."

"First of all, we're just friends, Mother." She was twenty-seven years old. And, based on the choices her mother had made, she shouldn't have to defend her own.

"Well, keep it that way."

It appeared Lillian was going to defend her own choices after all. "I might. I might not. I really like him. And his son, David."

"Oh, great. There's a child involved too?"

"He's eleven. He's a great kid, and—"

"Lillian, I have to run. Paul is calling from downstairs for me to hurry. I'll talk to you soon."

Her mouth was still open, midsentence, when she heard the line go dead. The false pretense of a normal conversation with her mother was nice while it lasted, but she could have predicted the final outcome.

The next morning Lillian swore she smelled smoke as she headed downstairs for breakfast. She looked at her watch. "Oops," she whispered. It was almost six o'clock. She'd probably missed breakfast. Cereal would have to do. Grandma was already headed to town by now.

That is smoke I smell.

Reaching the kitchen, she came to a sudden halt when she saw Grandpa casually puffing away on a cigar at the kitchen table.

"Grandpa! What are you doing?"

"Nothing like a fine cigar after breakfast." He flicked ash into a nearby coffee cup, his eyes twinkling with mischief.

"You can't do that . . . can you?" Amish people didn't smoke.

He chuckled. "We grow tobacco, my little Lilly. And some of us older folk partake in a cigar from time to time."

"Oh." She watched him take another puff. "But that's not good for you. I mean, you're sick. Maybe you shouldn't be smoking." She walked closer to him and frowned. "Does Grandma know about this?"

He sat up straighter on the wooden bench. As he held the cigar in one hand, he blew smoke and stroked his beard with the other hand. "Might be best not to mention it to her." He smiled with the sneaky satisfaction of a child.

"She's going to smell it." Lillian crossed her arms and shook her head.

"*Ya!* You'd think so! But every time she goes to town, I have me a smoke. Been smokin' me a cigar like this for months when she's afar. I open the windows and the doors." He pointed to the three open windows in the kitchen and the open screen door.

"Well, I could smell it coming down the stairs. Why don't you go on the porch?" Lillian knew she shouldn't be encouraging him.

"It's more comfortable in here, and near the coffee. Besides, I think Irma Rose has a bad nose. She don't smell good. I passed some gas the other day that would have knocked over a large cow. She didn't even give a flinch." He laughed as he took another drag.

Lilly blushed. "But, Grandpa, it's not good for you. You're sick and shouldn't be smoking."

"Lilly, I'm going to the Good Lord—soon. Ain't nothin' gonna change that." He grinned. "Just hope I go on a day when Irma Rose is in town, so I can go with a cigar in my hand."

"Grandpa, you might live many more years." She could only hope. The thought of him not there put her stomach in knots.

"Not gonna happen, my Lilly. I'm on my way out the door."

"Don't say that!"

He lifted his hairy chin, pushed back his straw hat, and gave her a hard look. With the cigar dangling from one side of his mouth, he said, "So, tell me about Samuel."

He clearly wanted to change the subject. And she supposed if it was going to get changed, she was glad it was to Samuel.

"He's nice. I like David too." She reflected on the hours of talking and laughing the three of them had shared the night before. It was nice. Although, based on Samuel's reaction, it might not be happening again.

"He's a fine man. The boy is a hard worker." He winked at her, the cigar still dangling to one side.

She wasn't sure how much to say. "Yes, he seems like a good father too."

"Gonna be spending more time with him?"

"Uh, I don't know. I'm sure I'll see him around." It was a vague answer but a truthful one.

"Well, it appears you'll be seeing him tomorrow."

"What? When?"

"It's his turn to have church service at his farm. You will be goin' to church?" His tone was an assumption she would be in attendance.

One thing at a time, though. "You have church service at a *home*? How did I miss that? I knew service was held every other week, but I must have missed the fact that it was at home."

"'God that made the world and all things therein, seeing that he is Lord of heaven and earth, dwelleth not in temples made with hands,'" he said. "*Ya*, we have church service in folks' homes. We each take a turn 'bout every ten months."

"Oh." She thought for a minute about the opportunity to see Samuel and where he and David lived. "I guess I can go."

Grandpa eyed her up and down. "Don't make a lick o' difference to me, but your Grandma sure would be pleased if you'd wear one of them dresses upstairs."

She frowned. "They're just not for me, Grandpa."

He sat quietly for a few seconds. "Maybe just give it some thought," he suggested.

Suddenly his face took on a fearful expression and he stuffed the cigar into the coffee cup. "Quick! Start fanning the room! Dump this out!" He handed her the coffee cup. "My hearing must be off too! I usually hear Jessie's hooves before he hits the dirt drive. Look at that! They're already in the yard!"

She grabbed the coffee cup and dumped the contents as instructed. Grandpa moved faster than she'd seen him since she arrived, waving his arms about, pushing the smoke toward the open windows. She watched with amusement at his wholehearted effort to keep his secret. Then, shaking her head, she said, "I'll go outside and try to stall Grandma. I'll show her the flowers I'm going to plant today."

With her grandpa still flailing his arms wildly around the room, she moved toward the open screen door. "I still think you shouldn't smoke," she whispered before she walked onto the porch.

"Hurry, child! Or Irma Rose will have my hide!"

6

LILLIAN HAD BEEN STARING AT THE DRESSES ON THE PEGS
for nearly ten minutes. She needed to make a decision soon. She
glanced toward the bed, where she'd laid out the only dress she
brought with her: a blue one, but much shorter and *way* more
stylish than the ones on the peg. All the other women would be
wearing dresses similar to those Grandma had put in her room.
Maybe it would be best not to stand out.

She pulled the dark blue dress from the peg.

"Grandma's already in the buggy, Lilly!" Grandpa yelled
upstairs. "You comin'?"

Changing quickly, she ran down the stairs to see her grandfather
sporting a wide-brimmed straw hat and a pair of suspenders she
didn't remember seeing before. His eyes lit up when he saw her.

"You'll make your *mammi* very happy, Lilly."

"Feeling good today, Grandpa?" she asked. He seemed to be
walking a bit taller this morning.

"It's a good day to go to church," he said, pushing back his
hat and taking another look at her. "What a fine Amish woman
you make."

"Thanks, Grandpa."

He made his way slowly down the porch steps and across the

front yard. A little wobbly, but all in all Grandpa seemed to be doing well. She stayed close by, occasionally offering her elbow for support. Grunting a little, he heaved himself into the driver's seat of the buggy while she went to go lavish a little attention on Jessie before they took to the road. "Hello, boy," she whispered as she stroked the horse's snout.

"Look at our Lilly. How 'bout that?"

Lillian poked her head around Jessie's. Grandma was sitting in the buggy and had her hands to her mouth as if overwhelmed by what she saw. After a moment's pause, she took a shaky breath. "I think you should drive us to worship this fine morning," she said, scooting off the seat. "I'll sit in the back. Jonas get up and push that seat forward so I can crawl in."

"Bossy, bossy," he snickered.

Thrilled, Lillian joined her grandpa in the front seat. With Grandma settled in the backseat, Grandpa handed over the reins. Lillian glanced over her shoulder. Grandma's hazel eyes shone with vivacity. If that's all it took for her to gleam like that, Lillian knew she should have worn the Plain dresses way before now. After all, they were just dresses.

Before she catapulted Jessie into action, Lillian reached into her apron pocket and pulled out the little white prayer covering she had stuffed inside. Hurriedly she wrapped her long brown hair into a tight bun and secured it with a hair band from her wrist. It was a last minute choice to bring along the hat, but she was glad she had. Her *Kapp* wasn't properly ironed, but she might as well wear the entire get-up.

She twisted in her seat and gave her grandma an "All set?" look. It warmed her heart to see the smile that stretched across the older woman's tired face.

"*Danki*, Lillian," she whispered.

Lillian smiled as she gave Jessie a giddyup. Why hadn't she just worn the silly dresses sooner?

As if sensing the women were having a moment, Grandpa lightened the mood. "Let's kick up some dirt, Lilly! Let ol' Jessie stretch his legs. Give a gentle flick with the reins. Jessie will do the rest."

Doing as her grandpa suggested, Lillian carefully maneuvered the buggy down the dirt lane to the main road. Then she looked at Grandpa again. He grinned and nodded.

"*Ya!*" she yelled, which thrust Jessie forward so fast Grandma fell backward against the seat.

"Thata girl, Lilly! A *wunderbaar* day to feel the wind in our face," Grandpa said as Jessie got comfortable in a quick gallop.

"Jonas, the Good Lord will still be there when we arrive!" Grandma yelled, regaining her composure as she adjusted her *Kapp*. "This is Lillian's first time to drive the buggy. She might not feel comfortable moving along so fast."

"Sure she does. Pick it up, Lilly! Another gentle flick of the reins."

Lillian glanced at her grandma, who was preparing herself for another increase in speed. But when she smiled in Lillian's direction, Lillian took that as the go-ahead and did indeed pick up the pace.

"Yee-ha!" Grandpa wailed.

Samuel's mother and two sisters, along with Katie Ann, had been busy readying the farmhouse for church service since the early-morning hours. Samuel, Ivan, and David were setting up tables and benches inside and out to prepare for the meal after worship.

"How did you meet the *Englisch* woman?" Ivan asked Samuel as they carried a bench from the barn.

"She was tryin' to find her way to Jonas and Irma Rose's farmhouse. She was walking along the road with only one shoe." He chuckled at the memory. "I gave her a ride."

"Is she planning to study the *Ordnung* in preparation of baptism? She is, after all, Amish by birth." Ivan placed the bench beside the long wooden table.

"I don't know. She says she wants to live a peaceful, quiet life for a while."

"Hmm, I see. The worldly ways of the *Englisch* are so different." Ivan shook his head.

"*Ya.*" Samuel wasn't clear about Lillian's plans, but he knew her heart was filled with compassion and kindness. That much was evident in the way she interacted with David, the way she reacted when the cow died, and her overall desire to lead a good life free of complications. Although misdirected in her attempts at finding such peace, Samuel knew her motivations were of God. She just didn't know it yet.

"Isn't that Jonas and Irma Rose coming up the drive?" Ivan pointed toward the dirt road leading to Samuel's farmhouse.

Samuel looked up. "That's Lillian driving," he said to his brother. "And . . ."—his heart did a somersault—"she's dressed in Plain clothes."

"It's a far cry from the boy breeches she wore when I saw her last." Ivan tipped back his straw hat and strained to have a better look at the approaching buggy.

"*Ya*," Samuel whispered, too stunned to say much else. He was pretty sure he'd heard her say she'd never wear one of the traditional Amish dresses.

As the buggy came to a halt, Samuel stifled a grin. Irma Rose's hair looked like she'd been through a tornado. Loose gray strands fell forward from beneath her *Kapp*, and she looked a tad pale. Lillian was sporting the same messy hairdo, but seemed to be bursting with pride.

"*Guder mariye!*" she yelled as they pulled up. "I drove the buggy!" Her contagious laugh even prompted a smile from Ivan.

"Good morning to you too," Samuel said as he walked toward the buggy. "How was the ride?" he asked Irma Rose.

"Lillian did a fine job," she said, stabbing strands of hair back under her *Kapp*, housed underneath a black bonnet. She drew in a deep breath, an obvious attempt to gather her composure.

Jonas popped out of the buggy. "I don't think I've been that fast in a buggy since my *rumschpringe!*" He paused and drew in a cleansing breath. "What a ride. And what a glorious day for worship." He shook Samuel's hand and made his way to one of the benches to take a seat.

Lillian slid off her seat and pushed it forward so Irma Rose could crawl out of the back. Samuel helped her out of the buggy. "Thank you, Samuel," she said, offering him a half smile. She headed toward Jonas, presumably to also take a rest after their adventurous ride.

Lillian couldn't have looked more beautiful. The crisp morning air tinged her cheeks a rosy pink, and her eyes were aglow with a passion for life. Her heavenly smile enhanced her dimples. In spite of his earlier resolve to keep things simple between them, he had to admit he felt strangely weak in the knees. He couldn't have been happier she'd chosen to attend worship service at his house on this fine Sunday morning. It was going to be a good day indeed.

As he had welcomed the others, Samuel extended his hand to her. "You look . . . lovely," he said. Surprised he'd verbalized the thought, he searched her eyes for a reaction. Her gaze met his, and she gave his hand a gentle squeeze.

"Why, *danki*, Samuel."

Samuel could hear faint rumblings and voices in the background, but he couldn't seem to decipher anything. The feel of Lillian's hand in his, the way her eyes connected with his . . . He was lost in her world.

"I dressed Amish," she whispered as she let go of his hand.

"And a mighty fine Amish woman you look." He couldn't seem to walk away from her, even though he heard someone calling his name.

"I think your brother is calling you," she said, obviously pleased she was diverting his attention.

He turned to see Ivan waiting for his help to carry another bench. "*Ya, ya*. Make yourself at home," he said to her and reluctantly made his way toward Ivan.

Samuel certainly seemed smitten with her this morning, and Lillian couldn't shake the smile he'd brought to her face. The way he held her hand and the look in his eyes left no question in her mind: he was glad she was here. She headed to where her grandparents were sitting. Grandma stood up right away.

"Let's head in with the other womenfolk, Lillian, and give a hand with the meal preparations." She grabbed Lillian's hand and continued holding it all the way into Samuel's kitchen.

"Hello," Lillian said softly when she entered the room. In addition to Katie Ann, there were two other younger women, and another woman about Grandma's age. They all paused at their respective chores and waited for an introduction. She was under the spotlight, no doubt.

"This is Lillian, *mei kinskind.*" Grandma's tone was proud. It touched Lillian's heart. Grandma gave her hand a squeeze. "And, Lillian, this is Mary Ellen, Samuel's sister." She pointed toward a woman about Lillian's age, who nodded in her direction. "This is Rebecca, another of Samuel's sisters." The slightly older woman also nodded and smiled. "And, this is their *mamm,* Esther."

"Lillian and I have met," Katie Ann spoke up. "Welcome to our worship service."

Lillian nodded. "Thank you for having me." She glanced around the kitchen, which mirrored her grandparents' kitchen, with the same white walls, table and bench, and wood-burning stove. Samuel's mother continued to study her as the other women returned to peeling potatoes, buttering loaves of bread, and arranging pickles on a tray.

"What church district do you come from?" Esther Stoltzfus finally asked.

"Uh, I don't come from any church district," Lillian said, unsure how Grandma would like for her to answer.

Grandma held her chin high. "Lillian comes to our district from the city—from Houston."

Esther looked confused.

"Lillian, maybe you could help me get the butter bread ready?" Katie Ann asked.

Grandma seemed relieved with the change of subject.

———— ❧ ————

It was a church service unlike any church service Lillian had ever attended. Not that she had attended very many. The men and boys sat by themselves in one room, and the women and girls sat in another room. There was a central room in between where the preaching took place. Since it was almost completely in German, Lillian understood very little of the two-hour service.

Her back ached from the backless bench. There was no organ or music, just songs that were sung unusually slow. When the service was over, the men left first, then the young women, and lastly the older women. Lillian tried to follow tradition as best she could.

Despite the awkwardness of the whole event, she came away from the service feeling a sense of fellowship and calm. While some of those in attendance gave her questioning looks, everyone was friendly. Sadie Fisher, however, didn't acknowledge her presence. She'd noticed the young woman sitting on the same row, at the far end from her. As they exited the service and moved toward the kitchen, Lillian caught Sadie watching her, but the woman quickly turned away when their eyes met.

Samuel, on the other hand, locked eyes with her several times. Each time, a smile swept across his face.

The men began to seat themselves at the benches outside while the women started to carry out trays of food. It seemed incredibly old-fashioned to her the way the women waited on the men. She had never seen Grandpa so much as serve himself a cup of coffee at home. And Grandma never seemed to mind tending to his every need, on good days or bad. Nor did these women seem to mind that the men were eating first. So she followed suit and helped carry out food trays and pitchers of sweet tea.

"Hi, Lillian."

After placing a pitcher of tea on the table, she gave David a hug. "Hi, David. How's it going?"

"*Gut*," he said.

Frowning, she pointed to a large bowl on a nearby table. "I canned some of those, but I have to tell you, I don't care for them."

"Those are *riewe*. Red beets. They're *gut*."

"Yuck. I don't think I'll be having any of those. But I'm going to have lots of that pie." She nodded her head toward one of the many desserts lining the table.

"That's *schnitzboi*. Snitz pie," he said grinning.

"Well, I'm going to be sure and have some. Where's your Pop?" she asked, looking around for Samuel. "Eating with the other men?"

David didn't say anything.

"What are you snickering about?" she asked playfully.

"Oh, nothing." He nervously kicked at the grass.

"It's my Amish outfit, isn't it?" Maybe it just didn't work for her, like she suspected. Although his father had sure seemed happy to see her wearing the traditional dress.

"No, that's not it. I think you look Plain."

"Well, *Plain* is good, right?"

Ignoring her plea for acceptance, he said, "Pop's in the barn.

He asked me to take him some sweet tea. But *you* can take it to him if you want." He reached for a glass of tea on the table and pushed it in her direction, still grinning.

She accepted the tea and winked at him. "I think I will." She walked toward the barn. "Save me a piece of that pie!"

"I will."

Samuel filled Pete's trough with oats. "There's a mighty crowd takin' over the house, ol' boy. Maybe I'll sit a spell with you." Knowing he should get back to the group with the extra chairs he'd been sent to retrieve, he took advantage of the opportunity to sit quietly for a minute. Taking a seat behind his woodworking bench, he eyed the many uncompleted projects. So much to do and so little time. Between caring for the boy, farming the land, and the many other chores necessary to keep the farm running, his favorite pastime was quickly becoming a thing of the past.

He picked up a birdhouse modeled after a plan his pop gave him before he died. It would be a fine home for the redbirds, if he could ever finish it.

He didn't hear Lillian walk into the barn. When he looked up, she was there.

"David said you wanted some tea," she said, handing him the glass.

"*Danki*. David could have brought it out here."

She remained quiet as he took several big gulps. He set the glass down, fearing he'd hurt her feelings with his comment. "I mean, I hate for you to have to get away from the other folks to bring me tea."

"I don't mind."

"What did you think about the church service?"

"Long." She sighed. "And my back's a little sore."

"The benches take some gettin' used to."

"But it was nice. I didn't understand most of it, but there was a certain something in the air. I don't know. I guess maybe a fellowship. It was like one giant family. I didn't really have a family growing up. It was just me and Mom."

"I reckon we're like one big family in most ways. Do you plan to study the *Ordnung* while you're here?"

"That's like the order of conduct, right?" She pressed her lips together and thought for a minute. "I guess if I'm really going to live the Amish life while I'm here, I should."

"It's not easy, Lillian. Especially since you come from worldly ways. Don't you miss television, electricity, and all the other modern conveniences?"

"Of course I do. But I don't miss living by myself and being afraid to go home alone at night. I don't miss my mother's reckless behavior and always needing something from me. I don't miss the busyness, the constant fast pace. I don't miss—" She caught her breath as vivid and painful memories of Rickie stabbed at her insides. "I don't miss a lot of things. All my life, I've sensed there was something else for me. I just didn't know what."

"Is this the something else you've been looking for?"

"I hope so. I don't know. I just know that I've felt lost for a long time, and something about being here, living with Grandma and Grandpa"—she paused—"and meeting you makes me believe maybe it is."

Alarms began to ring in Samuel's head. His fascination with

her aside, he knew it would be best to get things right in *both* their minds if they were going to stay friends.

"Lillian," he began.

"Yes?"

"I hope you find what you're lookin' for." She nodded and seemed to be waiting for more. "I mean, truly living our ways would mean a lot of studying and acceptance of God's will. It's not just about wearing the clothes, gardening, making bread, getting up early, or making quilts."

"Hey! I haven't thought about quilts. I want to learn that too."

She was missing his point. "Our way of life is *here*, Lillian." He held his hand to his heart. "It's a faith we carry without doubt and a way of life we practice with humility and selflessness."

"I know," she said as if trying to convince him.

He shook his head, realizing any feelings he had today at seeing Lillian in her Plain clothes were best put aside. No matter her intentions, they lived in two different worlds.

"Why are you shaking your head?"

It was time to clear the air. "I like you, Lillian. And I would like to be a friend to you." He hesitated; she seemed to hang on his words. "But for it to be anything more between us isn't possible. David seems to have taken a fancy to you, and I don't want to see the boy get hurt by an *Englisch* woman with no sense of our ways."

A little presumptuous of him, Lillian thought, as she weighed her options. There were two ways to play this. One, she could save face and say she completely agreed and then change the subject. Or two, step out on a huge limb and see if Samuel could practice what he was preaching.

Choosing option two, she said, "I think maybe *you* have taken a fancy to me, also, Samuel Stoltzfus." She lifted her chin and shot him a curious grin.

His eyes widened.

Sensing his shock at her comment, she decided not to back him into a corner where he might choose to not even remain friends. "But . . . okay," she said.

"Okay, what?" He pushed back the rim of his straw hat as though trying to see her better.

"We'll be friends. Nothing more. And we'll make that clear to David as well."

"I think that's a fine idea. I'll talk to David, so the boy doesn't get any misconceptions 'bout us spending time together."

"That's perfect. You and David are the only friends I have here, and I'd hate to lose that." She leaned forward a bit. "So . . . *friend*. Wanna come have another talk by the barn tonight?"

"There's chores to do and I think—" He stopped midsentence when his eyes met with her pleading gaze. "I reckon it would be all right. David and I will come over after suppertime, though. I don't want us to wear out our supper welcome with Irma Rose. Plus, that will give us time to catch up on some chores around here."

"Sounds good. I better head back. I'll see you and David later."

It was nearing six o'clock when Samuel walked downstairs that evening. David was at the kitchen table generously helping himself to leftover butter bread and pickles.

"David, Lillian asked us to come by this evening to talk for a while."

The boy grinned. "You're courting her."

"No, David. Lillian is a friend. Anything else wouldn't be right. I want you to understand that."

With the same maturity beyond his years that Samuel had noticed before, his son said, "I know our ways are different from hers, Pop. But she's here, and she's learnin' our ways. Whose to say God won't work a miracle? Maybe she'll realize she'd like to become Amish."

"David, you know that doesn't happen very often—an *Englisch* man or woman converting. And even if they choose our ways, most can't stick to it. I've told you before: don't be gettin' any silly notions in your head about Lillian. Now go get cleaned up, and we'll just go visit for a while."

Mischievously, David said, "Ivan is picking me up any minute. I told him after church service I would spend the night with him and Katie Ann so I can help him paint the fence starting early in the morning. Didn't he tell you?"

Samuel felt a slight pang of panic. Most of the time he'd spent with Lillian had been with David in tow. Safer that way. "Uh, no. No one told me."

The boy choked down a piece of bread and jumped up from the table. He reached the window and stared into the sunset. "Here comes Ivan now."

Samuel followed his son to the window and saw Ivan's buggy

coming up the driveway. "What am I going to tell Lillian? I told her we'd come for a visit. I didn't know you were going with Ivan."

David spun around on his way to the door. "Guess you'll have to go visit her all by yourself, Pop."

It wasn't right. Going to see Lillian by himself would seem like he was courting her. But if he *wasn't* courting her, then why was he worried about it? It was just a friendly visit, after all.

So why couldn't he control the buzz of activity in his belly at the thought of being alone with her?

7

LILLIAN CONSIDERED CHANGING OUT OF HER AMISH DRESS and back into her blue jeans, but she didn't. As she roamed the yard inspecting her gardening efforts from the previous day, she heard the screen door slam. Grandma took a seat in one of the wooden rockers on the front porch.

"The yard looks *gut*, Lillian."

"*Danki*, Grandma. It was fun planting all these." She waved her arm around, motioning toward her work.

She thought back to Samuel's comments about nurturing the land and how work could be healthy and enjoyable. Planting the flowers didn't seem like work, and it certainly brought her a sense of calm. She noticed she felt the same way after a successful day of baking, or when she mastered a particular sewing task. It was a sense of accomplishment, but there was something else too.

"How's Grandpa feeling?"

"He's resting. I'm thankful he was able to attend worship this morning, but I think he's paying the price about now." She shook her head. Lillian could see the worry in her tired eyes, magnified by dark circles underneath. "The *Englisch* doctors in town changed his medication. Seems to give him a boost of energy, but then he's down and out in the evening hours." She shook her head again.

"I'm sorry I didn't finish my other chores in time to help you with supper." She paused. Grandma was shaking her head as if it didn't matter. But Lillian knew she was going to have to start taking on more chores around the house and try to complete them in a more timely manner. Otherwise, Grandma was going to end up sick right alongside Grandpa.

"Grandma, I think maybe I should just make it a point to cook the meals. That includes breakfast. I've been getting up early, and I've seen what Grandpa likes to eat for breakfast. Why don't you start sleeping in a little bit, and let me handle the cooking?"

As if she didn't hear a word Lillian was saying, Grandma said, "Child, what are you watchin' for down that driveway?" She strained to see down the dirt drive.

"Huh?" Lillian was anxious for Samuel and David to arrive, but she didn't think she was that obvious.

"Are you waiting for Samuel and David?" Grandma wrinkled her nose.

"Oh . . . They're just coming by. For a quick visit." She shrugged her shoulders to signify it was no big deal.

Grandma's lips pursed together and she gave her granddaughter a stern look. "Now, Lillian," she began slowly. "You'd have to be thick as pea soup not to see that you and Samuel have taken a fancy to each other. But you need to be very careful. There's a child involved here, and it seems to me that the boy has taken a fancy to you as well."

So, it wasn't just her imagination. Samuel *did* like her a little more than he was willing to let on. Even Grandma had picked up on it. "We're just friends, Grandma. That's it."

In a tone indicative she wasn't buying it, her grandmother said, "*Ya.*"

"Really. We've talked about it." Lillian took a seat in the other rocker. "We're just going to be friends, and Samuel said he'd talk to David about it."

In spite of her obvious concern, Grandma chuckled.

"What?" She watched her grandma shaking her head.

"You've talked about it?" Grandma's face grew serious. "Lillian, if you've *talked* about it, then the notion for courting must be in both your heads. And you need to know it would be devastating to the community, and to Samuel and David, if he fell *in lieb* with you. You *aren't* Amish and it could cause a world of trouble for Samuel." Her mouth twisted as if biting on a sour grape.

"What?" Lillian couldn't believe what she was hearing. "Grandma, first of all, we barely know each other. No one is *in love*. We're just friends. And I would never allow Samuel to get into any kind of trouble."

"You say that now, dear. When two people are attracted to each other, reckless decisions can be made."

"I know all about reckless decisions, Grandma. I watched Mom make a whole slew of them over the years." She looked away, trying to avoid certain memories that crept into her dreams at night. Her own reckless decisions had stemmed from her attraction to Rickie. But unlike her mother, she refused to allow herself to keep making the same mistakes. She blinked her eyes, shook her head, and turned back toward her grandma. "I like it here. So I don't see why Samuel and I can't be friends."

A worried look still scrolled across the older woman's face. "I didn't say you couldn't be friends, Lillian. I'm sayin' you are both treading into dangerous territory. I'm pleased as punch you like it here and want to stay on for a while, but to live among us is to learn our ways and to give up many things you're used to having. Most people come here looking for something they don't find."

Lillian's chest grew heavy. "Don't you want me here?" She realized just how much she wanted to be here.

"Your *daadi* and I want you here very much." Grandma smiled, but the worry quickly returned. "But running away from something isn't always the answer either."

Lillian thought for a minute and tried to ignore the lump forming in her throat. Maybe Grandma was having second thoughts about bringing her into their community. "Grandma, I'm not running away *from* something—I'm running *to* something. There's been something terribly amiss in my life."

"Do you think you've found that something in Lancaster County?"

"I do, Grandma. Or at least . . . I might have. These last few days have been wonderful. But if you don't want me here, I would understand. I know I have a lot to learn." Tears were building, and she didn't want Grandma to see her cry. Then she'd feel obligated to say she wanted Lillian there.

Grandma reached over and cupped her hand over Lillian's. "Lillian, there is nothing I want more than for you to live with us—for as long as you like." She paused. "But the *something* you are running to won't be found through gardening, cooking, or making bread." She looked at Lillian's blue dress and black apron. "Or by wearing our Plain clothing."

"That's what Samuel said."

Grandma looked shocked at first that she and Samuel had

such conversations. But then she softened. "Well, Samuel's right. Find God, Lillian. The rest will follow."

Find God? And exactly where had He been hiding all her life? She'd tried praying, waiting to see if an all-powerful Being really existed, but her prayers had gone unheard. When she and her mother slept in the car when she was twelve, where was God then? Where was God when her mother begged the landlord for just one more day to pay the rent? When Rickie strode into her life and trapped her in a twisted maze of good and evil, why didn't this Supreme Being show her a path to safety sooner?

Find God. She had looked for God. And while she hadn't ruled out the possibility Someone had helped her through some tough spots, she hadn't ruled out the possibility it was all just coincidence either.

As if reading her mind, Grandma said, "Try to find *not* what the Lord has done for you, but what *you* have done for the Lord."

Lillian pondered her statement for a minute. What could she have possibly done for God when she wasn't even sure He existed?

But if He did exist . . .

Suddenly, it was as if every bad thing she'd ever done was rising to the surface and demanding to be heard. There was an inner conflict going on inside her head she didn't understand. It was confusing.

"Grandma, I want so badly to feel a calmness inside. I want so badly to live a good life." Her heart was heavy. "It's just hard for me to understand why sometimes things happen the way they do." She brushed away a tear.

"There, there, child," Grandma said, again reaching over and placing her hand atop Lillian's. "Some things are just God's will."

There it was again: God's will. That was the part she had the biggest problem with. "But I have doubts, Grandma. I have doubts, and I know that's not right. How can I find God with all these doubts in my mixed-up mind?"

Grandma lifted Lillian's chin up. "I think this is a very good start."

As Samuel turned onto the dirt driveway leading up to Jonas and Irma Rose's place, he'd made up his mind to stay only a few minutes. He'd say *hello*, talk briefly about church service, admire the flowers he knew she'd planted the day before, then be on his way. But all that changed when she met him at his buggy in the front yard. He didn't think he'd ever seen a more fragile-looking creature. Tears stained her rosy cheeks, and her eyes glazed over with emotion. Towering over his *Englisch* friend, he softly asked, "Lillian, what is it?"

She shook her head.

Idle chitchat wasn't on her agenda. Something had her all awhirl. "Lillian?" he asked again.

"I'm sorry, Samuel," she said, dabbing at her eyes.

"Did something happen?" Maybe Jonas had a bad spell. "Is it Jonas?"

"No, no." She took another swipe at her eyes. "Just ignore me. I was having a talk with Grandma . . . a talk about God. I just got kind of emotional and a little upset."

Wondering if this territory was best left alone, he asked, "What got you upset?"

"I have so many doubts about God, and I don't have a rela-tionship with Him. And I want to, Samuel. I really do. But I don't know how to go about it."

She was clearly waiting for answers. And he didn't have any. It wasn't his job to show Lillian the way to God. *Unequally yoked.* The phrase pounded away in his head. Missionary work was not part of the Amish way. Steering clear of nonbelievers in an inti-mate way—friendly or otherwise—was.

When he didn't respond, she turned her back toward him.

"Lillian?" he asked, unsure what to say or do.

After a few seconds, she turned back around. "Let's don't do this," she said after taking a deep breath. "I had a conversation with Grandma that got me thinking about things. About God. And then you got here. You just caught me during an emotional moment. Let's talk about something else."

"*Ya,*" he said relieved. They'd talk about something else for a short while, and then he was hightailing it home. He shouldn't be there in the first place. The *Englisch* woman was mixed up, all right. She was a downright mess.

But a beautiful mess.

What a whiny baby. Lillian hardly knew the man and yet she had gotten teary in front of him twice. Once over a cow and now about her lack of faith. She frowned as he followed her to their spot on the side of the barn. From now on, cheery conversation was in order.

"Sadie didn't acknowledge me at church service today," she said without thinking first. Not exactly cheery conversation.

"She was jealous." Samuel seemed to regret the comment the minute he said it. He glanced away when she met his eyes with a look of surprise.

"Really? Why would she be jealous? You and I aren't court- ing." She should have avoided empahsizing the word *courting*. He looked uncomfortable.

As silence formed a barrier between them, Samuel changed the subject. "The other evening we spent most of our time talk- ing about life here. Tell me about yourself, Lillian. Tell me about your life before Lancaster County."

She watched him place his straw hat on the stump nearby. His flattened hat hair did nothing to take away from his stunning looks. As she watched him stroking his beard, she tried to envi- sion the face underneath. "What do you want to know?"

"Whatever you're comfortable telling me." He shrugged.

"Hmm, let's see." She'd made so many mistakes. Surely he didn't want to hear about her failures. Better to focus on the posi- tives in her life. "I was a teacher in Houston. I wanted to make a difference in the lives of children, help them see their potential and feel good about themselves. I love kids."

"Well, David sure likes you."

"He's a great kid. You've done a good job with him."

"*Ya*, he's a *gut* boy. But, I can really only take credit for the past couple of years. Before that, I give credit to his *mamm*. After Rachel died, I've done the best I know how."

She wanted to know more about Rachel. But before she could say anything, he said, "So tell me more."

"I guess saying I'm a lost soul trying to find my way would sound a little dramatic." She cringed and forced a half smile.

"Less dramatic would be to say I needed to get away from my mother for a while, and I had a bad breakup with my boyfriend." She paused and looked up to see him hanging on her words. "So I'm trying something new."

"What happened with your boyfriend?" he asked.

This was veering away from the cheery conversation she'd hoped for earlier. She shrugged, unsure how much to tell Samuel.

"Did you love him?"

"I thought I did."

He was waiting for more. There was so much more. She hesitated, but the look on his face was kind and encouraging. "Rickie was great in the beginning. Very loving and kind."

His eyes were intently focused on her, and she wished she could finagle her way out of this conversation. She'd make it brief so they could move on to something else. "Then he just changed."

"What do you mean?"

Closing her eyes, she pushed the vivid details of her and Rickie's last confrontation out of her mind. She was far, far away from him and didn't want to dredge up the memories. "He just changed," she repeated as she shook her head. "I should have never moved in with him."

"You lived with him? And you weren't married?"

"It was a horrible mistake. I should have never moved in with him," she repeated. She meant it, but why all of a sudden did she feel like Samuel thought less of her with this confession?

She prepared herself for a turn in his attitude toward her, but he surprised her. "All of us make mistakes. God forgives us for those mistakes." His tone was gentle and kind.

Lillian shook her head. "He wouldn't forgive me, Samuel. I've made too many mistakes. I try to be a good person and live a good life, but I keep falling down. I've tried so hard not to make the mistakes my mother made. And yet, somehow, I let Rickie creep into my life. He wasn't good for me."

Samuel tilted his head to one side; she felt as though he was staring right through her. "Of course God would forgive you, Lillian. All you have to do is ask Him. The important thing is to get up when you fall down, and it sounds like you have."

"You make it sound so easy, Samuel."

In an unexpected gesture, he reached over and briefly patted her hand. "Maybe you should try it."

Something was going on inside her. Something she couldn't get a grasp on. All this talk about God and forgiveness stirred emotions inside that she wasn't familiar with. Grandma and Samuel—both so solid in their faith . . . Maybe there was something to it all.

Suddenly she felt cheated out of whatever insight they both seemed to have.

"I can't help but wonder how different my life might have been if Mom had just stayed and raised me here." Would she be privy to the same strong faith Samuel and Grandma had? She cringed at the thought of some of the situations she and her mother had endured over the years.

"Do you know why your *mamm* left?"

"No, I don't. Mom won't talk about it, and I don't think Grandma and Grandpa really know. I guess I'm looking for answers in several areas."

"Where's your father?" He balanced both elbows on his knees and leaned forward. Facing him, she did the same—putting their faces about a foot away from each other. As darkness closed in around them, she could see Samuel's features illuminated with interest.

"I don't know." This was another painful subject. Somehow they'd gone offtrack in an effort to keep things upbeat.

"We don't have to talk about this," he said softly, as if sensing it caused her discomfort.

"It's okay. I don't know where my father is because I don't know *who* my father is. Mom said she doesn't know. But she's lying. She does this thing with her eyes and nose when she's lying." She blinked repeatedly and crinkled her nose, to show him. "Like that."

He smiled broadly, amused by her imitation, which lightened the mood.

"I know. It looks funny. But I'm telling you, that's how I can tell she's lying. I can recognize a lie immediately. I've heard plenty over the years."

"It sounds like you had a hard childhood."

"Let's just say my mother wouldn't have received the Mother-of-the-Year award."

His bewildered gaze made her wonder if talking so intimately with him was a mistake. She'd probably shared too much about Rickie. And she'd barely touched on that painful part of her past. He probably had the perfect childhood. Great parents. A wonderful family. She, on the other hand, didn't know who her father was, had duplicated her mother's legacy by living with a man she wasn't married to, and wasn't even sure she believed in God.

"Parenting is a hard job." He pushed back his windblown

bangs and wiped his forehead. "So, if you weren't really *in lieb* with Rickie, have you ever been truly *in lieb*?"

Samuel had a way of changing the subject when he felt it was time to move on. Where was he going with all this? And if they were just going to be friends . . . why was he so interested? "No, I don't think I have," she said, realizing it was heartbreakingly true. She looked at the ground.

"It's a *wunderbaar* thing to be *in lieb*," he said.

She looked up at him. He looked as if he were a million miles away, presumably with thoughts of Rachel. She couldn't imagine losing someone so dear. Placing her hand atop his just felt very natural.

———❦———

Samuel knew he was in dangerous territory. Somehow his plan to keep the visit brief and be on his way hadn't panned out the way he intended. But the feel of her soft hand resting on his gave him comfort. Her touch ignited senses in him that he had buried along with Rachel. His blossoming friendship with Lillian was confusing. Wonderfully confusing.

Underneath the moonlit sky her face was radiantly aglow, as if the clouds parted solely for her benefit and bathed her in the magic of the night. He tried to put his apprehension at ease and just enjoy the moment. It had been a mighty long time since he'd felt this good. But as he attempted to bask in the present, visions of Rachel began to flash through his mind. How he'd loved her and missed her. The feel of her soft skin. Her passion for life.

Lillian had that same passion.

Scolding himself for comparing the women, he gently pulled

his hand from underneath Lillian's and sat up a little straighter, leaning away from her. Surely God would help him steer clear of such temptation. To hold hands, no matter how calming the effect, wasn't right.

As Samuel pulled his hand away, Lillian worried if perhaps she'd crossed a line she shouldn't have. Cupping her hand over his had been an unplanned expression of mild affection that just happened. She didn't mean anything by it. But she didn't recognize the emotion she was experiencing. It wasn't a physical longing, but a yearning of the heart. Her need to be close to Samuel was overwhelming.

"What are you thinking about?" she asked, fearful her small gesture might have caused him to withdraw. There was so much she wanted to know about him.

He shrugged. "I reckon I was just thinking about a lot of things."

"Rachel?" she asked softly, hoping he would open up to her.

But he shook his head. "Not so much."

His expression said otherwise, but Lillian wasn't going to push it. She decided to change the subject this time. "Are you curious about the outside world? I mean, have you ever been tempted to walk away from all this?"

"I know all about the outside world. During my *rumschpringe* I was allowed to experience the *Englisch* world. I watched television, went to movies, rode in cars with *Englisch* friends, drank beer, and kicked my heels up at the local dance hall." He paused. "You look speechless. And one thing I have learned about you is that you're usually not without somethin' to say."

She looked away, feeling a little embarrassed. "Yes, I tend to talk a lot."

"That's a good thing, though. You have a bubbly spirit."

"Which means I talk a lot."

Samuel reached beside him and retrieved his hat. Placing it atop his head, he stared intently at her. He gave her the strangest look, and Lillian couldn't decipher it.

"Just because I choose this life doesn't mean I don't know what's out there." He swung his arm toward the highway. "I hope you find what you're looking for, Lillian."

Jonas stumbled around the kitchen until he found some leftover butter bread. A slice of bread and some lemonade was in order. Irma Rose would be fit to be tied if she knew he'd made his way down the stairs by himself so soon after taking his pills. But he was hungry, and the poor woman was snoring so loud he didn't have the heart to wake her. The Good Lord had seen fit to give him the cancer, but he knew his wife was plumb worn-out from tending to him all during the night. She shouldn't have to be caring for him during the sleeping hours. Some things he could do for himself. A man should be able to walk down the stairs and get a slice of bread and some lemonade if he wanted them.

As he filled his glass up, he thought he heard voices. The wooden door in the kitchen was open, and he hobbled to the screen door. "Well, well," he whispered as he spotted Lilly and

Samuel out by the barn. "Looking mighty cozy." Jonas sighed. Irma Rose would have a fit about now.

Feeling a little light on his feet, Jonas headed back toward the lemonade pitcher he had left on the table. He topped off his glass and took a big gulp. Having another look outside, he couldn't help but share some of his wife's worry about Samuel and Lilly. They'd have a hard road ahead of them should they start court-ing. Straining to get a better look, he chuckled. If they thought they *weren't* courting, they were fooling themselves.

Knowing Irma Rose might stir and be all wound up he was gone, he finished off the butter bread and put the lemonade back in the refrigerator. Taking a step into the den, he looked up at the stairs. Going up was a mite more challenging than coming down. And it sounded like he had bees in his head. *Buzz, buzz, buzz.* A bothersome noise, getting louder by the second.

He reached for the back of the wooden rocker to steady him-self. Seemed like his legs were turning to jelly, and the bee noise was getting louder and louder. He took another couple of steps. *Just need to get back in bed, that's all.*

As everything went dark, he never felt his lanky body slam onto the wood floor. Nor did he feel it when his head caught the corner of the rocker. And he couldn't feel the rush of blood spill-ing into a pool beneath him.

8

LILLIAN RESPONDED TO SAMUEL'S COMMENT ABOUT FINDING what she was looking for by simply nodding. The tone of his voice indicated he might not be interested in playing much of a role in that process.

As he stood up, presumably to leave, Lillian tried to think of something to say, something that might make him stay. She wasn't sure, but Samuel seemed hesitant to go.

Say something. Anything. He appeared to be waiting for her to come up with a reason for him to linger. But maybe she was reading him wrong.

Before she could come up with anything, a loud noise from inside the house caused them both to redirect their attention.

"What was that?" she asked, turning toward the porch.

Samuel began to move toward the house. Lillian was right behind him. Sensing something was wrong, they both burst into a run, taking two steps at a time up the porch steps. As they moved through the kitchen, Lillian heard her grandma calling her name repeatedly.

"Grandma!" she answered, never slowing her pace behind Samuel as they entered the den.

Grandma was hurriedly making her way down the stairs toward her husband. "Lillian!" she yelled. "Lillian, help!"

The three of them rushed to Grandpa's crumpled figure on the wood floor. Grandma gently lifted his head. Tenderly cradling it in her lap, she brushed back his blood-soaked hair. "Jonas, wake up," she cried. "Oh, Jonas. Oh, Jonas, wake up." She looked up at Lillian and Samuel. "Lillian, he won't wake up. My Jonas won't wake up. Oh, Lillian . . . *do* something."

Lillian was frozen, legs glued to the floor. So much blood. Grandma's agonizing cries echoed through the old house, and Lillian felt like she might pass out. One thought consumed her. *Is Grandpa dead?*

Samuel ripped his shirt from his body before Lillian had time to gather her thoughts. Applying pressure to Grandpa's head, he turned to face her. With a calmness Lillian found incredible, he firmly said, "Lillian, bring me some wet towels and then go get your portable telephone."

"Jonas," Grandma cried. "Please, Jonas. Wake up, my love."

"Now, Lillian!" Samuel yelled, bolting her into action. She retrieved a wad of towels from the kitchen drawer and soaked them with water from the sink. Dropping the towels into Samuel's hands, she looked down at Grandpa. His mouth hung open, and his face was pasty white. He was dead. She just knew it. This couldn't be happening. She was just getting to know him.

"Not yet, God. Not yet," she silently prayed.

"Go get your telephone, Lillian," Samuel said, holding the wet towels against the gaping gash in Grandpa's head. "Hurry."

She bolted up the stairs, continuing to pray. Aloud she repeated, "Please, God, don't let him die. Please, God, don't let him die."

She repeated the prayer all the way back down the stairs, whispering as she neared the threesome. Samuel was holding his hand out for the phone. He grabbed it, fiddled with it, and handed it right back to her.

"I don't know how this works," he said, frustrated. Then he rattled off a number and instructed Lillian to dial it. When it started ringing, she handed it to him.

"Mr. Pierson, this is Samuel Stoltzfus. I'm out at Irma Rose and Jonas's place, and we need some help. Can you bring your car out here? Jonas is hurt, and we need to get to a hospital." He nodded and set the phone down as he turned his attention to Irma Rose. "He's on his way."

Lillian watched the way Samuel calmly handled a crisis. She, on the other hand, was fighting waves of panic, and she still worried she might faint. She sat down on the floor beside Grandma and put her arm around her. The woman's cries softened. But as she rocked back and forth stroking her husband's face with hands covered in blood, Grandma's lips moved in prayer. If ever there was a time to pray, it was now.

Lillian closed her eyes and pleaded with God for her grandfather's life. If there was a God, he wouldn't let her grandpa die.

"What's all the fuss about? Irma Rose, why in the world are you crying?" Jonas reached up and touched his head. Samuel sighed, feeling the relief wash over him. Lillian let go with sobs she must have been stifling the whole time, and Irma Rose looked toward the heavens and whispered softly, "Thank you, Lord."

"I think you gave the ladies a scare, Jonas," Samuel said,

continuing to apply pressure to Jonas's head with the wet towels. "Mr. Pierson is on the way with his car, and we'll get you to the hospital."

Jonas looked around at the three of them before honing in on Irma Rose. "You know I *hate* hospitals, Irma Rose. I'd rather you just fix me up here."

"You silly old man," she blasted. "I can't fix you. You need a doctor." She shook her head in exasperation. "What in the name of the Good Lord made you come down here by yourself?"

Samuel glanced at Lillian, who was still crying. Discreetly he reached for her hand and gave it a quick squeeze.

Jonas was glaring at Irma Rose as if he'd like to rip her head off. "I was hungry!"

"Why didn't you get me from my sleep then?" Irma Rose demanded, patting her eyes.

Ignoring his wife, Jonas looked over at Lillian. "Lilly, why are you crying?"

Lillian wiped her eyes. "You scared us, Grandpa."

Jonas patted her hand. "Thought I was dead, didn't ya?" Then he chuckled.

"That's not funny, Grandpa!" Lillian's tone of voice made it clear she was not amused.

"You scared us all, Jonas," Irma Rose belted out. "From now on, if you get a hankering for a late-night snack, you get me or Lillian."

"*Ya*, I'd have starved to death waiting on one of you."

Samuel tried not to laugh. He glanced at Lillian, who was also fighting a trembly grin. He was glad she'd stopped crying. Always a joker, Jonas was turning a bad situation around, with everyone laughing to keep from crying.

"You were snoring so loud, Irma Rose, the house could've fallen down and you wouldn't have taken a notice." Jonas turned his attention to Lillian. "And our *kinskind* here was busying herself with other things." He looked at Samuel and grinned.

Lillian picked up on the curious stares all around them at the hospital. True, they were all covered in blood, but she heard the occasional whispered, "Oh, look, they're Amish." She supposed it would have been worse if they were somewhere other than Lancaster County, where so many Amish lived.

"Thank you, Mr. Pierson," Samuel said, shaking the man's hand.

Lillian could tell right away the men shared a friendship. So Samuel had friends who weren't Amish. And a good thing too. Mr. Pierson had arrived within minutes of Samuel's phone call, and without his help it would have been difficult to get Grandpa up off the floor.

"I'm glad you called, Samuel. Any time I can help you folks, you let me know." The gray-headed man smiled. "I'm going to go call Mrs. Pierson and let her know everything is all right."

As they waited for Grandpa to get his head stitched up, Lillian looked at Grandma seated nearby. Her head was tilted back, and she appeared to be sleeping. Samuel leaned against the wall, looking as haggard as she felt.

"Thank God he only needs a few stitches and that he's okay otherwise," Lillian said to Samuel as she stood beside him. *Yes, thank God.* She had prayed, and Grandpa had lived. It worked.

When Samuel didn't respond, she asked, "Are you okay?" He didn't look okay.

He took a deep breath and blew it out slowly. "I haven't been here since Rachel died."

Instinctively, she reached for his hand. And as her fingers brushed against the top of his hand . . . he pulled away. And it stung.

Samuel recognized Ms. Morgan behind the desk. The nurse had stayed with him and Rachel right up until the end. For weeks, the woman had tended to Rachel's every need. Samuel hoped she wouldn't recognize him.

He scooted slightly away from Lillian. He should have never squeezed her hand when they were on the floor tending to Jonas. She had just looked so sad and scared at the time, and it was nothing more than a comforting gesture. But he needn't have her thinking his action was an open invitation for affection—particularly *public* affection.

Glancing at Lillian, he feared his deliberate action had hurt her feelings. She'd been through enough on this night. He didn't want to add to her upset, but this touching of the hands needed to stop. It wasn't proper, and it roused feelings in Samuel he shouldn't be having. Especially right now, only a little ways from where he'd said good-bye to his beloved Rachel in a small room down the hall.

"Samuel?" The tenderness in her voice warmed his heart and frightened him just the same. "I know it must be hard for you to be here. If you need to leave . . ."

He wasted no time accepting an excuse to leave before he said or did something he'd regret.

"I'm glad Jonas is going to be okay," he said abruptly. "Tell

Mr. Pierson I needed to head on home. I'll take a taxi cab. He'll wait for you all and take you home." His emotions were flailing and he needed out of there.

"Okay," she said. "I don't know what we would have done if you hadn't been there, Samuel. Thank you so much."

Samuel nodded and took a step away from her and toward the exit door. He'd almost made a clean getaway when he heard her call his name.

"*Ya*," he answered, turning reluctantly.

"Maybe you'd like to come over for supper tomorrow night? You and David." She paused when he didn't answer. "As a repayment of sorts for all you did tonight." She smiled as warmly as he'd ever seen.

He looked at her a moment, then shook his head sharply. "*Danki*, Lillian, but I can't." The woman was frustrating him, confusing him, and he was irritated with himself for allowing her to do so.

Her pleading green eyes made it mighty hard to walk away. But he did.

Irma Rose might close her eyes from time to time but seldom her ears. As Lillian plopped down beside her in the waiting room, she opened her eyes and looked at her granddaughter. She had heard the sharpness in Samuel's tone when he declined the supper invitation, and it saddened her to see her granddaughter unhappy. But it was bound to happen. Samuel was content with his world, willingly locked into his life among the Plain folk, and he was a smart enough man to recognize what was happening between the two of them. Probably best he put an end to anything before it got started. It would be more painful for both of them down the road if he didn't.

"It takes a strong man to walk away from something he might want but knows isn't right by God."

Lillian tucked her head in embarrassment, "You heard?"

Irma Rose patted her leg. "I did."

"It was just an invitation for a meal. But the way he spoke to me was rather harsh."

As Irma Rose suspected, her granddaughter was hurt. "Be true to yourself, Lillian. There's a spark between you and that Samuel, and it has nowhere to turn but into flames. And if it had continued, you'd both have been burned far worse than you are now."

"It's not what you're thinking, Grandma. We talked about it. We were just going to be friends."

"*Ya*, so you say. But I saw him squeeze your hand at home when we were tending to Jonas. And I saw you reach for his hand a few minutes ago." Wondering if she'd already said too much, she went on. "Has he kissed you yet?"

"Grandma! Of course not."

Lillian's incredulous look screamed guilt. If they hadn't kissed, she imagined it wasn't for lack of wanting on Lillian's part.

"Lillian, we might be Plain and not know much about worldly things, but we love and we have desires, just like the rest of the world." She could only assume her granddaughter was no longer pure. Living out in the world, she was bound to have succumbed to things that would be unheard of in their Amish community. There was no judgment. It was just a fact.

"Samuel isn't wise about worldly ways, nor are your *daadi* and me. Temptation to step astray is unheard of in our community. We live by the *Ordnung*."

Lillian's face took on a flush, and her eyes filled with tears. Irma Rose regretted instantly that she'd clearly said something to hurt the girl's feelings. "Lillian, I just meant—"

But her granddaughter interrupted her. "You think I'm *seducing* Samuel. You think I'm filled with impure thoughts and tempting him to go against his beliefs!"

"That is not what I said, Lillian. What I meant was—"

"Grandma, you really don't know me at all. I'm nothing like my mother." And with that the child stormed off, leaving Irma Rose with a heavy heart.

Irma Rose knew Lillian spoke the truth. She *had* been fearful Lillian would pull Samuel into her world, in every way. Apparently she'd been wrong.

After four days of not seeing Samuel and barely speaking to her grandma, Lillian decided it was time to make amends with everyone. Grandma had tried repeatedly to apologize for anything she might have said to hurt her feelings, but Lillian had made little effort to recognize her attempts. She and Grandma had continued on with their daily chores, often side by side, but the tension was thick. Samuel had come to the door asking about her the day before, and she refused to come downstairs.

Today was a new day, and she was going to start fresh.

"Grandma," she said as she walked into the kitchen early that

morning. "I told you I'd make breakfast. Sit down and I'll do it."
She gently pried the spoon from Grandma's hand and began to
stir the eggs.

"You haven't had much to say to me, Lillian. I'm feeling badly
about things," Grandma said. She sat down on the bench at the
kitchen table.

"I'm sorry. I got my feelings hurt, and I should have talked
things out with you."

"I am sorry, Lillian. For me to presume that by living out in
the world you had not made good choices was wrong of me."
Lillian turned around to see her grandma shaking her head.

"Oh, I've made bad choices, Grandma. Make no mistake. But
I've tried to avoid some of the same blunders I watched my
mother make over the years." She had to accept responsibility for
her bad judgment when it came to Rickie. But she planned to
better her life by learning from the experience, as opposed to
reliving the pattern via a repetitious string of men who were
wrongly suited for her—as Mom did.

Grandma seemed to be in deep thought, a place she retreated
to anytime there was mention of her mother.

"I want to study the *Ordnung*. I want to learn everything about
living Amish. Maybe it would help me to get my mind right."

"Lillian," her grandma began, then paused. "Nothing would
please me more. Please don't take offense by what I am about to
say . . ." She hesitated again.

"What, Grandma?" Lillian stopped stirring the eggs and
turned completely around.

"Just do it for the right reasons."

"You mean not for Samuel, but for myself?"

"*Ya.*"

"I am. And I'm going to talk to Samuel and set things right with him as well. I want him to know I'm not interested in anything more than friendship with him and that there is no reason why we can't get back on track with that." And she meant it. She'd had a few days to realize that she needed to realign her proiorities. Lancaster County represented a new beginning. She wanted to get back to making the right choices.

"Well, hello there," she said to David later that afternoon. "Hey, where've you been?" he asked. His tone indicated his feelings might be hurt.

"I've just been thinking about things," she said as she followed him to the barn. "Whatcha doin'?"

He was carrying a cardboard box with a lid on it. "These are old newspapers I found in the other barn. They were getting wet, though, so I was moving 'em in here."

"Are there any more? Want some help?" She eyed the box, thinking maybe she'd catch up on the history of Lancaster County when she had some spare time.

"That was the last box. There were three of them." He pointed at two other boxes stacked nearby. "This barn stays dry. The other one has a few leaks. Pop says we'll fix those one day for Jonas and Irma Rose."

"Speaking of your pop, here he comes." She watched as Samuel maneuvered Pete onto the dirt driveway. "David," she said hesitantly. "Do you think it would be all right if I talked to your pop alone for a minute?"

"I think if it will make him stop being so sad, then *ya*." David shrugged and turned to walk off.

"David, wait," she said, realizing things didn't seem the same between them. He turned around and faced her, and the look on his face confirmed her suspicions. "Things are just complicated sometimes, you know?"

He seemed to be thinking as he glanced up to see his pop getting nearer. "I reckon sometimes grown-ups make things complicated that needn't be."

"*Ya*," she whispered as he walked off. "You're probably right."

Samuel was glad to see Lillian waiting for him in the front yard. He smiled with newfound confidence as he approached her. He had done a lot of soul-searching and prayed for answers over the past four days. He was creating problems that need not be there and worrying about things he shouldn't. They'd discussed the terms of their friendship, and there was no reason they had to stray from that. Being attracted to Lillian didn't mean he had to act on it.

"Hello, Samuel," she said as he walked to where she was sitting in the grass.

"I tried to talk to you yesterday. I feel badly about speaking so harshly to you when I left the hospital." He sat down in the grass beside her.

"I think I understand, and there are some things I want to clear up." She paused, then started to wave her hand in front of her nose.

"What?" he asked as she edged away from him.

"You smell like you've been rolling in manure, Samuel

Stoltzfus." She crinkled her nose as he sniffed at himself, feeling highly embarrassed.

"I came straight from the fields spreading manure, and the wheels from the plow probably slung some my way." He went to stand up, but she put a hand on his arm.

"No, sit down. I can take it." She giggled, but quickly removed her hand. "I just wanted to tell you that I think maybe you have the wrong impression about something, and I want you to understand that—"

"No, Lillian. Me first," he interrupted. "My chores aren't the whole truth as to why I said I couldn't come to supper. I've been worried that maybe you and me were moving in a direction that might not be right in God's eyes. But I've prayed hard about it, and I think maybe it's still His will for us to be friends." There. He'd said it. Now, with the Good Lord's help, he'd live the life God meant him to live and be the man he knew he should be.

"That's exactly what I wanted to tell you."

Samuel sighed with relief.

"Only, I have one more thing to tell you. I'm going to be studying the *Ordnung*. Grandma is planning to teach me everything about the Amish faith. And I just want to make it clear to you that I'm doing this for *me*, no other reason. I seem to have gotten sidetracked from my original plan when I came to Lancaster County: to find a sense of who I am and my role on this earth. I don't understand about God, or having a relationship with Him. But I *want* to understand. And I prayed to God to let Grandpa live. And it worked."

It worked? She wasn't exactly fully on the road to becoming Amish, but she at least had a foot on the path. So instead of arguing that her motivation for prayer was still misdirected, he said, "I think that's a fine idea." Studying the *Ordnung* would be good for Lillian. And they seemed to be clearing the air about some things.

"What's your pop and my Lilly have their heads together about?" Jonas asked David as he took a seat in the other rocker on the front porch.

"Not sure," David said.

Jonas strained to have a better look. Lilly had been moping around ever since they came home from the hospital. He didn't know what had happened, but he was hoping they'd fix whatever it was.

"I brought you boys some sweet tea," Irma Rose said, walking onto the porch toting two glasses. She looked out toward Lillian and Samuel. "Nice to see them talking again," she said as David attempted to get up and give her his seat. "Keep your seat," she said, smiling. "I can see better standing up."

"Pop's seemed kinda down lately," David said.

"Well, our Lilly has been in a *baremlich* mood too." Jonas shook his head.

"Definitely not herself lately." Irma Rose sat down on the porch step.

"They'll both be better now," David said. "They just have to get things uncomplicated."

"What do you mean, David?" Jonas asked him, curious where the boy's mind was.

"Lillian said her world was complicated. And by coming here, she's complicated my pop's world. She didn't mean to. It just happened." The boy shook his head and frowned. "They're both just making things complicated for themselves, and they needn't be. It's all real clear to me."

"What's clear?" Irma Rose asked.

The boy took a sip of his tea and said proudly, "She's my new *mamm*. Her and Pop just haven't figured it out yet."

Jonas knew his eyes were bugging out of his head. But he also knew a person wouldn't have to look far to find eyes gaping even larger than his own. You could've mistaken Irma Rose for an owl. She sat motionless, eyes bulging, speechless.

"Take a deep breath, Irma Rose," Jonas said, hoping his wife wouldn't say too much to the boy. He had to agree with David. Samuel and Lilly were making things too complicated. One day at a time. Once Lilly completed her studies of the *Ordnung*, there was no telling what the Good Lord might have in mind for them. But if they took to courting, it would be a long road to travel. He hoped they both survived the trip in one piece. He hoped Irma Rose would survive it. The woman was looking a tad pale.

"Well, David, stranger things have happened. I'm sure God will guide both your pop and our Lilly in the right direction," Jonas said as he reached over and patted poor Irma Rose on the hand.

David smiled. "He already has."

9

"WHAT DO YOU MEAN THERE IS NO EQUALITY OF THE sexes?" Lillian asked Grandma the next morning as they began to tackle the *Ordnung*.

"It's very clear in the Bible, Lillian." Grandma dried another plate and handed it to Lillian to put in the cabinet.

"It actually says in the Bible that women are to be subservient to men?"

Grandma looked confused, and Lillian realized she didn't understand the question. "The women serve the men, so to speak?" she translated.

"'He is the image and glory of God: but the woman is the glory of the man,'" Grandma said with pride. "'For the man is not of the woman: but the woman of the man. Neither was the man created for the woman; but the woman for the man.'"

Lillian sat down at the kitchen table, pondering the biblical reference. "I might have some trouble with this one, Grandma. Relationships should be an equal partnership." She shook her head. "I've noticed the way the Amish women always sit in the back, eat last, and wait on the men hand and foot."

"We are proud to do so. We don't question the Bible." Grandma placed another plate in the cabinet and took a seat at the kitchen table across from Lillian. "It is our job to care for our husbands, the children, and the home."

"I understand that, and that part is fine. But to say there is no equality just doesn't seem right."

"The man is the ruler of the home."

Lillian chuckled. "Now Grandma, you seem to have a pretty strong thumb on Grandpa."

Playfully Grandma said, "*Ya*, but Grandpa doesn't know that." She paused. "But in our early years, things were different. And I'm still proud to do for your Grandpa, even in his silliness."

"When I get married, my husband is going to have a clear understanding that we are entering into a union as *equals*."

"*Ya*, as long as you don't marry an Amish man," Grandma said, tilting her chin upward. "To marry an Amish man, you would say in your vows that the man is the head of the household and that you are his helpmate."

"Who made this rule?"

Grandma seemed taken aback. "Why, God, of course. We don't question the Bible, Lillian. Let's move along."

Lillian was still wrestling with the literal interpretation of this particular Bible reference when Grandma continued, "The two most important things to understand are our rejection of *hochmut*, which is pride and arrogance, and that we are not forward, self-promoting, or assertive. We let things be."

Grandma folded her hands together and sat up a little straighter. "For example," she pressed on. "It is perfectly fine for us to ride in automobiles. But to own such a means of transportation would be arrogant and prideful. There are so many different kinds of cars. All the choices of price, color, and accessories could cause us to be competitive—which would be a breeding ground for arrogance and pride. We have to watch our young folks when they go through their *rumschpringe*. Many times they add radios in the buggies or opt to install flashy trinkets, which distinguishes one from the other. That is not acceptable in our way of life."

"Okay," Lillian answered softly, realizing Grandma was enjoying her role as teacher. However, this topic was clearly nonnegotiable.

"And when I say we let things be," she added, "that means we accept all things as being God's will. The *Englisch* often mistake our passiveness as not caring. That's not true. We do care. But we believe God will resolve a situation in a way that's best for all concerned."

As if checking items off on a mental list of things to teach Lillian, Grandma continued. "Our children become adults when they are baptized and make a lifetime vow of obedience to the *Ordnung*."

"How is the *Ordnung* different from the Bible?" Lillian didn't know a lot about the Bible. But at least the Bible was a book that could be studied. So much of the *Ordnung* was unwritten.

"Let me see how I can explain this so you will understand," Grandma pondered, pausing. "You really can't compare the *Ordnung* to the Bible, Lillian. We believe in literal interpretation of the Bible. Meaning we don't question it. That belief is part of the *Ordnung*, which is our governing system. The *Ordnung* is a means of making sure we all live by the Scriptures in the Bible."

"Shouldn't all the rules be written down for people to study and to prevent misinterpretations?" *You'd think over the many years someone would have done that.*

"The *Ordnung* varies from district to district. Governance is local."

"So why aren't the rules for the *Ordnung* in this district written down and studied?" Lillian had spent the better part of her life studying written texts, all the way through college. She'd made a career out of teaching others to do the same.

"We just know them," Grandma answered. "We begin learning the order of conduct in the *Ordnung* at a young age. It's passed down from generation to generation."

Seeing there was no hope for a written study guide, a practical question popped into Lillian's head. She knew the rule but hoped it could be bent. "Grandma, I don't understand why we can't cut our hair. It seems to me that as busy as we are, it would be a lot easier to manage, and—"

Grandma vigorously shook her head; it appeared that there was no questioning this rule. "No, no, no, Lillian. 'But if a woman have long hair, it is a glory to her: for her hair is given her for a covering.' This is in Corinthians, Lillian. We do not cut our hair."

Grandma abruptly jumped up. "I have something for you, Lillian. Wait here."

It was a couple of minutes before she returned from upstairs. Rejoining Lillian at the table, she handed her a black book. "Is this for me to keep?" Lillian asked. She'd never owned a Bible.

"It is. And you'll notice an inscription inside from me and your grandpa." Bouncing back in time, she said, "I bought it when you were born."

Lillian read the inscription: *This Holy Bible presented to Lillian Miller by Mammi and Daadi.*

"I've dreamed about this day." Grandma's eyes grew moist. "I'd hoped that maybe someday you'd come callin' for the Lord. I'd meant to give it to you when you were here last. You were young, but I meant to send it after you left." She shook her head. "And I forgot."

"Thank you, Grandma." Holding the book gave Lillian an unfamiliar sense of hope.

"You seem to need words to study," Grandma offered. "Study the Bible, Lillian. It is the contents of this book that we live by. To understand the *Ordnung*, you must first understand God's Word."

"I will, Grandma." She blinked back her own emotions.

The lesson continued for the rest of the morning while they baked extra loaves of bread for a sick friend of Grandma's. With a full plate of her own, Grandma never complained and always volunteered to help those around her.

For the next several weeks, Samuel and David ate supper once a week with Lillian, Irma Rose, and sometimes Jonas, when he was well enough. Lillian always cooked, and much of the menu came from Samuel's garden. It was the highlight of Lillian's week. Finally, she had a family. A *real* family. David and Samuel had become as much a part of her little group as Jonas and Irma Rose.

"How are your studies of the *Ordnung* coming along?" Samuel asked one evening after supper.

Lillian handed him and David each a piece of shoofly pie. "It's a lot to learn, but I'm getting there. It's hard because so much of the *Ordnung* isn't written down. Everyone here starts learning at such a young age and I guess it just sticks. I'm trying to absorb and store all the information as best I can."

She thought it best not to mention her constant questioning of their ways. Grandma spent much of their morning sessions exasperated by Lillian's inability to just accept complete obedience to God's will without all the questions. But with strained patience, Grandma continued to instruct her daily about the code of conduct they all lived by. She realized how hopeful Grandma was that she'd choose their ways.

"She's a fast learner," Grandma said, placing a piece of pie on a plate. "I'm going to take this upstairs to Jonas."

After waiting until Grandma was out of earshot, Samuel asked, "How is Jonas? I noticed he hasn't been at supper the past two weeks."

"I don't think he's doing so well," she said, taking a seat on the bench beside David and across from Samuel. "He's been in bed a lot during the day too. It's hard on Grandma. I've offered to help her with Grandpa, but she insists on taking care of him all by herself."

"Men are funny about things. Maybe Jonas wouldn't be comfortable with you tending to him," Samuel said.

"Well, he's going to have to get over that, or I'm afraid Grandma's going to just wear herself out."

"*Ya*, it's hard when you're a caregiver."

"You took real good care of my *mamm*," David said to Samuel.

"I did the best I could."

Samuel often looked uncomfortable at the mention of Rachel. Lillian sure wanted to know what the woman looked like and more about her. But she'd never know. Samuel offered up little information about Rachel and she'd learned the second commandment forbid photos: *Thou shalt not make unto thee any graven image, or any likeness of any thing that is in heaven above, or that is in the earth beneath, or that is in the water under the earth.*

She had been studying. And putting on her Amish attire had become as natural as brushing her teeth in the morning. But to go without *any* pictures the rest of your life . . . That particular rule, like several others, seemed to take things too literally. But literal interpretation of the Bible was the Amish way. There was no picking and choosing of the rules.

"It must be hard not to have any pictures to remember her by," she said, resting her chin in her hands. She glanced back and forth between Samuel and David. "I don't like that rule."

"I remember exactly what she looked like," Samuel said softly and in a tone she seldom heard him use. He seemed a million miles away with thoughts of Rachel.

Lillian's stomach twisted. For all her honest efforts to keep a healthy distance from Samuel, the thought of him having loved someone *that* much bothered her immensely.

"*Ya*, me too," David said, lost in the same world as Samuel.

"But wouldn't it be nice to have a picture of her?"

Both of them looked at her like she was crazy.

"We have a picture of her," Samuel said. He pointed to his head.

"It's not the same." She shook her head and paused. "When I have children, I want to have pictures of them growing up."

"It's not our way, Lillian," Samuel said, as if there was no room for further discussion.

"Do you want *kinner?*" David asked with a keen interest.

"Lots of them." She loved children. "And I'm going to be a much better mother than my mother." The mention of children caused her to reflect on her students at Northbrook High. She'd regretted having to leave her teaching job.

"I don't think she did such a *baremlich* job," David said.

Lillian nudged her shoulder against his and smiled. "*Danki,* David."

"I think you'll make a fine *mamm*." David glanced at Samuel. "Don't you, Pop?"

Samuel looked uncomfortable. "I'm sure she will," he said.

Lillian found the awkward way he made the remark touching.

She is so good with David.

There was no doubt in Samuel's mind Lillian would be a good mother someday. It was hard for him not to occasionally fantasize about a life with her. With each passing day, he found her more beautiful and more interesting. He'd allowed the occasional fantasy to float around in his head, but he always followed it up with a dose of hard reality. Lillian usually did or said something to remind him of their many differences or brought up one of the Amish "rules" she didn't agree with. She seemed to be going through all the motions by learning the *Ordnung*, attending worship, studying the language, reading the Bible, and following community traditions. It was just a mighty big change for her, and he had serious doubts she'd choose a life in their world. Her ideas about pictures were a good example.

"Why did your *mamm* leave here?" David asked.

"David!" Samuel said, reprimanding the boy. "That's *schnup-pich*." He knew it was a painful subject for Lillian.

"No, it's not snoopy," she said, pausing. "I don't know why she left. I think something happened, though. Something *big* that no one wants to talk about."

"Like what?" David pushed.

"David," Samuel warned. The boy should have no interest in such things. Plus, the look on Lillian's face told him that her bubbly spirit was taking a nosedive.

"I don't know." Her lips folded into a frown. But, in a forced effort, she sat up a little straighter and smiled. "And I'm starting not to care. She made her choices, and I'm making mine."

Her statement was strong, but Samuel knew it wasn't true. She cared a lot.

Lillian walked Samuel and David to the buggy, as had become the norm each time they came for supper. David always needed to go back into the house for something—either to go to the bathroom or because he'd forgotten his hat or needed a drink of water. It was always something, and he wasn't fooling anyone. Lillian could see right through his forgetfulness and last-minute potty breaks. His intent was for her and Samuel to spend a few minutes alone. And she had to admit: it was a welcomed gesture on young David's part.

This night in particular, David stayed gone longer than usual. Maybe it was the full moon, or maybe it was the way Samuel was looking at her, but Lillian's heart was bursting with emotion.

Despite their initial attraction, they'd pushed impure thoughts aside and a special friendship was blossoming. She was just about to tell him how much she enjoyed their weekly suppers when he hit her with a piece of news.

"I know staying for supper has become a regular thing on Wednesdays," he said, sounding hesitant to continue. "But next week David and I will be eating supper elsewhere." His gaze shifted from her to David, who was slowly making his way back to the buggy.

She was disappointed, but tried not to sound as let down as she felt. "All right," she said, and then added, "But you know you're always welcome to change your mind."

"Change his mind about what?" David asked as he walked into earshot.

Samuel crawled in the buggy and shut the door, motioning for David to do the same thing. "I was just telling Lillian how we wouldn't be havin' supper here next week."

David let out a big sigh. "*Ya*, we have to have supper with Sadie Fisher." He shook his head in obvious disappointment, but Lillian doubted his unhappiness equaled her own sense of displeasure.

No wonder Samuel hurried into the safe haven of his buggy; probably afraid of her reaction. The thought of him having supper with anyone other than her—much less Sadie Fisher—was a hard blow. But she kept her thoughts to herself. She and Samuel weren't courting. How could she justify such jealous thoughts?

"It's even worse we have to go on a picnic with her the next Saturday," David said as he frowned and continued to shake his head.

"What? A picnic?" she asked, foregoing her plan to keep her thoughts to herself. "How cozy," she added sarcastically, shooting a look of disapproval at Samuel.

"She kept asking to cook for me and the boy," Samuel said defensively, "so I finally accepted her kindness." He shrugged, signifying he owed her no further explanation.

Kindness? There was nothing *kind* about it. She bit her tongue so hard it hurt. When she didn't respond, Samuel added fuel to the fire.

"The elders think I should at least give courtin' Sadie a try. So she's cooking supper for me and David next week. And we're going on a picnic the following Saturday."

"*Courting?* You're going to court her?" Her tone was demanding and laced with angry bewilderment.

"I don't know, I just . . ." He paused briefly, but his tone firmed up. "*Ya,* I am." As he sat up a little straighter, his look challenged her to argue.

Trying to stare him down, she was having a much harder time controlling her emotions. She knew what that meant: tears were not far behind. "Fine," she said. She turned her back and walked briskly toward the house. "Just *fine.*"

"I told you she'd be real mad, Pop," David said as they headed toward home.

"No need for her to be. We're only friends." Samuel really didn't want to have this conversation with his son. He knew exactly how the boy felt about Lillian. And how David felt about Sadie.

Maybe Sadie wasn't the one for him and David, but Samuel knew he needed to go through the motions, at least.

Whatever it took to keep Lillian from creeping into his dreams at night.

But Lillian's reaction to his news only made him want to be with her that much more. She was as jealous as she could be, and it warmed his heart. And to have such notions made him wonder if he was doing right by Sadie. His intentions were mostly in the right place. But was he really being fair to her? Agreeing to give it a try because the elders thought it was a good match didn't seem the best way to approach a courtship. If he was true to his heart, he'd have to admit that courting Sadie would distract him from the person he really wanted to be with but couldn't have.

Samuel refused to set himself and his boy up for heartbreak if Lillian chose to leave the district.

"I'd rather be havin' supper with Lillian next week," David snapped. "And I sure don't want to go on a picnic with Sadie either!"

Samuel stopped the buggy with a sharp pull on the reins. He turned to face his son, whose face was shriveled into a scowl. "I did not raise you to speak to me in that tone, David." He'd never heard his son use such an angry voice. Yet another reason he needed to put some distance between not only him and Lillian, but *David* and Lillian. The boy was way too attached to her.

Samuel prepared to reprimand the boy even more, but stopped when he saw David's scowl shifting into a look of hopelessness. As his son's eyes clouded with tears, he hadn't the heart to scold him further.

"I miss my *mamm*," he said softly, turning to face Samuel.

"I know."

"And if you court Sadie, I'll miss Lillian." His tone pleaded for Samuel to reconsider his plan.

He gave Pete a flick of the reins and bolted back into a trot down the dark dirt road. How could he tell his son how much he'd miss Lillian, too, and still make him understand that it was best to put some distance between them? He didn't want to send the boy mixed messages.

"Please don't court Sadie, Pop. Please!"

In a tone harsher than Samuel had ever used with the boy, he said, "This talk is over!"

Lillian was glad her grandparents were upstairs asleep. She lit the propane lantern above the kitchen table and rummaged around for a snack. Grabbing some butter bread and a glass of tea, she plopped down on the bench and stuffed herself silly. It was misery eating, she knew. And she didn't care. "I'll just be a big fat Amish woman," she whispered angrily, stuffing another piece of bread in her mouth. It was a flippant statement, and she was glad no one was around to hear it. One thing she'd learned since her arrival was that all the hard work allowed for extra calories. It was a healthy balance.

How could Samuel even think about courting Sadie? She shook her head. It was fine being friends with him as long as it was an exclusive arrangement. Sharing him with the likes of Sadie Fisher was another thing. And this was worse than just breaking their friendship bond. He was actually going to pursue a romantic involvement with Sadie. Courting to the Amish meant a prerequisite to marriage. Surely Samuel was not considering marrying this woman? She shoved another piece of bread in her mouth.

"How's my Lilly?"

She hadn't heard Grandpa come down the stairs. "Grandpa!" she scolded. "You're supposed to get me or Grandma before you come down the stairs by yourself."

He waved her off and took a seat across from her at the kitchen table. "I was hungry."

"Well, you should have gotten Grandma up."

Frowning, he whispered, "She's cranky, Lilly, when she gets woke up." He leaned in and helped himself to a piece of the bread she had piled on a plate. "Hungry?" he asked sarcastically, eyeing the mound before her.

"I'm eating my misery away," she said, stuffing in another piece of the moist buttery bread.

"And what does my Lilly have to be miserable about this fine evening?"

"Samuel is going to court Sadie Fisher," she said around a mouthful.

"*Ya*, I heard there's a rumor about that going 'round town." He shook his head. "And this makes my Lilly feel like she has to eat a loaf of bread?" He shot her a questioning grin.

"I know how things stand with Samuel and me, Grandpa. Really, I do."

"Do you now? Because it sounds to me like you're jealous." His grin transformed into a look of disapproval. "And jealousy is a sin, Lilly."

"I'm not jealous, Grandpa. There's no reason to be. Samuel can certainly court whoever he wants. We share a friendship. Nothing more."

"Who you tryin' to convince, Lilly, me or you?"

"Well, of course I know we're just friends. It's just . . . well, if he's courting Sadie, I won't get to see him and David as much. We're buddies. That's all. Samuel and I agreed it was best to keep it that way."

Grandpa smiled broadly. "My silly little *kinskind*. I may be a Plain man who's been married longer than I remember, but the only two people who don't know you and Samuel are *in lieb* are you and Samuel."

"We're not in love, Grandpa! But we have a special relationship."

Grandpa frowned, as if he knew she was lying. "A courtship with Samuel would be filled with challenges," he said. "But the Lord sometimes makes the good things worth the struggle."

"Well, there's no courtship going on with me. He's courting Sadie."

"Maybe that's for the best, then," he said softly.

"How can it be for the best when—" Stopping abruptly, she knew what she'd almost done.

"When *what*, Lilly?"

She looked down at the half-eaten loaf of bread and sighed. Was she fooling herself by thinking she could remain friends with him? If the thought of him courting Sadie sent her into this much of a tailspin—well, perhaps she *did* have feelings. But no one had to know. "I just got used to having them around. They've become like family."

"*Ya*," her grandpa said as he sat up a little taller and stroked his beard. "They surely have."

It took a couple of days for Lillian to adopt a more mature attitude about the prospect of Samuel and Sadie courting. After a good cry, she concluded that at this point in her life she wasn't worthy of Samuel's affections. It was only right he should seek someone better suited for him and David. So after keeping her nose in the air and ignoring Samuel those first two days, she spent the rest of the week making polite small talk when he arrived to pick up David— if she happened to be outside when he showed up. Funny thing, she always seemed to be outside when he arrived.

But she made it a point to stay in the house when she heard Samuel coming up the drive to pick up David the following Wednesday. As she peeked out the window, her heart was breaking. The thought of Samuel and David spending an evening with Sadie was almost enough to make her run outside and beg them not to go.

The temptation was mounting when she heard her cell phone ringing upstairs. Knowing Grandpa was sleeping, she jetted up the stairs two at a time. Grandma met her at the top of the stairs with a frown. "Sorry," she whispered, offering her grandma a sheepish smile. She'd meant to turn it off and just check messages to save her battery. Charging her battery in town was a hassle, and she knew it irritated Grandma to hear it ringing in the house. Although her mother hadn't called her in weeks—not since she'd called and said she was sending Lillian money. Money that never arrived.

"Hello," she said breathlessly into the phone.

"I miss you."

She sat down on the bed and pushed back her hair. She recognized the voice immediately. "Hi, Rickie."

"Did you hear me, Lillian? I miss you." His humble tone filled her with memories. In the beginning, things had been so good between them. It took a while for him to show his true colors. But he did. More than once.

As if reading her mind, he went on. "There's nothing we can't fix, Lillian. I want you in my life, and I'm willing to do whatever it takes to make things right between us." He paused, then continued when she didn't respond. "It's been weeks, Lillian. I've left you alone like you asked in your letter. And that was really hard. I wanted to call you so much, but I thought if I gave you some time, you'd come around. Come home, Lillian. Please. I promise—"

"Rickie," she interrupted before his tone tempted her to believe him. She knew better. "I've started over in a new place. I have a new life."

"I know," he said. "And I think that's great. Putting some distance between us has made me realize how much I love you. Please, Lillian, come home."

"I *am* home, Rickie." And she realized she meant it. Her feet were firmly planted, and she wasn't going anywhere.

"Then I'll come to you. I'll get on a plane tomorrow. Your mom said you're in Lancaster County with your grandparents."

She'd specifically told her mother she didn't want Rickie to know where she was going. *How could she do that?* "No, Rickie!"

"Just for a short visit," he pushed on. "We just need some time together to sort this out."

Rickie was a born salesman. He might sell expensive cars for a living, but he wasn't about to sell her his story that he was a changed man. "No," she repeated.

An uncomfortable silence brewed, and Lillian said, "Rickie, I need to go."

"Is there someone else?"

She didn't say anything.

"Oh, I see," he said after a while.

"There's no one else, Rickie. But I've changed my life."

"I heard. Your mom said you're living with the Amish. Surely you haven't become one of them?"

She would have flown through the phone line if she could have. How dare he say *them* as if they were from another planet? "As a matter of fact, I have," she said firmly. She wasn't sure if this was true, but she hoped it would deter Rickie.

"So you're all into God now?" He sounded disgusted.

Her first instinct was to yell at him, to defend her actions. But . . . *That isn't the Amish way.* As soon as the thought registered in her mind, she realized it stemmed from the hours of time she'd spent with Grandma studying the *Ordnung.* She had a long way to go, but some of it was sinking in. The way she might have handled Rickie in the past no longer seemed appropriate.

"I'm learning to live a different life, a better life. I think the way to do that might be through God."

She could hear him yelling at her choice of lifestyle, but it became fainter and fainter as she realized the implications of what she just said, and the fact that she *meant* it. She *was* giving God a shot . . . for the first time in her life. Trusting that He was there.

"Good-bye, Rickie," she said softly, and she hung up the phone.

When she returned downstairs, she gazed out the window in the den. Samuel and David were gone, and Sadie would be cooking for *her* family tonight. A combination of bitterness and despair crept through her like a virus, targeting her heart and landing in the pit of her stomach. She'd grown to love Samuel and David, and with that love came a new sense of unselfishness unfamiliar to her. How could she deny Samuel and David a life with someone who might be better for them?

"I'm trying, God. I'm trying to have faith. I'm trying to live a good life. Please help me to trust that You will provide what's best for me," she whispered, "and for Samuel and David."

She felt a hand on her shoulder.

"Grandma, I didn't hear you come downstairs. Is everything okay?" She was embarrassed that Grandma might have heard her praying. She wasn't entirely comfortable with her evolving relationship with God.

"*Ya*, Jonas is sleeping soundly," Grandma said, sighing. "He isn't feeling well."

Her gray hair was bound tightly in a bun on her head. Deep wrinkles spiderwebbed from the corners of her eyes and trailed downward, burrowing into sunken pale cheeks. The circles under her eyes were more prevalent than usual, and her stance indicated sheer exhaustion might cause her to surrender to gravity at any minute.

"Grandma, you can't go on like this. You have to let me help you with Grandpa." She grabbed her grandmother's elbow and walked her to the nearby rocker. All the while Grandma was shaking her head.

"Why not?" Lillian asked.

"Your *daadi* is a proud man, Lillian. Sometimes he gets down in a bad way. He wouldn't want his Lilly to see him like that." She kept shaking her head.

"Irma Rose!"

Grandma jumped when she heard him calling, but Lillian gently grabbed her shoulders. "Grandma, let me go to him. I can handle it. You have got to get some rest."

She watched her Grandma eyeing the staircase as if it were Mount Everest. "But he might need—"

"Whatever it is, I will handle it. Go have a snack or something. I'll take care of Grandpa."

Before Grandma could refuse, she headed for the staircase. Halfway up the stairs he cried out again. But it wasn't Grandma's name or Lillian's name he was calling. Lillian froze in her tracks on the staircase, her legs trembling.

10

FORCING HER FEET TO MANEUVER UP THE STAIRS, LILLIAN eased into her grandparents' bedroom, dimly illuminated by one small lantern on a nightstand by the bed. On a wooden hutch across the room there were at least a dozen pill bottles, a pitcher of water, a glass, and a Bible. Grandpa was tucked under a brown-and-red quilt, his eyes closed. His thinning gray hair was tousled and flattened against a feather pillow, and his breathing was labored, his mouth opened wide.

Taking a seat on the wooden chair beside the bed, she said, "Hi, Grandpa." She reached over and touched his arm.

Twitching his pale face, he slowly opened his eyes and smiled. "Sarah Jane," he said softly. She'd hoped maybe she heard him wrong when she was walking up the staircase.

"Grandpa, it's Lilly," she said. She gently squeezed his arm and leaned in closer to make sure he could see her clearly.

"I've missed you," he said tenderly.

"I saw you at breakfast this morning, Grandpa."

"*Ya, ya,*" he whispered. "Is the pond frozen up? Reckon we'll have to shine your skates up."

"Grandpa, it's summertime," she said hesitantly, resisting the urge to cry. *What is wrong with him?* He'd been frail since she arrived, but his mind was always sharp as a tack.

He laughed. "I'm a silly old man. I know you're a might too old to be skatin' on the pond." He leaned in close and his eyebrows lowered as he reached over and gently clutched her arm. Gazing hard into her eyes, he said, "You'll be breakin' your *mamm's* heart if you leave us, Sarah Jane. I know something's goin' on with you. Talk to your Pop."

"Grandpa," she whispered, "it's Lilly."

He was looking right through her with a glassy expression. "It's the *Englisch* man, ain't it?"

"What?"

"*Ya.* Your *mamm* ought not know 'bout this, Sarah Jane. But I reckon' I've seen the newspapers you've been stashing in the barn. The *Englisch* man writes of worldly ways, Sarah Jane, things best not learned. And you ought to stay away from him."

Her mind was awhirl, thinking about the boxes David moved into the barn. "What *Englisch* man?" she asked.

Grandpa released his grasp on her arm and pushed back gray bangs that were too long and had fallen forward. Swiping his brow, he frowned and shook his head.

"Grandpa, what *Englisch* man?" she asked again. But, he closed his eyes.

"Grandpa?"

Within seconds, the labored breathing returned, and she realized he was fast asleep. Lillian sat quietly for a few minutes, until she heard footsteps coming up the stairs. She turned to see Grandma entering the room.

"What did he need?" she asked.

"I don't know." Lillian paused. "He thought I was my mother."

Grandma patted her shoulder. "It happens. I reckon it's those pills the doctor gives him." She waved her arm toward the hutch. "Sometimes he thinks I'm *his* mother."

"Does he just snap out of it?" She hoped so.

"*Ya.* He mostly acts up like this right after he takes the pills."

"Oh," she said softly, contemplating whether or not to share the conversation with her grandma. Deciding she wasn't up for such a discussion, she excused herself.

She barely choked down her breakfast the next morning. After cleaning up the kitchen, she told Grandma she was going to the barn to brush Jessie and lavish a little attention on him for a while. Giving her loose strands of hair a final tuck under her white *Kapp,* she asked, "Need me for anything else right now?"

"You go on," Grandma said. "I'm going to take these *dippy eggs* on up to Jonas." She poured a glass of orange juice and toted everything up the stairs.

On the way to the barn, Lillian pondered on what Grandpa had said the night before. Between that and thoughts of Sadie cooking for Samuel and David, she hadn't gotten much sleep.

"Hello, Jessie," she said, prying the barn door open. Giving the horse a quick stroke on the snout, she made her way to the stacked boxes in the corner and heaved the top box down to the dirt floor. In the dim light of early morning, she saw *The Intelligencer Journal, November 2, 1980* folded neatly on top. Lifting the newspaper up, she could see the box was filled with past issues.

Why did Mom save all these? And what Englisch man was Grandpa referring to?

The Intelligencer Journal was a daily publication. But upon further inspection, she noticed they were all thick Sunday editions. *Why only Sunday papers,* she wondered.

The Budget was the choice of newspaper for the Amish in Lancaster County—the national Amish publication coedited by both the Amish and English. Grandma read *The Budget* every Wednesday. Grandma also read *Die Botschaft*—strictly for Old Order Amish—every week. But she'd never seen *The Intelligencer Journal* in the house.

Placing one of Jessie's saddle pads on the dirt floor, she took a seat with the November 2 issue of *The Intelligencer.* She scanned the headline. "U.S. President Jimmy Carter and Ronald Reagan Debate in Cleveland, Ohio."

"Wow," she whispered as she flipped through the pages to the entertainment section. *Star Wars: The Empire Strikes Back* and *Friday the 13th* were movies featured at the theatres. Both movies were made before she was even born. "Sailing" by Christopher Cross was the top record. And everyone wanted to know who shot J. R., evidently from some TV show named *Dallas.* The headline said the November 21 conclusion was expected to draw more viewers than any other show in TV history.

She set the paper aside and retrieved the next issue in the box. *November 9, 1980.* Ronald Reagan won the presidential election in a landslide victory. The NASA space probe Voyager 1 made its closest approach to Saturn and sent the first high-resolution images of the world back to Earth. And people were still talking about who'd shot J.R.

While all this was fascinating, why did her mother save all these papers? Clearly, it had something to do with an *Englisch* man who wrote about worldly events, as Grandpa put it. Continuing to flip through each Sunday edition, she looked for something each issue had in common.

After an hour, she was starting to doubt the newspapers had anything to do with anything. But July 27, 1980, offered up a clue. As she had been doing, she scanned the front page headlines. "Former Turkish Prime Minister Nihat Erim Killed by Two Gunmen in Istanbul, Turkey." And "Pope John Paul II Visits Brazil—Seven People Crushed to Death in Crowd."

No wonder the Amish didn't read the daily papers and stuck with *The Budget* and *Die Botschaft*. Bad news was everywhere.

The most interesting items to her were what movies were showing and the top albums. She scanned the entertainment section and almost closed the paper when something in the columns section caught her eye. Actually, not the column itself, but the inscription beside it. She couldn't be sure, but it looked like her mother's handwriting. *Daniel and Sarah Jane forever.*

She pulled the newspaper closer to her face to get a better look. Daniel Foster looked to be in his late twenties. Maybe thirty. Although it was hard to tell from the black-and-white photo above his column, he looked to be a handsome guy. Sporting clean-cut short hair and a pair of large, gold-rimmed glasses, he smiled above his column, entitled "Outside the Box." She read:

The road to happiness is filled with paths of self-discovery. One slip, and you can end up going down the wrong path with no map to guide you back to the main road. How do we as individuals choose which road will fulfill our destiny with the least amount of challenges? Are we born into a predetermined plan? Is it fate? Or do the choices we make render us capable of creating our own destiny?

These are questions I have pondered. In the end, I believe we create our own destiny. But notwithstanding an occasional trip down the wrong path. The key is realizing when it's the wrong path and having the courage to do a little backtracking until you are back on the road to the life you were meant to live.

Were all his columns this *heavy*? She grabbed the next paper and read:

Dreams are the manifestations of our daily thoughts. Although some dreams might seem like they came out of nowhere, that's not true. We have but one mind, and the thought processes—whether in waking hours or asleep—belong to us exclusively. So the next time you have a bizarre dream that makes no sense, take the time to dissect it. There might be a message in there somewhere.

Lillian tossed the paper aside and went on to the next issue, thinking about her mom reading the columns twenty-eight years ago. Clearly, his message had intrigued Mom.

Religion and spirituality—are they one and the same? I think not. I know people who are religious and who lack a shred of spirituality. Then there are those who never attend church but possess more spirituality than most . . .

She read at least ten more columns. Two of the ten had hearts drawn around them. All thought-provoking in some way, she could see why her mother would have a crush on the guy. But she wasn't naïve and she'd done the math. Her mother would have been eighteen in 1980. Mom left the Amish community in 1981. Lillian was born in 1981. Could this guy be her father?

Her heart was pounding against her chest. Maybe, just maybe, she'd be able to find her father. He was handsome, a good writer, deep, and apparently spiritual.

Her heart raced faster. Finally, after all these years . . . just maybe.

There was only one way to find out.

———

"Hi, Mom," Lillian said. She'd retrieved her cell phone and headed back to the barn without Grandma's knowledge.

"Lillian, what a surprise. Is everything okay?"

"Yeah, everything is fine."

"I know you're probably wondering about the money, Lillian. I had it all ready to put in the mail to you, and I—"

"It doesn't matter, Mom," she interrupted. "I want to talk to you about something else."

"What's that?"

"Who's Daniel Foster?"

The line was silent so long, Lillian wondered if her mother was still on the other end. "Mom?"

"Yes, I'm here."

"I found the newspapers in the barn. I read his columns, and I saw where you wrote—"

"Lillian!" her mother interrupted hastily. "I don't know where you're going with this, but just leave it alone."

Her mom's voice was quivering, and Lillian knew she'd hit the nail on the head. "He's my father, isn't he?" She knew her tone was demanding, but she'd been denied any knowledge about her father because her mother had refused to discuss it, always saying she just didn't know who he was. Lies. All lies. She knew exactly who he was.

"Is *he* why you left Lancaster County? Is he, Mom? I have a right to know who my own father is. It's him, isn't it?" She realized her voice rose to a near yell.

"Lillian. Please let this go." Her mom was crying, but Lillian pushed on. She felt it was her right to know.

"Mother," she said sharply. "You said you never knew who my father was. If you covered this up for all these years . . . That is *so* wrong. You owe me this."

"I was young, Lillian. I was just so young." She was crying full force now.

Lillian softened her tone. "Mom, please. Please tell me. I'm trying so hard to start a new life. I'm trying so hard to find answers and fill the voids. This is part of the process for me. You have wonderful parents. You can't deny me the right to even know who my father is." Her own tears began to flow as she realized she needed to know, but at the same time was afraid to know.

"DNA does not make a person a parent, Lillian."

Confirmation. "Oh, Mom. So Daniel Foster is my father."

"Yes."

Lillian grabbed her chest, sure that her heart was going to leap through her skin. "Why didn't you ever tell me?"

When her mother didn't answer, Lillian went on. "Is that why you left Lancaster County? You were pregnant with me? Why didn't you tell someone? It would have been hard, but I don't think Grandma and Grandpa would have—"

"Shunned me?" her mother interjected with a sharp tone. "No, Lillian. They would not have shunned me in the traditional sense because I wasn't baptized. But I was eighteen years old, and I had premarital sex with an *Englisch* man. Reprimanding by the community would have been equally as harsh as a shunning. I couldn't have stayed. The embarrassment for your grandparents . . . I just couldn't stay. It was best to leave and never say anything."

"All these years, Grandma and Grandpa never understood why you chose to leave the district." She paused. "And what about me, Mom? You let me believe that you didn't know who my father was. How could you do that? How?"

"Lillian," Mom cried, "you don't understand."

"Then explain it to me!"

"I made a horrible mistake and I didn't know what to do. Daniel gave me some money, and I left to start a new life."

"Why couldn't you have started a life with him?"

Mom wept harder. "He wouldn't have me, Lillian. He wanted nothing to do with me or having a baby. Daniel said he would deny the entire thing, that I would be an outcast in my community, and that it would be best for me to leave town."

"And you never saw him again? Did he ever see me? Did he know you had a girl?"

"I never heard from him or saw him again. Please, Lillian. Now you know. Let it go."

"I'm going to find him. He'll want to meet me after all these years. I'll find him, Mom, with or without your help."

Sobs were vibrating through the phone lines. "No, Lillian. It was a long time ago. Please don't do this. I doubt he even still lives near Paradise."

"Mom!" she cried. "That's three miles down the road. I could have bumped into him on the streets in town. How could you not have told me?"

"Lillian, leave it alone."

"Good-bye, Mom."

She hung up the phone, nervous anticipation flooding over her, commingled with fury and sympathy for her mother. As angry as she was with Sarah Jane Miller, hearing her mother relive that painful part of her past pulled at her heartstrings in an unfamiliar way.

Samuel eyeballed a big wooden table outside a shop in Paradise. It wasn't as nice as the one in Intercourse—the one he would buy someday. He wondered if that day would ever come. Lately his visions of the table in his kitchen came with a detailed picture of him and David sitting at the table with several other children—and Lillian cooking supper. It was a notion he couldn't seem to shake.

Telling Sadie the night before that a courtship wasn't going to work had been hard. Extra hard when she started to cry. But carrying on with her when he couldn't shake his feelings for Lillian wasn't fair. Not even the elders could push him into a courtship with someone he didn't think he could ever love. And it wasn't fair to the boy either.

He'd rather hold out hope that maybe Lillian could find her way to the peaceful way of life she was longing for. That maybe she'd find God in her heart. She'd so lovingly accepted him and David into her heart. Why was it so hard for her to accept God's will in her life? It wasn't his way, but maybe he should help her more. After all, she'd had no upbringing that would teach her such things.

It was a difficult situation—compounded by the fact he could list all the reasons Lillian wasn't right for him and David. But the bottom line was she brought out feelings in him he'd only ever had for Rachel. And allowing himself to indulge usually resulted in guilt. Guilt that he shouldn't have such thoughts when Rachel was the love of his life. He still dreamed of her. Only now, not as often. It was both comforting and worrisome when Lillian showed up in his dreams more often than Rachel these days.

As he continued to fantasize about a life with Lillian, he caught a glimpse of her out of the corner of his eye. Was she looking for him? She was sure looking for something. He headed toward her.

She appeared frazzled. Her hair looked like she'd been on another high-speed buggy ride, tousled and dangling about her beautiful face. But something was wrong. Her eyes were swollen and registered an uncharacteristic seriousness.

"Hello," he said as he walked up to her.

"Hi, Samuel," she said with little emotion. He was being punished, which he probably deserved. He'd need to set her straight about Sadie right away.

"What are you looking for?"

She shot him a look that confirmed what he suspected, and didn't answer. Yeah, she was mad all right.

"Are you not speaking to me?" he asked, leaning down.

"Where's Sadie?" she blurted out. "I figured the two of you would be planning your picnic for Saturday."

He grinned. He couldn't help it. She was jealous. And it felt so good. "*Ya*, the picnic," he teased.

"What are you grinning about?" She put her hands on her hips and attempted to stare him down with her big green eyes. Swollen eyes.

"What's wrong?" he said, changing the subject. "I can tell you've been crying."

"Don't worry about it," she said harshly. "I'm fine."

"You don't look fine."

"Well, I am."

"What do you think would be good to take on a picnic?" He was toying with her, and in light of her current mood, he knew he was stepping on thin ice.

"Samuel Stoltzfus, what you and Sadie decide to take on your picnic is of no concern to me." She leaned in and cut him down to the bone with her look.

"You like tuna salad, don't you?"

"Who cares what I like. Go ask Sadie what she likes!" Her tone was getting really mean. Better tell her.

"Why would I ask Sadie what she likes when it's you I'm taking on a picnic on Saturday?" He shot her a wide smile, hoping to cheer her up.

"What?"

"I told Sadie last night after supper that I just wasn't going to be able to court her. It just wasn't right to even try."

Her hands dropped to her side and her look softened, but he still had a sense something was wrong. "Oh," she said softly. "And why's that?"

A loose strand of hair was sweeping across her face. Wanting desperately to push it back into place, wanting an excuse to touch her . . . he did nothing.

"It just didn't feel right."

"But I thought that's what the elders wanted?" she asked, backing away from him somewhat.

"In the end, the elders want me to be happy. I have to make choices that are best for me and David."

She smiled, but not the fullface smile he was used to seeing from her. "Are you asking me to go on a picnic with you and David on Saturday?"

"Nope," he said, playing with her again.

Those hands landed right back on her hips, and she opened her mouth to say something . . . but stopped, straightened her apron, and took a deep breath instead. Samuel thought he better tell her the truth. "I'm asking you to go on a picnic with me. Alone. David will be helping Ivan do some work out at his place."

"Oh," she said softly.

"And me and the boy have more vegetables than we can ever eat. I thought we might bring some for supper tonight, if you think that would be all right."

"That's fine."

She lacked the enthusiasm Samuel hoped for. Not that he expected her to run into his arms for changing his mind about Sadie. But . . . something more than this.

"Lillian, what's wrong?"

She motioned for him to follow her. Away from a group of tourists chatting in the street, she sat down on a wooden bench outside a small Dutch bakery. He took a seat beside her.

"I just found out who my father is," she said, fighting tears.

"And I'm going to find him and meet him. I'm sure he's wondered about me all these years, like I've wondered about him. I think it will help me to put some things behind me, so I can have the life I'm looking for." She paused and looked him hard in the eyes. "And, Samuel, yes, I'm trying to find a place for God in my heart. I have a lot to learn, but I'm working very hard to find my way. Finding my father will fill a void I have in my life."

It was music to his ears that Lillian was working to accept God into her life. And if it would help her to make peace with her father, well he was all for that.

"He lived right here in Paradise. Evidently, he and my mother had a love affair. She became pregnant with me and knew people in the district would look down on her, so she left. I don't know why she couldn't have told me sooner." A tear rolled down her cheek as she shook her head.

His need to comfort her was overwhelming. But he didn't move. Fantasizing about Lillian was a safe secret he could live out in his dreams. The reality of actually touching her, even as innocent as that might be, would imply intentions he was still unsure of.

"That was twenty-eight years ago. He was a young writer who worked for *The Intelligencer Journal.* Who knows where he might be now."

"*Ya,* that's true," he said as he continued to fight the urge to put his arm around her, offer her hand a squeeze . . . something. "So, what's his name?"

She sighed. "I'm still in shock that I have his actual name. And I can sort of put a face to the name, from the picture in his column. It's just all very surreal."

"Do you want me to help you find him?" It wasn't his way to pursue anyone or anything outside the district, but if it would fill the void in Lillian's life and help her to move forward, then he was going to help her.

She sighed, looking down at her hands in her lap. "His name is Daniel Foster."

Samuel tried not to react, but he was stunned. Grimacing, he shifted his position on the bench. How in the world would he tell her that she wasn't going to have to look very far for her father? Not farther than about twenty yards. Samuel could see Daniel Foster's shop from where they were sitting.

11

LILLIAN WAS THINKING ABOUT THE SUPPER THEY'D HAVE later, about their picnic on Saturday, about finding her father, and what her future might hold. Hopeful thoughts were flying around in her head. It seemed odd when Samuel jumped up and began to pace in front of her.

"What's wrong?" she asked. He was nervous as a cat.

"I don't exactly know how to tell you this, Lillian." He paused and sat down beside her again. But the words didn't come.

"Samuel, you're scaring me. What is it?"

"Daniel Foster," he said softly.

"My father. What about him?"

Samuel removed his straw hat and ran his hand through his hair. Placing it back on his head, he began to stroke his beard as if in serious thought. Lillian couldn't help but notice his huge arms underneath the blue shirt and the way his suspenders draped across his solid chest.

"What?" she asked again. "Samuel, what is it?"

"Lillian, stay calm."

"Samuel, you better just tell me whatever's on your mind because you are *really* scaring me!"

"Daniel Foster is standing right over there." He pointed toward their right.

Lillian jumped up and peered in the direction he was pointing. "What?" She sounded confused.

"He owns that shop," he said hesitantly, knowing it would be a blow to her to find she'd walked past her father's shop dozens of times in the past couple of months.

"What?" she asked again, staring down Lincoln Highway.

Samuel stood up and reached for her arm, fearful she might take off running in that direction. That probably wasn't the best plan. He watched Daniel arranging a table full of wares right outside his antique store. "He's the owner of Outside the Box," he told her.

"The name of his column," she whispered. "I've been in that shop." She pulled away and headed toward her father. The closer they got, the faster she moved.

"Wait, Lillian." He grabbed her arm and brought her to a halt. "Have you thought this through?"

She turned briefly to face him. "No, I haven't thought it through. But I've imagined a million times what it would be like to meet my father. I can't wait another minute." She picked up her pace again.

Samuel knew very little about Daniel. Besides exchanging friendly greetings over the years, the only thing he knew about the man was he'd been married for a while but later divorced. As they neared the store, he couldn't help but wonder if Lillian was entering a hornet's nest.

Lillian was bursting with anticipation. Part of her wanted to run into her father's arms and tell him how long she'd waited for this moment. However, about ten feet from the store she stopped. Her mother's words flooded her like a rushing river. *"He wouldn't have me, Lillian. He wanted nothing to do with me or having a baby. Daniel said he would deny the entire thing, that I would be an outcast in my community, and that it would be best for me to leave town."*

That was a long time ago though. Surely he had wondered over the years if he had a daughter or a son. So many times she'd wondered if she had brothers and sisters. So many questions.

"Lillian, this might not be the best time—"

"I'm not waiting. I've waited my whole life." But her feet weren't moving. What would she say? She scanned the table full of antique trinkets and household items on the display table outside the shop. A FOR SALE sign hung in the window. Maybe he was retiring. People bustled by her, seemingly in slow motion.

"Are you sure about this, Lillian?" As Samuel shook his head, clearly indicating *he* wasn't sure about it, she wondered how this moment had crept up on her so quickly. Years of imagining, dreaming. And now, all in one day, she'd discovered who he was and where he was. Swallowing hard, she stood stiffly in place watching the man arrange items on the table outside his shop.

Her father. Standing not ten feet away from her.

It wasn't just her life that would be changing forever, but his too.

Placing her hand on her chest, she took a deep breath. Her heart was beating much too fast. She could faintly hear Samuel—

"Lillian, are you okay?"—but she couldn't peel her eyes from Daniel Foster. Maybe Samuel was right. Maybe she needed to think things through and plan things out.

But she knew she wouldn't. She was going to meet her father. Today. Now. Her lifelong vision would be a reality in a matter of minutes.

Gradually, she uprooted her feet and eased her way forward. She'd only taken a couple of steps when she stopped. Realizing this was the most important moment in her life to date, she sidestepped to the wall of the shop next to Daniel Foster's, leaned against it, and closed her eyes. She could feel Samuel next to her as she attempted to block out the noise of passersby, cars, the clippity-clap of horse hooves, and the conflicting voices rambling around in her head. *Stay. Go.*

God, she prayed silently, pressing her eyes closed even tighter, *I don't know You very well. And it might be wrong of me to ask for Your help right now. But this is so incredibly important to me. Please help me to say the right things and to accept whatever it is that's Your will.*

Her plea for help and guidance sent a flood of emotion running through her. Fighting tears, she went on. *I'm so sorry. I'm just so very sorry for all the things I've messed up in my life. Please help me to do this right.*

It seemed wrong to ask for His help when she'd been absent from Him her entire life. Was it a selfish request? Did He even hear her?

No sooner than the thought registered did she feel a sweeping wave of courage. More profound was an unfamiliar sense of guardianship surrounding her, as if Someone wrapped her in a blanket of protection and love. *Is this You?* she silently asked.

As a tear trickled down her cheek, she allowed herself to feel the glory of prayer. "Thank You," she said as she opened her eyes and wiped the tear from her cheek.

She looked over at Samuel standing by the wall next to her. His eyes were closed. Was he praying for her? She watched him intently, presumably offering up prayers on her behalf. This moment on the busy sidewalk of Lincoln Highway would be with her a long time.

"Are you ready?" he asked, opening his eyes.

"I am."

Side by side, they eased their way toward Daniel Foster.

"Good afternoon," the man she now knew to be her father said. "Can I show you anything in particular?"

"We're just having a look," Samuel said when she didn't respond.

Lillian could see he still resembled the picture. He was a handsome man. His dark hair was now salt and pepper and receding, and he had replaced his gold-rimmed glasses with smaller ones that hung low on his nose. Considerably shorter than Samuel, he still towered over her. He had a friendly smile, and Lillian knew right away that everything was going to be fine.

"I'm Lillian Miller," she said, wondering if the name Miller would ring any bells. Maybe she should have planned this conversation out. Too late. She was there and waiting for any recognition from him.

"I'm Daniel Foster." He extended his hand to her as though she was any new customer wandering up to his shop. "Welcome to Outside the Box."

It had been twenty-seven years and there were tons of Millers. She'd have to be more clear. "My mother is Sarah Jane Miller."

Instantly Daniel took a step backward. His smile faded, and he gave her an odd look she couldn't decipher.

"I, uh . . ." She stumbled. "I . . . think you're my father."

Samuel was stroking his beard and pacing slightly. Daniel just stared at her.

"I'm so happy to finally meet you," she went on. "I've waited my whole life for this moment, and I didn't think I'd ever find you. And, here you are, three miles from where I'm living with my grandparents. It's just so good to meet you." She instinctively stepped toward him.

"What do you want?" His tone was more than abrasive and sent chills up her spine, halting her in her tracks.

"I, uh, don't want anything. Just to know you." She felt Samuel gently touch her arm. It gave her little strength; her knees were buckling with the weight of the moment. "You still look a lot like your picture from the column you wrote years ago. I see you named your store after it." She was rambling. "Maybe we can have a cup of coffee and get to know each other when you have time and—"

"I don't know you. I don't want to know you. Whatever your mother told you is a lie. Sarah Jane Miller has lied to you." He took a step back.

"So you do know my mother, then?" she asked, resisting the urge to cry. "Are you my father?" It was a simple question that she felt deserved an answer.

"I just sold my shop; I'll be moving from here in two weeks. If you try to find me, I'll call the law on you." His face drew into a raging scowl, and his posture became aggressive. He leaned forward as if he might dive for her.

Every wonderful fantasy she'd had about meeting her father was stolen from her in less than a minute. On instinct, she stepped back from him. She wanted to run. To go back. To start over. Resisting the urge to flee, she spoke again.

"Sir, I'm not here to cause you any trouble at all."

"Is it money you want?" His fists were clinched at his sides and he stared her down as if she were threatening his life.

"No!" she said emphatically. "Of course not."

"Lillian, let's go," Samuel gently took her elbow and attempted to guide her away from him.

"Yes, I think you better go," the man said. The man who couldn't *possibly* be her father.

"But, I just . . ." The words weren't coming. The fantasy was over. She now understood why her mother had chosen to avoid even an informal community shunning. She'd never felt more abandoned in her life. A bastard baby, with a father who didn't care if she was alive or dead.

"Lillian, let's go," Samuel said again, pulling her farther away from Daniel.

She yanked free of Samuel's hold. As a tear rolled down her cheek, she walked toward her father. He didn't step back this time. She couldn't read his expression, but she was not going to leave without letting him know how she felt.

"I dreamed about meeting you my entire life. I dreamed about this moment since I was a little girl. In a few short minutes, you have not only denied me my dream of what it would be like to meet you, but you've discarded me as if I were dirt." She stepped closer to him, and this time he did step back. "Well, I'm not dirt. I am a wonderful, vivacious woman. I'm smart. I graduated from high school at the top of my class, and I went to college and became a teacher. I am a fabulous cook. I care deeply about other people." By now she was sobbing almost uncontrollably, and she struggled to form the words so he could understand her. "I'm sorry that you won't have the opportunity to know me."

She paused. His expression softened, and the water forming in the corners of his eyes pushed her to go on. "So go ahead and toss me aside. It's certainly your choice. But I am a good person, and it will be your loss."

And with that, she spun around and ran down the sidewalk.

Samuel kept up with her until she was away from the crowds. When she crossed the highway and headed down Black Horse Road, it appeared she might keep running all the way home. He grabbed her arm. "Lillian, stop," he said. "Did you come in the buggy?"

She pulled free, shook her head and kept on walking until she was a good piece down the road. "Well, I brought my buggy. I have to go back," he yelled. She waved him on and didn't stop. "I'll be back to pick you up."

Fast as he could run, he headed to where he'd parked his buggy and got on his way. A few minutes later, knowing he was going a bit too fast through town, he still gave Pete an extra flick of the reins. It didn't take long to catch up with her.

"Get in," he said, guiding Pete to a stop.

She wouldn't look at him as she crawled into the buggy. It didn't seem like she was going to stop crying any time soon. Maybe he needed to just let her get it all out.

"I'm sorry," he said softly.

She didn't say anything and continued to stare off into the pasture. When he passed Irma Rose and Jonas's farm, she spoke up.

"Where are we going?" She swiped at her eyes.

"To my favorite place."

Samuel hadn't been to the overlook since Rachel died. He used to go there when he wanted to be by himself—just him and God. He'd never taken anyone there. Not even David. Today he was going to take Lillian. She needed all the spiritual guidance she could get right now, and Samuel knew God would be waiting there for her with open arms to comfort her in her time of need. Aside from the incredible view of the valley below, it was where Samuel felt most connected to God.

She'd stopped crying by the time they reached the overlook. He helped her out of the buggy and toward the edge of the cliff. "Don't get too close to the edge," he said as he pulled her to the ground with him. "Let's sit here a while."

For a split second, a hint of happiness swept across her face. "This is the most beautiful place I have ever seen," she said before placing her hands over her face. She started to cry again.

"I'm so sorry, Samuel."

"What do you have to be sorry about?" he asked, turning to face her.

"That I cry a lot."

"I think I heard you say earlier that you care deeply about others," he said. "That's nothing to be sorry about."

"Thank you for being here with me."

As he watched her staring at the ground, fiddling with a

blade of grass, he worried how she was going to handle all this. But one thing he knew for sure. He wouldn't let her handle it alone.

"There's nowhere else I'd rather be," he said.

***

Samuel's words warmed Lillian's heart, and his presence eased her pain somewhat. The meeting with her father had been a setback. A painful, heart-wrenching setback. But now she knew. She'd put it behind her and move forward.

"There's something about this place, Samuel. It's very . . . I don't know. I mean, it's beautiful here, but there's something else. It's very calming. Serene. It's like I feel . . . I feel . . ."

"God?" He asked.

She speculated for a moment. "Yes, I suppose that might be it." She recalled the feeling she'd had while she prayed before meeting her father. She'd had the same feeling then.

"And that's only the beginning. I have my strongest sense of Him here too. But one day you'll take that feeling with you everywhere you go. When that happens, it will become easier for you to accept things as God's will."

"It's hard for me to accept what happened earlier as God's will. I would think God would have preferred things to go differently." She cringed and shook her head as the memory of her father's look and words came flying to the forefront of her mind.

"We don't question God's will."

"That part is hard for me. And I want to, Samuel. I want to accept all things as God's will." She paused. "And I'm working on it."

"I can see that. It'll come, Lillian. Talk to Him. But more important, listen to Him."

"What do you mean? I've said my prayers, but I've never heard a response."

"Are you sure?"

"I've never heard God talking to me." She shook her head, quite sure of that one.

"Ever have a thought or feeling and wonder where it came from? A thought that just seems to come out of nowhere, or a comforting feeling?"

"Sometimes." She recalled again how she'd felt when she prayed before she met her father. Leaning against the storefront wall, she'd felt an overwhelming sense of calm. "Is that God?"

"I believe it is. I think some people are so busy talking to God that they forget to listen too." He bumped his shoulder gently against hers. "I'm sorry about what happened today, Lillian."

He'd changed the subject again, as she had gotten used to. "I'm sorry too," she said. "Sorry for me. Sorry for you. And sorry for my mother."

Wow. It was the first time she'd thought about her mother since all this had happened. For the first time, she saw her mother in a whole new light—as a young Amish woman who got involved with an *Englisch* man, got pregnant, was afraid of becoming an outcast in her community, and decided to venture out into a world she knew nothing about. Maybe there was enough compassion in Lillian's heart to forgive her mother for her childhood.

"Are you gonna be all right?" he asked.

"It's not the storybook reunion I'd hoped for by any stretch of the imagination. But I'll have to put it behind me. Now, at

least, I know. I'm not completely sure how I feel about all of
it, but . . ."

As she and Samuel sat together at the overlook, Lillian trailed
off, trying to push the events with her father out of her mind.
While she knew it would take a long time for her to completely
heal, a new sense of calm and peacefulness seemed to be slowly
seeping into her heart. It was a welcomed feeling. For the next
hour they sat at the overlook. Mostly they were quiet.

"I'm sorry that Sadie cried when you told her you wouldn't be
courting her," David told Samuel on the way to Lillian's that
evening.

"How'd you know she cried?"

"I heard her from upstairs."

"I thought you were sleeping."

"Nope. But Pop, she just wasn't the one. You know that, *ya*?"

Samuel nodded, unclear exactly what he thought these days.
But he knew it wouldn't be right to court Sadie.

"Well I'm glad we're going to Lillian's house for supper. I like
being around Irma Rose and Jonas too."

Nodding again, Samuel wondered if Lillian was feeling any
better. Time healed so many things. Time and God. But it had
only been a few hours. A blow like this would take a long time
for her to get over. He knew all about pain, healing, and the time
it took.

As his thoughts drifted to Rachel, David came out of the
clear blue with a direct question not suitable for a boy to ask
his pop.

"Are you going to marry her?" David's eyes grew wider and wider as he waited for a response.

"Not right for you to be asking me that, boy."

"But it could happen?"

Samuel could handle his own feelings, even if they were all mixed-up. His thoughts about a life with Lillian were his secret. But, he knew what was right and wrong. "No, David. I've been tellin' you for weeks that Lillian and I are friends. Just like she's a friend to you."

"But she's studying the *Ordnung.*"

"So do a lot of people who come from worldly ways. And I think the *Ordnung*—and God—will help Lillian to find her way. But outsiders don't stay, David. It's rare. So you need not be thinking about things that may not happen."

This was exactly what Samuel feared—David getting too close to Lillian. And he sure couldn't be telling his son that he had allowed himself to get too close to her.

"But it *does* happen sometimes. Besides, aren't people good friends before they get married?"

Samuel glanced at his son. The boy's youthful optimism caused him to briefly contemplate the possibility. "I guess, David. It does happen sometimes. And, *ya, gut* marriages start out with friendship first."

Nonetheless. He shook his head as doubt resurfaced.

Lillian was glad to see Grandpa down for supper. She'd prepared one of his favorites: roast with potatoes and carrots. The events of earlier that afternoon weighed heavily in her heart, but her family was all together. It was cause for happiness and she refused to let Daniel Foster take that away from her.

"Boy, what are you *rutschich* about?" Grandpa asked David when they all sat down to eat. Unless there was a problem with his meds, Grandpa never missed a beat.

"Jonas, leave the boy alone. He's not squirming," Grandma said.

"*Ya*, he's *rutschich*. And grinning like he's got some business for sharing. What's on your mind, son?" Grandpa leaned an ear inward, waiting for an answer.

"David, why don't you give the blessing," Grandma said as she shushed Grandpa.

They all bowed in prayer.

"Dear Lord, thank You for this food before us and the many blessings You have given to us. Thank You for the land that provides us with this fine food, and we know all things are God's will. *Aemen*."

"*Ya*, God's will. *Aemen*. Thank you for that offering, David," Grandma said.

"And one more thing!" David said, bowing his head again. As everyone else hastily lowered their heads, he added, "*Danki* for bringing Lillian to Lancaster County and for Pop deciding not to court Sadie. *Aemen*."

All eyes shot to Samuel, whose embarrassment—and anger— were apparent. Planting clenched fists slowly on the wooden table, he scolded his son with his eyes to the point Lillian feared a trip to the woodshed for David when they got home. That wasn't fair, though. It was such a sweet thing for him to say— about *her*, anyway.

Grandpa chuckled, but quickly stopped when Grandma fired him a look like she might take *him* out to the woodshed for a lashing. As Grandpa pursed his lips together and frowned, Lillian tried to lighten the mood.

"I'm glad God brought me here, too, David." She reached across the table and patted his hand. "That was a very sweet thing to say."

Maybe that would keep him out of trouble with Samuel. But by throwing out the fact that Samuel wasn't courting Sadie in the same breath as his comments about her . . . Well, it *was* cause for speculation by all of them.

It took him a few seconds, but Samuel's scowling look softened and his fists unclenched. *Whew.* Maybe David was in the clear.

Grandma still had a visual hold on Grandpa, warning him not to speak. But as was Grandpa's nature, he spoke anyway. He was looking down when he said it, almost in a whisper, as if a tiny bit afraid of Grandma. But everyone heard him loud and clear.

"Don't know why you kids keep hee-hawing around and don't just take to courtin'." He shrugged.

"Jonas Miller!" Grandma snapped. "This is not your place to talk of such things!" She turned to Samuel. "It's his medications, Samuel. Makes him all cuckoo."

Samuel nodded and opened his mouth to say something, but Grandpa beat him to it, turning toward Grandma. "Irma Rose, if you don't quit blaming them pills for everything I say, I'm gonna stop takin' 'em!"

"Don't take that tone with me, Jonas Miller!"

David's eyes widened in amusement. Glancing at Samuel, Lillian was glad to see him suppressing a grin. He winked at her.

Everything was going to be just fine. And she wondered if maybe, just maybe, Samuel might be toying with the idea of them actually courting. It was always hard to tell with him.

"Irma Rose—" Grandpa prepared to fire back, but stopped and cupped his hand to his ear. "Somebody's here," he said, leaning back to see out the window.

"Jonas, watch yourself. You're gonna fall right over," Grandma said.

"We expecting company? It's the supper hour," Grandpa growled as he shoveled another load of roast onto his plate, seemingly fearful he might not get his share.

"Jonas, I declare. There's nothing wrong with your appetite, 'tis for sure." Grandma wiped her mouth with a napkin, indicating she'd get the door.

"I'll get it, Grandma," Lillian said as she stood from her place on the bench, which was next to Samuel. She smiled in his direction, glad to see he wasn't going to take offense at Grandpa's comment.

Smile still on her face, she contemplated the evening's excitement as she pulled on the wooden door and peered through the screen door. What she saw turned her legs to rubber. Suddenly she was struggling not to suffocate on the air around her. Air poisoned by the past that now found her.

"*Rickie*, what are you doing here?"

12

"ARE YOU GOING TO LET ME IN?" RICKIE ASKED, GRINNING as he studied her from head to toe.

Lillian opened the screen door onto the porch and closed both doors behind her. She couldn't believe Rickie was actually here. Always perfectly groomed, his neatly clipped blond hair accentuated his golden tan. Deceptively charming deep blue eyes scanned his surroundings. Dressed in khaki pants and a yellow golf shirt, he appeared to be the epitome of the perfect man. His looks were undoubtedly what had attracted her to him in the first place. Oh, how he had fooled her, though.

"What are you doing here?" she asked him again between clenched teeth, not wanting anyone to see him.

"That is not your best look, baby," he said, shaking his head and taking in her Amish attire. Him calling her *baby* turned her stomach. "I know you said you've started a new life, and I can see that—but it's hard for me to understand how you could just leave without even talking to me first. That's cold, Lillian. I provided you with a home. I've taken care of you. How could you do this?"

"Taken care of me?" she asked in a loud whisper. "Go home, Rickie. You should have never come here."

Ignoring her, his eyes darted over her shoulder. "Going to let me come in and meet your grandparents?"

"No. We have company tonight. You just need to leave!" Panic was starting to set in. She didn't want any of them to see the kind of person she used to be with. It was hard for her to believe she ever dated Rickie, much less lived with him.

"Lillian, I came a long way to talk to you," he said. "You owe me that much. I love you, and you just took off."

"You know why I left, Rickie." She glanced over her shoulder. The faint voices coming from inside crippled her thought process. Somehow she needed to get rid of him, at least for now. "We can talk tomorrow," she said as she backed up toward the porch door, hoping he would venture back to his rental car.

"Lillian, please," he begged, standing steadfast. "I know I made mistakes, but do you realize what a mistake you've made by coming here? You can't possibly want to live this life. When you get this God thing out of your head, I'll be waiting for you to come home." Walking toward her, he added, "But I won't wait forever, Lillian."

She took a step backward. "I don't want you to wait for me at all, Rickie. It's over. You should have never come here!"

She heard the rustling of feet inside. She dreaded introducing Rickie to anyone.

"I don't believe you, baby," he said, closing the gap between them.

"Don't call me that! I'm not your 'baby.' Please, Rickie, just . . . go home. I don't love you." She held her arm out to keep him at a safe distance.

"What's wrong with you?" His voice spiked up a notch. "And

what's with the freaky clothes? Have they brainwashed you or something?"

How dare you. But fighting with him would only heighten the risk of someone coming out on the front porch. She needed him to just go. "If you'll leave now, I promise we will talk tomorrow. Where are you staying? I'll call you in the morning."

"Lillian, it's only five o'clock in the afternoon. I'm *not* going to wait until morning to talk to you."

"Then let me at least finish supper with my family. I'll call you when I'm done. I can meet you in town or something."

"Fine," he said as he turned to head down the porch steps. He'd almost hit the grass when he called over his shoulder. "Change your clothes too. You look ridiculous."

Her pulse quickened. Thoughts of tackling him to the ground raced through her mind. But he was leaving, and that's all that mattered. She made an about-face and opened the screen door about the same time Grandpa opened the wooden door.

"Who's our company?" he belted out, causing Rickie to spin around and head back up the porch steps.

"Hello, sir, I'm Rickie." He extended his hand, and Lillian's panic settled in even further when Grandpa eased past her and shook his hand. "I'm a friend of Lillian's," Rickie added.

"It's suppertime. Come in and fix yourself a plate." Grandpa turned to go back in the house, obviously anxious to get back to his roast more than anything else.

"Thank you, sir," Rickie said, making his way past Lillian. She flinched as his arm brushed against hers.

"Lilly, come make the proper introductions," Grandpa said over his shoulder.

A sense of dread accompanied her as she followed Grandpa and Rickie into the house.

"This is a friend of Lilly's," Grandpa said, resuming his place at the table. "David, maybe you could scoot that rocker from the den over here to the table for this man."

"No, thank you, sir. Actually, I ate on the plane. I just came to see Lillian." An arrogant smile swept across his face—the same smile that had won her over in the beginning but now was making her stomach turn. "I need to make her realize how much I've missed her." He paused. "I don't want to interrupt your Amish dinner."

Lillian wanted to gag. The look on Samuel's face was one of confusion mixed with irritation.

"I imagine it's about the same as an *Englisch* dinner," Grandpa said sarcastically, still stuffing roast in his mouth. "Lillian, best you introduce everyone to your friend."

Grandma's facial expression resonated with sympathy. David seemed oblivious, or was just as preoccupied with the meal as Grandpa.

"Uh, Rickie, these are my grandparents, Irma Rose and Jonas." She pointed to each respectively. "And this is Samuel and David."

Samuel stood first and shook Rickie's hand, followed by David.

"Nice to meet all of you. I see you really don't use any electricity, just like in the movie *Witness*."

Lillian wondered if anyone saw her cut her eyes in Rickie's direction. Could this day get any worse?

"Well, we don't shoot at people like I hear they done in that movie," Grandpa said. "Or protect shot-up detectives. Right silly, if you ask me."

Lillian was still standing near the doorway, hoping she could coax Rickie back out the door—and then out of her life forever. Mom was going to hear about this.

"David, I reckon we better be on our way," Samuel said, standing up. He walked directly to the hat rack and retrieved his hat without even looking in Lillian's direction.

"No!" she blurted out. "We haven't had dessert."

"Me and the boy have chores to do. *Danki* for supper," he said, still barely making eye contact. "We'll let you and your friend catch up." The way he said "friend" revealed more than just a slight irritation.

"Nice to meet you both," Rickie said, nodding at Samuel and David as they headed toward the door.

"Likewise," Samuel responded, almost pushing David through the doorway.

"I'll be right back," Lillian said in a frenzy, leaving her grandparents with Rickie. That in itself was probably a mistake. No telling what Rickie might say. Or Grandpa, for that matter.

"Samuel, wait," she said, scurrying down the porch steps.

"David, tell Lillian thank you for supper and go wait for me by the buggy."

"*Danki*, Lillian," David said hesitantly, as if he knew something was wrong.

"Don't go," she said, touching Samuel's arm. "I thought you and David might stay for a while."

"Your company came a long way to see you."

"He should have never come here," she said firmly. She wanted to throw herself into Samuel's arms, a place she knew would be safe.

"*Ya* . . . but he *is* here." He raised his brows as if asking her what she would do about it.

"Not for long. As soon as I go back inside, I'm going to make sure he gets on the next flight home."

"I have to get David home, Lillian."

She could hear the remorse in his voice, and she worried to what extent he was feeling it. Did he regret leaving so early? Did he regret ever befriending her in the first place?

As he turned to walk toward the buggy, Lillian followed him. "Samuel."

He turned around to face her. "*Ya.*"

"Thank you again for being with me today."

Samuel shook his head and then gazed intently into her eyes. "Lillian." He paused. "I'm glad I was there for you today."

She definitely sensed there was a "But" coming.

"But, you have . . ." He hesitated.

"I have what, Samuel? Just say it." Although she wasn't sure she wanted to hear it.

"A lot of things going on that I don't understand. All this with your father, the problems with your mother, and now this. These are all worldly conflicts I'm just not used to." He shook his head again.

The regret was still evident in his tone. In a defensive explosion, she tried to redeem herself. "What my mother did is *not* my fault. What my selfish father did is *not* my fault. And Rickie showing up here this way is *not* my fault. Are you going to punish me for these things I have no control over?"

He gently grabbed her shoulders and leaned down. "Lillian, I'm not punishing you for anything. I'm just being honest and telling you I'm not used to all this."

She didn't know what to say. It seemed no matter how far she traveled, drama was determined to follow her.

"Make peace with all the confusion, Lillian," he said softly. "It's the only way you'll find the happiness you're looking for."

"I'm trying! I found my father, which answers a lot of questions. I understand a little better about why my mother left here, and I broke up with a boyfriend who is a jerk! He should not be here."

Samuel didn't say anything, instead looking over her shoulder. She clenched her teeth as she slowly turned around.

"A *jerk*?" Rickie was standing on the porch step and had clearly heard her last remark.

Lillian glanced back and forth between the men. Samuel dropped his arms to his side. Rickie folded his arms across his chest.

"Exactly what's going on here?" Rickie went on. "Are you involved with this Amish guy or something?" His voice deepened to a growl as he spoke—a sound she'd grown to recognize and fear.

"He is my friend, Rickie."

She clasped her hands together and momentarily closed her eyes. *Please God, don't let Rickie hurt the people I love*, she silently prayed.

"Are you *praying*?" Rickie asked, a disgusted look sweeping across his face. "Give me a break!" As he came flying down the porch steps, Lillian instinctively backed up. His eyes were ablaze. "Get in the car, Lillian. I'm taking you home," he said softly as he forcefully grabbed her arm above the elbow and began dragging her toward the car. "We will get all this straightened out at home, sweetie."

Lillian glanced over her shoulder at Samuel, who hadn't moved. His feet were firmly planted in the grass a few feet from the porch steps as he watched Lillian's life unraveling. She looked around for David. To her horror, he was standing by the buggy as Samuel instructed, taking it all in with a look on his face Lillian would carry with her for a long time.

"I'm not going with you, Rickie," Lillian said as she tried to wiggle out of his grasp.

"Oh, but you will. Did you really think I wouldn't come get you?" He spun her around to face him, tightening his grip on her arm. "I just wanted to enjoy my freedom for a little while." He chuckled.

"You'll never get me on a plane, Rickie," she said.

"Oh, I know that. But I'm going to get you back to my hotel room. I don't know who you think you are! Leaving me a cheesy little note and walking out of my life without so much as a warning! This is something we need to talk about."

"I've had one too many talks with you, Rickie."

"Well, you've got one more talk coming," he threatened, opening the car door. "And quit looking over your shoulder. Do you really think that Amish guy is going to come to the rescue?" He snickered. "His kind would let someone shoot up the place, rape his wife, and kill his dog without doing anything. They're *passive*." He paused and glanced briefly at Samuel as if to confirm he was indeed still in the same spot. "Now, get in the car, Lillian," he growled. "We are going to talk."

"No, Rickie. I'm not going." She struggled to pull away, looking toward Samuel. She knew Rickie was right. No matter how strong her friendship with Samuel was, she knew he would remain non-assertive. She was not going to make it any harder on him by begging him to help her. Plus, she couldn't bear the thought of Rickie going after Samuel—and David having to witness such a horrible event.

Rickie swore. "I left my cell phone in the house. Get in the car, Lillian, if you don't want any trouble for your new friend. I'll be right back."

She crawled into the front seat. The car door slammed shut, along with her hope. Facing forward, she couldn't look back at Samuel. She just couldn't. Resting her head in her hands, her body trembled with the realization of what was happening. She'd just take it, one more time. Then she'd come home. She'd be humiliated, but she'd survive. Somehow she always survived.

"God, give me the strength," she said aloud, "and please get Rickie out of my life forever."

After a while, she wondered what was taking Rickie so long. She slowly turned around, still unsure if she could bear to look at Samuel. No one was in sight.

Sitting up a little straighter, her eyes darted across the yard toward the house, then to her right, her left. Where was he?

David was nowhere in sight either. Where was Rickie? Her heart raced, fearing a confrontation between Samuel and Rickie. She opened the car door and bolted out.

She was running toward the house when the screen door swung open. Grandpa walked out on the porch holding a glass of tea as if he had not a care in the world. At the same time, she heard the clippity-clop of Pete's hooves and watched as the buggy spun around. David was driving.

"Grandpa! Where's Samuel?" She scrambled up the porch steps in time to catch the strained look on Grandma's face before Grandpa closed the door behind him. She turned to watch David galloping down the dirt driveway. "Grandpa!"

"Samuel thought it best for David to run over to Ivan's for a bit. Katie Ann has a shoofly pie she made 'specially for them. He'll be right back."

Confusion. Panic. Where was Samuel? She saw Grandma peek out the window. Her face resonated with pity. Lillian wondered if Grandpa was utilizing his authority as head of the household, instructing her to stay in the house—for her own safety.

"Grandpa," she said frantically, gently grabbing his arm. "Where is Samuel?"

"Why, he's in the woodshed right here beside the house." Grandpa took another sip of tea.

"What?" She turned to venture in that direction, but Grandpa stepped forward.

"Lilly, I think it best if you come sit with your ol' Grandpa on the porch." His expression turned solemn. "Do what your *daadi* says."

"But, I—"

"On the porch, Lilly." Grandpa pointed to one of the rockers, taking a seat in the other one himself.

She reluctantly sat down. "Grandpa, listen to me. Rickie is not a very good person. Samuel could be in trouble. I have to go to him." She looked toward the woodshed.

Grandpa tilted his head back and stared into the yard. "Lilly, you will have to trust your grandpa and do as I say," he said firmly, before cutting his eyes in her direction. "And we will not speak of this again."

A rustling to her right drew her eyes. There came Samuel, walking side by side with Rickie. As they reached the front of the house, Samuel headed toward the porch and Rickie walked to his car. Rickie never looked her way. Samuel said nothing as he walked up and took a seat on the porch step.

"I'll have Irma Rose bring you something to drink," Grandpa said to Samuel. "We'll have us a nice glass of tea. David should be back shortly."

"Samuel, what——" Lillian started ask.

"Maybe you'd like something cold to drink, Lillian?" Grandpa interrupted as the three of them watched Rickie's car ramble down the dirt drive. Rickie looked none the worse for wear, but something had happened to make him tuck his tail and run.

Lillian turned back to look at Samuel. His face was as solemn as Grandpa's.

"Samuel, are you all right?"

Before he could say anything, Grandpa spoke up one more time. "He looks mighty fine to me." His look left no question in Lillian's mind that there were to be no more questions. Now . . . or ever.

———

"Who was that man, Pop?" David asked Samuel when they pulled into the driveway.

"You heard Jonas," he said. "An old friend of Lillian's."

"Pop, I'm almost twelve. I know what's going on."

"Do you, now?" Samuel brought Pete to a halt and hopped out of the buggy. David followed him into the house.

"It's her old boyfriend," David said, watching Samuel light the lantern above the kitchen table.

Samuel eyed the kitchen, again picturing the table at his favorite shop. As was the case recently, the image in his mind included Lillian. But it was hard not to have doubts that such a notion was ever going to happen. The thought of Lillian being involved with the likes of that Rickie fellow brought on a rage that was not in line with his upbringing.

As Samuel poured him and the boy each a glass of cold milk, David said, "I didn't like him. I saw the way he tried to drag Lillian to the car. He's not a *gut* man."

"Only the Good Lord can pass judgment, David."

Samuel reflected on the judgment he himself had just passed on the man out in the woodshed.

"*Ya*, I know."

Samuel regretted the boy saw as much as he did. Especially Rickie pulling Lillian to the car like a rag doll. Sending David to Ivan's was a good move. The boy needn't ever know why Rickie hightailed it back to the city. For that matter, no one ever had to know. But Samuel would know, and he'd have to live with it.

It was hard for him to imagine what life must have been like for Lillian, living with a man like that. He imagined things must have been even worse behind closed doors. No one to see him doing her harm. Cringing, he recalled her fearful expression when Rickie dragged her off—a look that shifted from dread to compliance to embarrassment, all in a split second. Her face had revealed a painful past not fit for any human being. Lillian would never cause harm to another person. It sickened him to envision anyone hurting her. That Rickie fellow sickened him for sure.

He couldn't help but worry how many more skeletons from Lillian's closet might show up in Lancaster County.

Grandma and Grandpa were sitting at the kitchen table when Lillian walked back into the house.

"Mighty fine mess we had here, Lilly," Grandpa said, uncharacteristically somber. "I don't think we'll be seeing that pretty *Englischer* again."

"I hope not, Grandpa." Lillian hands trembled as she poured herself a cup of hot tea and took a seat beside her grandma at the kitchen table. "I'm sorry about all this."

"*Ya,*" Grandpa said. "We will put this behind us. No talk of it again."

Grandpa spoke with a conviction Lillian hadn't heard before. Grandma had temporarily taken her place as a traditional Old Order Amish woman, allowing Grandpa to rule the roost. Her expression was distant and staid.

"I hope Samuel will still want to be friends after all this," Lillian said, fighting tears.

Her grandparents didn't answer, as if they were harboring the same thought.

"I think I'll head upstairs," she said finally, feeling defeated by the events of the day. She barely heard her grandparents wishing her a good night's sleep as she headed up the wooden steps. She was almost to the top of the stairs when Grandpa called to her. "Lillian."

"Yes, Grandpa?" She turned around, not sure if she wanted to hear what he had to say. His voice still resonated with the same somberness.

"God does not judge us by the actions of others," he bellowed. "And me and your Grandma don't either."

Lillian tried to muster up a smile. She nodded, turned back around, and headed upstairs feeling embarrassment and regret. Everything she'd been working to attain seemed to be teetering toward failure. Feeling herself curl up into the place she often went after an encounter with Rickie, she realized she could either allow herself to revert back to the person she used to be—or fight for the peaceful life within her grasp.

"Guess who showed up on the doorstep this evening, Mom?" Lillian asked her mother when she answered the phone.

"Lillian, I think Rickie deserves another chance, and that's the reason I told him—"

"Mother! I decide who I am going to be with. You made a terrible mistake sending Rickie all this way!"

"Rickie is a very nice-looking, well-mannered man with a good job, Lillian."

"He has you so fooled, Mom."

"Is this about the Amish man?" Her mother's tone resounded with disapproval. "Are you not giving Rickie another chance because of this other man?"

"It has nothing to do with Samuel."

"You should give him another chance."

Sensing her mom's complete and utter disappointment in her, she considered setting her straight about Rickie. But her mom had introduced her to Rickie, and she knew her mother would blame herself. Yet again, Lillian found herself in a role reversal, feeling the need to protect her mother. But she wondered when her mom was ever going to be a mother to *her*.

Still, she and her mother had sufficiently hurt each other enough over the years, and she wasn't going to rub this in her face. Besides, she felt humiliated that she'd let it go on for as long as she did.

She recalled the parting of ways between Samuel and Rickie, wondering what exactly had happened out in the woodshed.

"Samuel and I are just friends, but Rickie could never be the man Samuel is."

"Oh, Lillian! I can hear it in your voice. You've fallen for this Amish man." She heard her mother's sigh.

Lillian took a deep breath and decided to change the subject. "I met my father today."

No response. "Well, Mom?"

"I'm trying to imagine what that must have been like," her mother replied.

Lillian thought back to her meeting with Daniel Foster. Shattered dreams. Suddenly, she didn't want to talk anymore.

After a while, her mother said, "I'm sorry, Lillian. I really am."

Again she didn't respond.

"I was hypnotized by Daniel's writing. He was wise about the world. He was forbidden. Just like Eve, I bit the apple. When he found out I was pregnant with you, I saw his true colors. Sweetie, I tried to warn you about him. Did you tell him who you were? Was he horrible?"

"Yes, I told him who I was. And yes, the whole thing was horrible." She paused, trying to imagine what it must have been like for her mother. "I suppose it was horrible for you, too, Mom. But you should have told me much sooner who my father was."

"I just wanted to protect you. How did you find out about the newspapers? I can't believe they're still in the barn after all these years."

"Grandpa thought I was you one night. He said he knew you were saving newspapers, and it would be best to stay away from the *Englisch* man. I had already seen the boxes of newspapers, so I looked through them. You made little notes beside some of his columns."

She heard a sniffle on the other end of the line.

"Mom?" she asked when there was no reply.

"How is Grandpa?" Now Mom was changing the subject, but she was also crying.

"He's okay, most of the time. I think his medicines cause him to get confused at night sometimes."

And, then, as if it had been building for years, Sarah Jane Miller wept uncontrollably. Lillian had never heard her like this. Thank goodness she hadn't told her about Rickie. "Mom? Are you okay?" Her own tears began to build. "Mom?"

"I'm so, so sorry, Lillian. I'm sorry I've been a bad mother. I'm sorry I didn't tell you about Daniel." She wept harder. "I miss my *mamm* and *daed* so much."

It was the first time Lillian had ever heard her mother speak any *Pennsylvania Deitsch*. It was the first time she remembered her mother apologizing for the way she had raised her.

"I miss them so much, Lillian," she went on. "And I'm so sorry for everything I've put you through."

Lillian tried to gain a level of composure before she said anything. The whole day had been an emotional disaster. Now she just felt sick about everything. She needed a hug. Oddly, she needed her mother.

"Mom," she said softly, choking back sobs. "You're not a bad mother. You made mistakes. We all do. I'm sorry for everything you went through."

"You don't have to try to make me feel better, Lillian. I know what kind of life I've led and how it affected you."

But I want to make you feel better, a little voice screamed. *I really do.* "It's okay, Mom." She sniffled and attempted a smile. "Besides, I think I turned out pretty good. And you get some credit for that."

"Oh, I don't know about that."

"Well, I do. Remember when I was in first grade and all the kids were going to the roller skating rink? We didn't have any money, and I knew that, but I wanted to go so badly. It was Cheryl Henston's birthday party. Remember?"

"Yes, I remember," her mother responded softly.

"I knew you pawned something important to get me a new outfit and a present to take to the party." She paused. "And Mom, I remember you singing to me when I was little. I remember you hugging me, bandaging scrapes, brushing my hair—" She stopped when she heard her mother sobbing again.

As Lillian's own cries of forgiveness leaped forward, she realized she'd been so busy thinking about the ways her mother had wrecked her life, she hadn't stopped to realize all the good things her mother had done. It wasn't as if she forgot the good things. She just had allowed the bad things to dominate her memories.

"I love you, Lillian. I'm sorry about telling Rickie where you are."

"I love you, too, Mom. I really do."

"Give your grandpa an extra big hug from me."

Both of them still crying, Lillian hesitated before saying, "Mom, why don't you come give him a hug yourself?"

"Oh, I can't face them, Lillian. I just can't. Do they know about Daniel? Did you tell them? They knew who he was back then. He lived in Paradise. Do they know?"

"No, no, Mom. They don't know. It's up to you to tell them if you want to. But either way, come to Lancaster County. Come see your parents."

She pleaded several more times with her mother, and her mother's response was consistent: "I just can't, Lillian. I can't."

The next morning, Lillian awoke with puffy eyes. It had taken effort to talk to God before she fell asleep. She couldn't help but feel like He had let her down. And she could feel doubt about His existence creeping in. But she had prayed just the same, like she had been doing each night.

She'd prayed for her mother: "Please God, help me and Mom to both make good decisions and heal from the bad ones. And help us to be close, the way mothers and daughters should be. Please help Mom to find the peace she is looking for and keep her safe."

She'd prayed about Samuel and David: "I pray that maybe there is a place for me in Samuel and David's life, God. Please keep them both safe."

Next were Grandma and Grandpa: "I'm so thankful for my grandparents and the relationship You've given me with them. So very thankful. Please keep Grandpa in my life. I pray his medications will keep him from being in pain and that he'll be able to live many more years. I pray that Grandma will get more rest, and that we will continue to grow closer. I've learned a lot from her."

Those were the easy ones. Much harder was to pray for Rickie: "I pray that Rickie will find his way to You and make the changes necessary for him to live a good life." That was all she could muster up on Rickie's behalf.

Her father was the toughest of all and she kept it simple: "Please let me forgive him."

She had put all her worries in one big bubble and blown it up to heaven for God to handle. Her last words before falling asleep were, "I'm putting it all in your hands, God."

This morning, as she forced herself out of bed and dressed, she wasn't sure if Samuel would show up for their planned picnic around noon. She wouldn't blame him if he didn't.

——

As Samuel guided Pete down the dirt driveway a few minutes before noon, he still worried if Lillian would be able to shed her worldly ways and past boyfriends. He had spent several long, sleepless hours last night raging with bitterness at the thought of that Rickie fellow. And several more questioning his feelings for Lillian. Now those concerns resurfaced.

But as he neared the farmhouse, he saw Lillian sitting on the front porch. And he realized one thing was for sure: despite everything, no matter her past, he couldn't stay away from Lillian.

She ran to meet him. As he stepped out of the buggy, she stopped right in front of him. "I was afraid you might not come."

"I invited you on a picnic. Why wouldn't I come?" he said, feeling a little guilty that he considered not showing up.

"Because of yesterday, I thought you—" she blurted out.

He forcibly shook his head, hoping they could put things behind them. "Let's forget about it." He paused. "You look different."

It was true. She glowed with a radiance that made her more beautiful than she already was. How was that so? He'd expected she'd still be a mess.

"I look just the same as I always do," she said beaming. She scanned her outfit and pointed toward her feet. "Right down to my black leather shoes!"

Seeing her so lighthearted set Samuel's heart and mind to rest. It was going to be a good day after all. Something was different, all right. He wasn't sure what. But he need not pay it any more mind. His heavy heart from the prior night, along with his worries, were beginning to wash clean.

"The picnic basket!" she said. "How can we have a picnic without any food?" She ran back into the house, returning with a large basket in one hand and a small knapsack in the other.

"I invited you on the picnic. I should have brought the food," he said, thinking back to when Lillian had offered to pack the basket. "What's that?" He pointed to the knapsack.

She smiled. "It's a surprise." She handed him the basket but kept hold of the knapsack.

"What kind of surprise?" he asked, intrigued.

She winked at him. "You'll see."

13

LILLIAN FELT LIGHT AND CAREFREE AS SHE AND SAMUEL exited the buggy and walked toward the lake. It was a beautiful summer day without a cloud in the sky, and the clouds in her mixed-up mind were slowly clearing as well. And Samuel was with her. Despite the horrors of the previous day, she wanted to face her future with hope and determination. She'd come too far to let Rickie or Daniel Foster deter her efforts.

"What are you thinkin' about?" Samuel asked, walking alongside her.

"What a beautiful day it is." Her eyes twinkled. "And how lucky I am to have you for a friend. Plus, I'm clearing the baggage in my heart that I've carried around for such a long time. I'm breathing in the blessing of this new day."

"We can talk about yesterday if you want," he offered, apparently regretful he'd avoided the subject earlier.

"No. I think I've figured out a way to put it all behind me."

Obviously curious, he nodded. As they moved closer to the lake, he asked, "What'd you think? Is this a good spot?"

"Perfect," she was quick to say. "It's beautiful here." And it was. The "lake" looked more like a large Texas pond. Tall pines surrounded them and a small pier edged across the water.

"It's quiet here most of the time. The tourists don't know it's here."

"Well, this is a great spot. Let's go get the blanket and picnic basket."

"And you can tell me what's in that bag," he said as they returned to the buggy. His eyes widened hopefully.

"I told you it's a surprise," she teased. "First we dine on this fine meal I have prepared—tuna-salad sandwiches, potato salad, some nasty beets, and funnel cakes for dessert. And, *ya*, I made the funnel cakes."

Samuel spread the blue and gray quilt on the ground. Lillian set the picnic basket on the quilt but kept guard over the knapsack, giving him a grin.

He was glad to see it. It had been a rough couple of days, especially for her. The sight and sound of her carrying on the way she was today reminded him of the first time he'd met her, toting the red suitcase and laughing up a storm. What a beautiful mess she'd been.

Now, as he watched her dishing out their lunch onto paper plates, he thought about how far she'd come. She looked Amish, and she sounded Amish. And she had gone a long way toward learning the *Ordnung* and some *Pennsylvania Deitsch*. She just might make it if she didn't let her old life get in the way.

They settled down to eat, chatting about nothing in particular, each of them careful not to bring up unpleasant topics. Lillian frowned when all of the food was gone. "I don't think I made enough. I should know by now how much you eat."

"I'm plenty full. It was the perfect amount. And tasted mighty fine too."

Shining with delight, she stowed food containers, plates, and the like back in the picnic basket.

"Now, let's have a look at the surprise in that bag." He rolled his eyes toward the heavily guarded knapsack.

Looking a bit embarrassed, she explained, "It's not really that big of a deal. Just something I wanted us to do . . . together."

"You've got all my attention."

"You might think it's kind of silly, but it's something I want to do." She reached for the bag and opened it. First thing she pulled out was a gardening spade.

"Are we digging a hole?"

"Yep. We sure are."

"Hmm . . . Mind if I ask what for?"

Leaning her head to one side, she shot him a serious look. "To bury this." She held up the knapsack.

Samuel sat up a little straighter. "Do I even dare ask what you've got in there? It's not like a dead critter or something, is it?"

"Yes, it's a dead animal, and I'm going to perform a pagan ritual."

He couldn't believe his ears.

She slapped him playfully on the arm. "Samuel! I'm kidding." She was eager to press on. "But we have to dig a hole."

"How big a hole? And more important, what are we burying?"

"Stop looking so scared," she said, letting out another round of giggles. "I have a few things I want gone, that's all. It's symbolic of a new beginning for me. No dead animals, I promise."

"What's in there?" He reached over and attempted to have a peek.

She quickly snatched the bag and pulled it to her chest. "You'll see," she said, once again embarrassed. Whatever the girl had the notion to get rid of, it sure seemed important to her.

"What about over there for your hole, where there isn't any grass?" He pointed to a nearby patch of ground.

"Perfect!"

He heaved himself up and offered her a hand. Once on their feet, he shook his head. "I sure am wondering what you're up to."

"You'll see," she said, heading toward the grassless spot a few yards away.

She watched Samuel digging her hole, his muscles bulging beneath his blue cotton shirt. His physical strength was evident, but it was his emotional strength she found most attractive. In addition to his unquestionable faith in God, his faith in her seemed to be growing. And his extreme sense of discipline did not overshadow his ability to enjoy life. He was able to play and have fun, but he took his responsibilities as seriously as his faith. Hard work was part of the Amish lifestyle, and Samuel worked harder than most. His role as David's father only added to his attributes.

A few inches down, the ground was moist, and it wasn't long before Samuel had a hole in the dirt about two feet deep and a foot wide. "Big enough?" he asked, wiping his brow.

"*Ya.*" Still toting the knapsack, she went to retrieve the quilt from where they had eaten. She spread it beside the hole and motioned for Samuel to take a seat, then joined him. As she reached into the knapsack, she glanced his way and smiled. "As I said, this might seem silly to you. But it will help me to move forward."

"If it's important to you, then it's not silly at all."

She reached into the bag and pulled out the first item she planned to discard. Retrieving the small diary, her thoughts traveled back to a time when she was fourteen—a mixed-up teenager harboring hateful thoughts about the life she was forced to live because of her mother's decisions. With no extras and living in a run-down shack, she'd saved her occasional lunch money to buy the diary. Absent of hopes and dreams, woeful accounts of her daily challenges filled the small book. Her plan: to show it to her mother someday and say, "Read this, Mother, and don't shed a tear because I have shed enough for both of us."

Samuel sat patiently as she scanned the pages. February 3, 1995—a particularly painful day. She silently read:

Dear Diary, today is possibly the worst day of my life. I haven't seen Mom in two days. She has a new boyfriend. There's no food in this place we call a house. And Mitzi died. I buried her in the backyard. I don't know what happened. I found my precious kitty lifeless on the front porch. She was skinny, but I'd been feeding her whatever we had in the house. I don't think that's why she died. Her eyes were open and her white and black fur was wet. She wasn't breathing, though. I brought her in the house and cried for almost two hours. I loved her. When Mom never showed up, I just dug a hole in the backyard and put her in it. I don't know much about God, so I didn't really say any prayers or anything. Then, it started to rain, so I went back in the house. This was a very bad day.

She jumped forward to July 23:

Dear Diary, something is wrong with Mom. I don't think she's drunk, but something else is wrong. She's slurring her words. I'm not sure if it's drugs or something. I told her I was hungry, but she just cried and mumbled something I didn't understand.

September 12:

Dear Diary, I'm feeling very sad because I want to go to the dance at school. Henry Webster will be there, and I really like him. I think he likes me too. But Mom says I can't go. It costs five dollars to get in. I don't have anything to wear anyway. I hate my life. I hate my mom.

Lillian cringed, recalling the events of that year. Hard to believe it was thirteen years ago. So much had changed. She had changed. And her mother had changed as well. Continuing to allow the bad memories to override the good memories was only hurting her. After her recent conversation with her mother, she knew the only way to continue along in her quest for peace was to replace resentment with forgiveness. She tossed the book into the hole.

"I forgive you, Mom," she said softly.

Samuel's expression was solemn, but he offered her a comforting smile and nodded his head. She reached into the knapsack for the next item. Opening the envelope, she pulled out the newspaper clipping she had cut out the day before. Studying the young face of her father, she read his column—such heartfelt insights on the page. Why couldn't he have made a place for her in his life?

She glanced at Samuel, who was studying her actions intently. He acknowledged that he saw the clipping, and she tossed it in the hole.

"I forgive you, Daniel Foster."

She blinked away tears, determined not to cry. If she continued to weigh herself down with the years behind her, she would never be free to experience the life before her with joy and happiness. The peaceful life she longed for—a life where she didn't harbor any resentments—was within her grasp. Releasing the burdens of her heart, forgiving those who hurt her, and turning her life to God would free her soul to be the person she wanted to be.

She reached into the bag.

"Are you sure about this, Lillian?" Samuel asked when he saw her retrieve the next few items. His forehead creased with worry.

"*Ya*, I am. This represents all my worldly clothes, along with a few other things." She folded the blue jeans and placed them in the hole, followed by a bag of makeup, several pieces of costume jewelry, a small battery-operated radio, and two books she no longer felt were suitable reading material. Some of the jewelry was from Rickie. She didn't see the need to mention that.

There was one thing left in the bag—her last tie to the outside world. As she pulled out her cell phone, Samuel said, "What about talking to your *mamm*?"

"I'll do what everyone else here does. I'll go to town and use the pay phone, or the shanty at the Lapp farm."

Samuel seemed leery about the cell phone, her final separation from the outside world. The lines in his forehead became more evident.

"It's fine," she replied as she tossed the phone atop the pile. "Grandma hates that thing. She winces every time it rings."

Samuel knew that giving up her worldly items and forgiving those who hurt her was all part of Lillian's plan to move forward in her new life. But he also knew it wasn't easy for her. Just like it wasn't going to be easy for him to add his own piece of the past to the pile.

"Okay, that's it." She twisted her hands together in a nervous sort of way. He reckoned he'd feel nervous in her shoes too.

"Wait," he said when she reached for the spade, preparing to refill the hole. He reached into his pocket. "I have something to add."

He'd been thinking about it the whole time he watched her giving up her worldly possessions and letting go of the things that haunted her. The item in his pocket didn't haunt him, but it would be equally as hard to give up.

He pulled out the wallet-sized picture of Rachel and handed it to Lillian. The edges were worn, but her face as beautiful as ever.

"Samuel," she whispered, as if she couldn't believe her eyes. "But I thought . . ." She paused, looking at the photo. ". . . pictures aren't allowed."

"I'm not perfect, Lillian." He thought back to the day his

Englisch friend Carl Johanson from the supermarket gave him the
picture a few days after Rachel died. "We don't have to tell anyone
about this," Carl had said as he slipped him the picture of Rachel.
Carl adored Rachel and evidently had sneaked in a picture when
she wasn't looking, knowing she had the cancer real bad and that
someday Samuel might want it. He'd carried it in his pocket ever
since. No one knew he had the picture, not even David.

"She's beautiful, Samuel," she said, taking note of the woman's exquisite facial features. Her eyes were a warm hazel color,
and her tightly wound hair a honey-brown shade. "Wow." She
handed the picture back to him.

He took one last look at the woman from his past, then looked
at Lillian. Her face was as serious as he'd ever seen her. And she'd
never looked prettier.

Slowly, his hand made its way toward the hole. But Lillian's
hand was quickly on his arm. "No, Samuel," she said, shaking
her head. "No."

"She's part of my past." His arm wavered over the hole in the
dirt. "And pictures aren't allowed."

Lillian disagreed. "It's not the same, Samuel. Rachel is a wonderful part of your past, someone to remember. You loved her,
and she's David's mother. I don't want you to ever forget her. I
would never allow you to mix her picture with these things I
want to bury forever." She continued shaking her head in a very
determined way.

Samuel froze. He wasn't sure what to do. His hand held fast
to the picture, still hovering over the hole. The whole while he
watched Lillian make peace with things from her past, he'd
thought burying the picture would be the right thing to do. He
wanted to be able to move forward too.

"Put the picture back in your pocket, Samuel," Lillian instructed, guiding his arm away from the hole. "We won't tell anyone. But I think you need to keep the picture."

"I reckon it's not right, though."

"It'll be our little secret." Her eyes sparkled with warm sincerity.

As he placed the picture back in his pocket, his gaze locked with hers in mutual understanding.

That night at supper, with her entire family assembled at the table, David offered the blessing, and everyone dug into the feast Lillian had prepared. She'd mastered *Yummasetti*, a traditional Pennsylvania German dish—ground beef, Amish noodles, bread, butter, onion, peas, chicken soup, mushroom soup, sour cream, and lots of cheese. Her city life would have sent the high-calorie meal straight to her thighs, but there was always enough work here to keep a nice sense of balance when it came to worrying about weight gain.

Everyone loved the meal, and she'd even made rhubarb pie for dessert.

"Our Lilly has turned into a fine Amish cook," Grandpa announced. "*Appeditlich!*"

"It's real *gut*, Lillian," David said. Although Lillian noticed he'd been awfully quiet since he came in from his chores outside. Maybe he felt left out, knowing she and Samuel had spent the day together.

"Are you ready to start school soon?" she asked. "Let's see, you have two more years left, right?"

"I reckon," David said softly, barely looking up. Lillian

glanced at Samuel, who shrugged slightly, also sensing David's solemn mood.

Lillian knew Amish children only attended school through the eighth grade. Weeks ago, Samuel had shown her David's school. The one-room, red schoolhouse was within walking distance of every child who attended. There were rows of wooden desks facing a long blackboard. There were no televisions, computers, or any other type of electronic equipment. It was like stepping back into another time period. Samuel explained that Amish teachers taught lessons in English.

Reflecting on her trip to the schoolhouse with Samuel, she thought about her twelve years in public school, plus her four years in college. In her mixed-up world, teaching had been the one goal that had remained constant. Once again, she recalled her regret at having to give up her teaching job.

"What are we gonna do when young David returns to school?" Grandpa asked. "We've become mighty dependent on him 'round here."

"David will still come around after school," Samuel said. "And Jonas, I'll do whatever I can to help too."

Grandpa sat up a little straighter. "*Ya*, well, I've been feelin' downright well here lately. Whatever medical concoctions those *Englisch* doctors are given' me tend to make me wanna tackle that yard with the push mower."

"Jonas, you will do no such thing!" Grandma snapped.

"Irma Rose, don't go bossin' me." His tone was equally firm. "I know yard work is for the womenfolk, but I'm gonna do it since I ain't been able to do much else."

"If I catch you mowing that yard, I'll do more than boss you,

Jonas Miller." She shot him a look that would've had everyone else at the table cowering, but Grandpa just sat up even taller.

"After I be done mowing the yard with the push mower, then I'm gonna go after the repairs to that hog pen. Thinkin' about takin' on a few hogs this next year."

"Jonas! We have more than we can say grace over to take care of 'round here. I'm pleased as punch you are feelin' better, but you can get those crazy notions out of your head."

Lillian glanced at Samuel, who was trying not to laugh. Even David was stifling a grin. When Grandma and Grandpa got going, it was always an amusing display of misdirected affection.

"I'll do whatever I want," Grandpa muttered, diving into some rhubarb pie.

Grandma rattled off a bunch of *Pennsylvania Deitsch* Lillian didn't understand, but Samuel and David looked shocked. And Grandpa didn't say another word.

As the men ate their rhubarb pie and began their own conversation, Lillian and her grandma cleaned the supper dishes.

"I think I smelled cigar smoke in here this morning when I returned from the supermarket," Grandma whispered. "Do you think that grandpa of yours would be silly enough to be smokin' with his bad health?"

Lillian figured Grandpa was in enough trouble for one day. She shrugged.

Whispering again, Grandma said, "Those medications have his mind all amuck. Do you know what he told me last night?"

Whatever it was, Grandma looked appalled. Her lips pursed together as she leaned in close to Lillian's ear. "He said he wants to have more *kinner*," she groaned in exasperation. "Now, is that not the silliest notion you've ever heard of in your life? First of all, Jonas knows the Good Lord was only able to bless us with one child. I couldn't have any more. Secondly, has that silly ol' man looked in the mirror lately?"

Lillian tried not to smile. Grandma was clearly upset.

"He's just been saying and doin' the craziest of things. It's those pills." She glanced over at her husband and frowned. Swiping a plate dry with the cup towel, she placed it in the cupboard.

Grandpa didn't notice. He was well into his second piece of rhubarb pie, as were Samuel and David.

"Well, at least he's feeling better," Lillian said, trying to cheer up Grandma.

"And I praise God for that. I just wish it wouldn't make his mind so cluttered, where he's not thinkin' like he should be."

As they whispered to themselves in the corner of the kitchen, Grandpa interrupted them. "Oh, Irma Rose and Lilly!"

"What, Jonas?" Grandma asked with a sigh. She glanced his way.

"I almost forgot to tell you both somethin'."

"What, Grandpa?" Lillian asked.

"No tellin'," Grandma whispered under her breath. She turned her back to dry another dish and place it in the cupboard.

Lillian watched while Grandpa swallowed his last bit of rhubarb pie. A big smile stretched across his wrinkled jowls. "Sarah Jane will be here on Wednesday."

Grandma spun around, sending the plate in her hand crashing to the floor.

14

LILLIAN PULLED THE BROOM FROM THE PANTRY AND BEGAN sweeping up the pieces of the broken plate. She'd begged her mother over the phone to come to Lancaster County. Had she finally decided to make peace with her parents?

"While you were out tending to your pretty flowers in the yard, Lilly, that noisy portable phone kept ringin' this morning," Grandpa bellowed. "It took me a few tries, but I finally was able to talk into it." He paused. "I told Sarah Jane she needed to come for a visit. She'll be here on Wednesday."

He made the statement as nonchalantly as if he saw his daughter all the time. When no one said anything, he went on. "Lilly, I say you prepare a special supper for your *mamm*. Show her what a fine Amish cook we've turned out 'round here. Said she'd be here by suppertime."

"Jonas, are you sure about this?" Grandma asked in a skeptical tone.

"Irma Rose, our Sarah Jane will be here on Wednesday." His announcement left no room for argument.

It was quiet for a bit before Samuel stood up to retrieve his hat from the rack. "That's great news, Jonas," he said, placing the hat on his head.

"*Ya, gut* news! Isn't it, Irma Rose?"

"Of course," Grandma said. Emotion flooded her face. "That's *wunderbaar* news."

"I'm going to walk Samuel and David out," Lillian said, not wanting to voice her concerns in front of her grandparents.

Once they were outside, Lillian told Samuel and David, "I begged my mother to come see her parents. She was adamant about not coming. I wonder what Grandpa said to change her mind?"

"Whatever he said, I think it's great she's coming," Samuel remarked.

Lillian shook her head. "You don't know my mother. She probably just *said* she would come. Grandpa is so excited about her coming, and she'll probably never show up. That will break his heart."

"People change their minds," Samuel said. As they headed to the buggy, he continued. "Think positive. It'll mean the world to Jonas if your *mamm* comes for a visit."

"It'll mean *everything* to Grandpa. And that's what worries me." She paused. "And another thing: Grandma said Grandpa has been saying all kinds of crazy things lately, mostly due to his medication. What if he didn't even talk to her? I'd better go into town tomorrow and use a pay phone." A guilty feeling swept over her; she was beginning to regret disposal of that one worldly item. How much easier it would be to walk inside and call her mother from the comfort of her bedroom.

"Pop, did you tell her about next weekend?" David asked, changing the subject.

"I was gettin' around to it." He turned toward Lillian. "I

know you've been around my *mamm* and the rest of my family at church services, but they want to have a big shindig next Saturday and have you, Irma Rose, and Jonas to the house for supper. They know me and the boy eat supper here a lot, and I think they'd like to do something for your family."

Lillian got along well enough with Samuel's family, but she knew they still regarded her as the *Englisch* outsider. Conversation was always polite, but limited. Neither his two sisters, nor sister-in-law had allowed her into their inner circle. Several times after church service she'd tried to make conversation with them. They were cordial, but guarded. His mother barely acknowledged her.

"And, of course, your *mamm* is welcome too," Samuel added.

"I wouldn't count on her being here."

"You never know," Samuel said optimistically. "People change."

She started to say, "Not my mother." But that would be the old Lillian talking. She had to admit: people could change. She had changed. And she had buried any bad thoughts she'd harbored about her mother in a hole by the lake. Plus, she'd had some hard but good conversations with her mom lately that helped her see her mom in a new light.

Her eyes glistened with hope. "I pray she does come." And she meant it. She just doubted it.

The next day, she set out to go talk to David. She sensed something was bothering him. It was a beautiful day for a walk and it was an off Sunday. Alternating Sunday worship services was one of the "rules" she wasn't about to argue with. While the service always left her with a sense of fellowship and heightened spirituality, it was incredibly long.

Walking down the dirt road toward Samuel's farm, she reflected on the events of the past few days. Deep in thought about her mother, she heard a buggy approaching from behind. She spun around and watched the buggy slowing down.

Of all people . . .

Sadie Fisher let out a "Whoa, boy" that any man would have been proud of. As she coaxed her horse to a stop, she yelled, "Need a ride?"

She didn't really. However, Sadie's expression was nonconfrontational and it seemed safe enough.

"Heading to Samuel's?" she asked, guiding her horse back into motion after Lillian crawled in.

"*Ya.*"

"I heard you were learning the *Ordnung* and some *Pennsylvania Deitsch.*" Her tone was neither sarcastic nor condescending.

"Yes, I am."

"Are you thinking of converting and staying in our community?" Again, her tone wasn't bitter.

"I'm learning as much as I can so I can make a good decision." *Why does this seem like dangerous territory?*

"That sounds like a *gut* plan." Sadie issued a pop of the leathery strap and picked up the pace.

Lillian didn't know what to say. The woman was being nice. She just nodded.

"It's no secret I was hoping to marry Samuel someday."

Uh oh. Here we go. "Maybe you still will," she replied.

Sadie shrugged. "*Ach*, don't be silly. He took a fancy to you, and I'm happy for the both of you."

"What?" She didn't mean her response to sound as surprised as she was. "No, no," she added. "We're only friends."

"Sure you are."

The woman didn't seem the least bit jealous or upset. Maybe it was a trick.

"I'm actually on my way to Samuel's as well."

Ah ha! She knew it.

"Levi Zook's barn burned down and a barn raising is planned for Saturday. I was going to let Samuel know, so he wouldn't make any plans."

"Oh," Lillian responded, wondering how that would affect the family shindig planned for both their families on the same day. She had heard about the Amish barn raisings. The whole community participated and framed and roofed-in a barn all in one day.

"And I know Jonas isn't well, but it'd be nice if you were able to come help tend to the menfolk."

Sadie's tone was sincere. She didn't seem to harbor an ounce of resentment that Samuel and Lillian had become friends. "I'd be glad to help," Lillian replied.

As they pulled onto Samuel's driveway, Sadie asked, "Can I tell you a secret?"

"Sure." What kind of secret could she have to tell her?

Lillian took in Sadie with fresh eyes. Sadie was a feisty red-head with ivory skin and sky-blue eyes. Tiny creases in the corner of each eye hinted she might be a few years older than Lillian. She was tall and thin. Her striking appearance was unique to the

Old Order district. Lillian had noticed almost all the women had dark hair and olive complexions.

"I've been writing letters to a man in Texas."

The look on Lillian's face must have revealed her shock.

"Not to worry—he's an Amish man. I'm going to travel there to meet him!"

"Really? Is that allowed?" Lillian wasn't sure. "I'm from Texas," she added.

Skipping past her latter comment, Sadie said, "*Ya*. My husband died three years ago and Samuel was my only prospect for marriage here. My biological clock is ticking, as the *Englisch* would say." She glanced at Lillian and smiled for the first time. "I have no bad feelings about it, Lillian. Once I found out that Samuel carried no interest, I rested my efforts."

Lillian doubted Sadie's biological clock was ticking too much ahead of her own. She knew the Amish started their families early. She couldn't help but wonder why Sadie had no children. It wasn't proper to ask.

"How did you meet him?" Lillian knew there were scattered, small Amish districts in Texas.

"His family traveled here for my cousin's wedding. That's how I found out 'bout him. His wife also died about three years ago. But he wasn't able to attend the wedding. So I haven't actually met him. We've just been exchanging letters. No one knows, either, except for my cousin."

They were now parked in front of Samuel's farmhouse. Lillian could see David on the front porch. "Sadie, I have to say I'm a little surprised that you're telling me your secret."

Sadie shrugged again. "I guess I wanted to show you I wasn't going to stand in your way." She kept going over Lillian's protests. "But I'll ask that you keep it to yourself for now, if you don't mind."

"Sure. I won't tell anyone."

Sadie nodded. "Listen. I don't reckon I need to come in. Can you just let Samuel know about the barn raising?"

"I will. And I'll come help."

"That would be *gut*." Sadie guided her horse in the other direction. Before she pulled out, she yelled out the window. "Lillian?"

"*Ya?*"

"Come for a visit anytime. I'd love to hear all about Texas." She smiled and headed down the road.

Lillian decided she liked Sadie. Who would have ever thought? An unlikely friendship, but one Lillian felt she would pursue.

By the time Lillian reached the front porch, Samuel was outside with David. "And to what do we owe the pleasure?" Samuel asked as he walked toward her.

"Actually, I came to see David."

"*Ya?*" David asked, sounding alarmed.

"I wanted to talk to you. How about taking a walk with me?" she asked.

"Can I, Pop? I did most of my chores."

"You can do the rest when you get back," Samuel said, firing a questioning look in Lillian's direction.

Offering no explanation, she smiled at Samuel and motioned for David to walk beside her. Halfway down the driveway, she said, "Something was bothering you at supper last night. Anything to do with me?"

"No," he said. Although he didn't deny something was wrong.

Lillian thought for a minute and decided honesty would be best. "I thought maybe you were upset that your Pop and I spent the day together without you. Most of the time, it's the three of us together."

David shrugged, but didn't say anything.

"*Ya*, that's it, isn't it?"

"No. That would sound like I was a kid."

"You are a kid."

Once on the main road, she said, "I think me and your pop are just trying to get to know each other better. Is that okay with you?"

"*Ya*, I reckon so."

"Sometimes me and your *daed* might want to spend some time alone, getting to know each other." She paused. "But it doesn't mean that I don't still want to do things with you. Like this—our walk. This is our time to talk. So there will probably be times when it's just me and your *daed*, or just you and your *daed*, or just me and you. See what I mean?"

"*Ya*, I know."

He seemed to understand. Maybe he just needed to hear it from her. "So, everything is okay?"

Before David had time to answer, they both heard a blaring noise coming from down the road. As the buggy drew closer, Lillian was surprised to hear music blasting from within it. That certainly wasn't allowed. As the speeding buggy came frighteningly close to running them over, a frantic boy inside struggled to turn down the music. His blond bangs were slicked back and he was wearing blue jeans and a black T-shirt.

"Did he steal that buggy?" Lillian asked alarmed. "And what was that he was drinking?"

David didn't seem worried. As they watched the boy disappearing down the road, he said, in an envious tone, "That's Milo Yoder. It's his *rumschpringe.*"

During *rumschpringe*, the community expected a certain amount of misbehavior from a teenager. But all this? Loud music, blue jeans, and whatever the boy was drinking in the brown bottle?

"Wonder where he's going in such a hurry and dressed like that?" she asked, frowning. She thought it tainted the Amish reputation for him to be acting like that.

"I can't wait until my *rumschpringe!*" David said as Milo Yoder's buggy disappeared completely, leaving only a dusty cloud behind him. "I'm gonna go to the movies, wear *Englisch* clothes, watch television in town, listen to loud music . . ." He paused. "And smoke cigarettes."

"Oh, David, I hope you won't smoke." She realized right away that it wasn't her place to speak to him in such a harsh tone, but the thought of David smoking bothered her. Turning to face him, she asked, "Why would you want to do all those things anyway?"

"Because you can do all those things during your *rumschpringe*," he said sheepishly, as if her tone surprised him. He looked down at the ground and kicked the dirt. "Besides, I bet you've done all those things."

Ouch. She certainly had. But that was different. David hadn't been exposed to any of those things, and she didn't want him to be. She wanted him to stay exactly as he was—free of complications and worldly ways. The outside world could snatch his innocence away before he realized what happened.

"Yes, I have done all those things," she answered. "And, it's not all it's cracked up to be either."

Standing on the side of the road, David pushed back his hat and gave her an inquisitive look.

"If there's something you want to ask me, go ahead." She folded her hands in front of her. "I'll tell you whatever you want to know."

"Have you ever drunk beer or smoked cigarettes?" His tone was almost demanding, but she'd started it.

"*Ya*, I have." *And please, don't do either one.*

"And I reckon you've seen lots of movies," he hesitated before he went on. "With all kinds of stuff in them."

"*Ya*, I have."

"Gone to a shopping mall and hung out with your friends?"

"Yep."

"Played an instrument?"

Lillian thought back to her short stint as a flute player while in middle school. Even though she had to give it up when Mom couldn't afford to buy her a flute of her own, she had loved making music. However, she knew the Old Order Amish community forbid instruments. Music was worldly and contrary to the Amish ways and was said to stir up emotions.

"I played the flute for a while," she finally said.

"Drove a car?" He crossed his arms, his tone still demanding. She should have never instigated this conversation.

"Yes," she answered. "But, David . . ." She wanted to tell him what a horrific childhood she'd had and how she wished she could have grown up right here. He wasn't done, though.

"Danced to band music?"

"*Ya*. I've done all those things, David. They may all sound fun and exciting to you, but you don't understand that—"

He was quick to interrupt her. "I'm going to do all those things during my *rumschpringe!*"

"Well, maybe just be choosy and make wise decisions when you go through your *rumschpringe.*" Fearing his exposure to the outside world, her emotions spilled out in an unplanned confession of sorts. "I'm sure all those things sound exciting, David. Driving a car, hanging out with your friends, drinking beer, smoking . . . but let me tell you what else can go along with all that fun-sounding stuff."

David was hanging on her words.

"Have you ever woken up and not had any food to eat? Ever slept in a car overnight because you didn't have a home to sleep in? Has anyone ever pushed you or threatened to beat you up at school? Anyone ever stolen from you? What about a terrible crime; ever witnessed anything like that? Been in a car accident that was so scary you didn't drive for six months?" She paused. "There is just a lot of bad stuff out there. That's all I'm saying. I wish I could have grown up here."

David wasn't saying anything. Maybe she'd said too much.

"I'm sorry. I should have never said all those things," she said with regret. She sat down on the side of the road in the grass. Slowly he followed her, his eyes begging for answers. "But living here seems to come with an invisible protective barrier that keeps you safe from everything out there." She waved her hand aimlessly to indicate a far-off place filled with worldly evils. "I told you before, it's complicated. And where there's all that stuff you think is so cool, there's a whole lot of ugliness too. I just don't want you to go through all that—*rumschpringe* or not."

They sat quietly for a few minutes.

"I won't do all those things, Lillian," he said softly. His big blue eyes were warm and tender, like Samuel's.

"Outside of this peaceful, tranquil, wonderful place is a world very different from yours. It might sound fun and intriguing, but trust me—it can steal from you, rob you of all the wonderful qualities that make you special. I just don't ever want to see that happen."

"It's all right, Lillian. I reckon I don't need to do all those things." It was quiet for a while before David said something Lillian felt sure she would remember for the rest of her life.

With a maturity way beyond his years, and possibly *her* years, he said, "Pop says when God closes doors, other doors will open. I had to think 'bout that for a while—like if I was in a big room with lots of doors." He paused. "I reckon sometimes we might not pick the door God woulda picked for us. But I think the door is like a two-way mirror. You best be happy with whatever ya see, no matter which side of the door you're on." He turned toward her and smiled. A smile she affectionately returned. "I reckon it'd be better to just try to pick the right door in the first place."

He couldn't have been more right.

Samuel noticed right away that the boy's frame of mind seemed much improved after his talk with Lillian. Neither one of them offered up any details, but that was all right. He reckoned they were forming their own special bond.

Lillian headed home after she filled him in about the barn rais-ing on Saturday. He figured all his kin would be there, so maybe they'd find some time to visit with Lillian there, as opposed to the private shindig they had planned. A barn raising was a whole bunch of work, but a festive occasion just the same.

He found it a little worrisome that Lillian and Sadie might be pursuing a friendship, but he knew Lillian needed some womenfolk as friends. Sadie was a good girl; she'd just never been the one for him.

It was later that afternoon that his son shared some troublesome news. "Me and Lillian had a real *gut* talk today," David said. He settled into a rocker on the front porch next to Samuel.

"And what did you two have your heads together about?"

"She's done a whole bunch of stuff in her life. Sounds like she had a pretty hard time growing up."

"*Ya*," Samuel said. "But I think she turned out real fine."

"Hard to believe she's smoked cigarettes, drunk beer, seen crimes and all kinds of bad stuff." David took a swallow of his lemonade, unaware of the can of worms he'd just opened up. "She's even slept in a car and seen people get beat up."

How could she? Had Lillian learned nothing through her studies of the Amish ways? *"Come out from among them, and be ye separate, saith the Lord."* In her studies of the *Ordnung*, did she bypass 2 Corinthians 6:17? Samuel wasn't naïve. He knew the boy would be entitled to a *rumschpringe* in a few years, just as he had been. Along with that would come some misbehaving as he took a peek at the outside world. It wasn't Lillian's place to encourage such behavior, though. Those kinds of things were best not talked about. And it sure wasn't her place to expose his son to behaviors Samuel wanted him to have no part of.

His blood was pumping and bubbling to a boil. David's

next comment sent it rushing through his veins like whitewater rapids.

"I'm real glad she told me all about her times in the *Englisch* world, about all the things she's done. Now I know what to do when my *rumschpringe* comes 'round." He placed his lemonade on the table between them. "I'm gonna go get washed up before we head to Lillian's for Sunday supper. She always makes something extra *gut* on Sunday."

Samuel nodded. They'd been having supper mostly twice a week with Lillian—Wednesdays and Sundays. Tonight, if it was up to him, they wouldn't be going anywhere for supper. He planned to tell Lillian exactly how he felt about exposing his son to her worldly past. It wasn't his way—to get all stirred up about things. It wasn't proper. But she'd crossed the line when she shared her colorful past with his son. Smoking cigarettes, drinking beer? What was she thinking?

15

"Answer the phone, Mom," Lillian whispered. Somehow she and Grandma had let the pantry run dry of flour, so this quick trip to town was a good opportunity to call her mother. She needed to hurry, though. Samuel and David would be heading over for supper soon.

"Hello."

"Hi, Mom."

"Lillian! How are things going?"

"Everything is fine. Did you tell Grandpa you were coming here on Wednesday?" Might as well get to the point.

"Yes, I did. And I'm really going to try, Lillian."

"Mom! What do you mean, you're going to *try*?"

"Well, Lillian, I do have a job. Hopefully it will work out where I can come."

"What made you change your mind? I thought you didn't want to come for a visit?"

"I just . . ." She paused. "I just need to see my parents. And when your grandpa asked me to come, well, it was just hearing his voice, I guess. I know he's sick, and I didn't want to disappoint him. He suggested Wednesday. Where are you calling me from? I've tried to call you on your cell phone several times."

"I don't have my cell phone any more. I'm calling you from a pay phone in town. Mom, Grandpa is counting on you coming. He will be very upset if you don't show up. You were so adamant with me on the phone the other day about not coming. Don't disappoint him, Mom."

"Don't take that tone with me, Lillian. I will do the best I can. I have to get someone to cover for me at work and see if I can get a flight."

"Mother, you should have thought about all that before you told Grandpa you're coming."

"I'm going to do the best I can, Lillian. That's all I can do."

"You're not coming." She wanted to reach through the phone line and—well, that wasn't the Amish way, so she tried to toss the thought.

"I don't know, Lillian. I'll try. I'd like to. Things with Paul aren't going very well either. I'm not sure if it's a good time to leave."

"I have to go, Mom."

"Wait, Lillian. Tell me about your Amish man. How are Grandma and Grandpa?"

"Come to Lancaster County and see for yourself." She slammed the phone down, knowing again that her behavior was not reflective of her newfound faith. Grandpa was going to be heartbroken.

Grandpa was sitting at the kitchen table when Lillian returned. Grandma was placing a loaf of homemade bread on the table. "Sorry it took so long," she said, checking on her beef stew she'd left simmering on the wood-burning oven. "I wanted to call Mom." She turned around and looked at her grandpa. "Grandpa, I'm not sure Mom's going to make it." She thought it best to prepare him.

"She'll be here," he said confidently. "Sarah Jane will be here on Wednesday."

"Jonas, did you hear Lillian?" Exasperated, Grandma evidently doubted the arrival of her daughter on Wednesday as well. "Sarah Jane might not make it."

Grandpa rattled off a round of *Pennsylvania Deitsch* Lillian didn't understand, but Grandma scowled, walked to him, and poked him in the arm.

"We don't talk like that in this *haus*, Jonas." She leaned down closer to him. "Sarah Jane has not been to this house in seventeen years. You needn't go gettin' your hopes up. That's all I'm saying."

Grandma was on the same page as Lillian.

"Lilly, what will you be cookin' for your *mamm* on Wednesday?" Grandpa questioned, obviously pretending he hadn't heard a word either of them said.

"I'll come up with something *gut*, Grandpa."

"Where's Samuel and the boy? I'm hungry," he belted out. Grandma rolled her eyes.

Samuel and David arrived about ten minutes late. Uncharacteristic. They were always on time. Samuel looked tired and bothered about something throughout the entire meal.

"Didn't you like the stew?" Lillian asked, noticing that although everyone else was about finished, Samuel still had quite a bit in his bowl.

"The stew was fine. Can I talk to you on the porch, Lillian?"

Something was wrong. Everyone at the table shot Samuel a questioning look.

"*Ya*," she whispered softly. "Do you want some peach pie first?"

"No, *danki*," he said, standing up.

This isn't good. Why was he so bothered? Everything was fine when she left his house earlier.

"You kids run along," Grandpa said. "David, I've been needin' me a chess partner for a long while. Your grandma won't play."

"Jonas, someone has to keep this house running," Grandma said. She stood up and began to clear the dishes.

"I'll help you in a minute." Lillian stood up to follow Samuel to the door.

"No, no. You go on. I've got it," Grandma replied.

"Let's be headin' into the den, David. A good game of chess will help settle our full bellies." Grandpa shuffled out of the kitchen.

———

Out on the porch, Samuel didn't waste any time. "I don't know what you were thinkin' when you told my boy all the things you did in your world. I don't want him to know anything about your world. Bad enough he witnessed that *baremlich* scene here with your friend, Rickie. I'm not sure I want you around him." He knew his eyes were ablaze and his tone sharp.

Instantly, her eyes glassed over. She looked shattered. Samuel realized right away he should have eased into the conversation, or at least toned it down a notch.

"What?" she asked. Her legs appeared wobbly before she folded into one of the rockers. Samuel took a seat in the other rocker.

"I don't want David exposed to your world, Lillian." He shook his head, but could hardly look at her.

"But this is my world." Her voice was cracking. This was harder than he'd reckoned it would be.

"But your worldly ways are spilling into our ways, Lillian. What were you thinkin' when you told David about drinking and smoking?" He paused. "And all that other stuff you told him about life in the city? The boy needn't be hearing any such things. It will be right hard enough when he has his *rumschpringe*. He doesn't need any encouragement from you to try all those things."

Her hands were on either side of her cheeks and her eyes were all watered up. His first instinct was to go wrap his arms around her, but that wasn't going to help things. Refocusing on what was best for David, Samuel knew he couldn't let her reaction muddle his thinking.

"But I don't want him to do *any* of those things. The reason I—" Her voice was still cracking, but he didn't want to hear her excuses.

"There is no reason for any of it, Lillian. And, I'm sorry to say, I just would rather you not spend so much time with David."

"Samuel, you don't mean that. You and David have become like my family."

He knew she was crying, so he just avoided looking at her.

Didn't she realize his heart was breaking too? But he had to do what was best for the boy.

"Don't you care about me?" She sounded pitiful. He wasn't sure he could respond without his own voice breaking up.

"*Ya,*" he said softly, forcing himself to look down at the ground and not at her.

"Samuel," she reached for his hand, and it took every bit of his might to pull away from her.

"I'm gonna go, Lillian. And I think it's best if me and David stop comin' for supper." He stood up, but this time his eyes were drawn to hers like a magnet. He had trouble looking away, but he did. If he didn't go now, he'd never be able to.

She was all curled up in the rocker crying hard. Walking away from her would be difficult.

"Samuel, please . . ."

"I'm real sorry, Lillian, that you're hurtin'."

"Just let me explain."

He could barely understand her for the crying. He walked back into the kitchen. As the door slammed behind him, he worried how he'd keep his emotions inside. He just kept telling himself it was the best thing for David.

"David, we need to be goin'," he said as he walked into the den where Jonas and David looked like they'd barely gotten started on their chess game. Irma Rose wasn't around.

"We're just getting started," Jonas said, sounding disappointed.

"*Ya,* Pop. I figured you and Lillian would be talkin' for a while." David smiled, but it quickly faded when he saw the look on his pop's face.

"Come on, boy. We've got things to tend to. Sorry, Jonas." He grabbed his hat off the rack and headed for the door.

Lillian was still curled up in the rocker. It took everything he had to make his legs walk down the porch steps and leave her like that.

"Lillian, what's wrong?" David made his way onto the porch and was standing behind Samuel, his eyes dark with worry.

He turned around in time to see Lillian jump out of the rocker and run into the house.

David didn't move. "Pop, what's goin' on?"

Samuel motioned for David to come along. It was going to be a hard conversation to have with his son. But it was for the best.

"But, Pop, she was just tryin' to tell me not to do all those things," David said later. "I think she was just tryin' to protect me."

He knew David was suffering right along with him and Lillian. "It's not right to talk about such things, David."

"But I want her to be *mei mamm* someday!"

Samuel had suspected the boy harbored the same hopeful image of the future he did: all of them as one big happy family. "Watch your tone, boy," Samuel said, careful not to scorn him too much. He was hurting for sure.

"But, Pop—"

It was tough to see his son's eyes welling up with tears. But someday he'd realize that this was the best thing for him. "On up to bed now," Samuel said, fighting his own emotions. Couldn't let the boy see him watering up.

David ran up the stairs without saying another word. Samuel put his head in his hands. He couldn't shake the image of Lillian crying.

"Lillian, can I come in?"

Lillian attempted to control her crying, to no avail. "*Ya,*" she said to her grandma, through the bedroom door.

How could Samuel do this? Was his friendship so limited that there was no room for mistakes or forgiveness? She thought she was helping David see how bad choices could turn out. Samuel didn't even want to hear her explanation. Obviously, he didn't care about her the way she cared about him. If he could give up on their friendship so easily, then maybe it truly wasn't meant to be.

No. She just didn't believe that. It *was* meant to be. It had to be. He and David were in her life. And she'd prayed so hard about it. Wasn't God listening? How could this be happening?

"There, there," Grandma comforted, taking a seat on the bed.

Lillian wept in her arms. "He didn't even let me explain, Grandma," she said after telling her what happened. "I want David to make good choices when he has his *rumschpringe.* He'll be exposed to so many evils out in the world. I was just trying to prepare him so he'd know what to avoid. I would never encourage him to make any of the mistakes I made." She cried some more while her grandma held her.

"I know you wouldn't lead the boy astray, Lillian. Maybe just give Samuel some time to think things out."

"He was so cold, Grandma. He just left me there, in pieces. It was horrible—like he didn't care about me at all. How could he do that? I don't understand."

Grandma gently pushed her away and cradled her cheeks with

her hands. "Let me try to explain something to you in a way I reckon maybe you can understand. I know you love me and your grandpa. I know you love Samuel and David. But when you have *kinner* of your own, you'll understand a whole different kind of love. It's a love so powerful that you'll cause hurt to yourself if it means protecting a child."

"David doesn't need protection from me. I do love him. I would never, ever do anything to hurt him." She pulled away from her grandma and threw her head on the pillow.

"I know that, dear. I think when Samuel talks to David and thinks this through, in his mind he'll come to know that too." Stroking Lillian's hair, she went on. "Sometimes, we think we're doin' right by our young ones. Maybe sometimes we don't always do so."

As Irma Rose tried her best to comfort Lillian, she couldn't help but wonder why her own daughter had left so abruptly—if it was something she did. There was no handbook for raising children, and she reckoned she'd done the best she could. Her heart went out to Lillian. And to Samuel. He was only trying to do what he thought was best for the boy. Hopefully he'd come to reason that Lillian only had David's best interest at heart.

"Did you call your *mamm*?" she asked when Lillian seemed to be a little better.

"*Ya*." She sat up on the bed and dabbed at her eyes. "She said she's going to try to come. But I know her, Grandma. She won't come and it will break Grandpa's heart."

And mine. As nervous as she was to see Sarah Jane, it was all

Irma Rose had thought about since Jonas shared the news of her visit.

Three days since his conversation with Lillian, Samuel wasn't feeling any better. To worsen things, David was barely talking to him. Maybe he'd acted too harshly. If he did, it was out of love and fear for his son. He thought back to his own *rumschpringe* and cringed, doubtful he'd experienced hardly a tad of what Lillian must have experienced in the *Englisch* world. Should he fault her for that? No. But sharing her past with his son was strictly off-limits. She should have known that.

Lost in regret and confusion, Samuel realized it was nearing four o'clock. He'd need to stir up some supper for him and David. Normally they'd be heading to Lillian's on Wednesday. His heart was heavy as he thought about facing each day without Lillian in his life.

"Have you talked to Lillian?" he asked, sitting down at the kitchen table across from his son.

"*Ya.*" David bit into a cookie. It didn't appear he was going to say anything about it.

"Is she okay?"

The look David fired at him surely deserved a trip to the woodshed and some discipline, but he let it go.

"No, she's not *okay*. And she fears talking to me—afraid she'll get me and her in trouble."

Samuel hung his head. "I was just trying to protect you." *Maybe I made a mistake.*

"Pop, I'm gonna be seeing the *Englisch* world in a few years. She was just trying to tell me not to make some of the same mistakes she made."

"*Ya*. But such *Englisch* things are best unspoken." He shouldn't have to justify his actions to David.

"Why? If her blunders might help me to not walk a bad path, then why should they not be talked about?" David's tone was bordering on rude, and Samuel didn't like it. But he considered the possibility that maybe his son was right.

"Maybe I should talk to her." Samuel stroked his beard and thought about what he would say. He was having a world of trouble trying to figure out how he was going to reconcile this situation.

"I don't think she wants to talk to you, Pop. I think she's gone from being real upset to real mad." David paused and bit into another cookie. "Besides, she's got worry in her heart about Jonas. She's fearing he's going be real upset when her mother doesn't show up today."

Samuel had been so focused on how much he missed her he'd forgotten that Wednesday was the day Sarah Jane Miller was due to arrive. It was gonna break Jonas and Irma Rose's hearts if she didn't show. And Lillian's. He should be there to wait with her or comfort her if her *mamm* didn't show up. What a fine mess he'd made of things.

"Your grandpa hasn't moved from that rocker on the porch for the past two hours. It's nearin' six o'clock, way past the supper hour," Grandma said. "He needs to accept that Sarah Jane isn't coming."

Lillian could hear the regret in her grandma's voice. Honestly, she wasn't sure who was more upset, Grandma or Grandpa.

"I'm sorry, Grandma. Maybe I should go talk to Grandpa." She stood from the kitchen table and headed toward the door. Grandma just shrugged.

How could everything have fallen apart like this? She missed Samuel so bad it hurt, but she was equally angry at him for snatching away their friendship as if it meant nothing. And now this. She knew her mother wasn't going to show. Just history repeating itself.

She took a seat in the other rocker on the porch. "Grandpa," she said hesitantly. "How long are you going to sit out here?"

He stared down the dirt driveway. "Until Sarah Jane gets here."

Lillian started to ask him how long that would be, but he spoke first.

"So, when are you and Samuel going to mend your ways?"

"I don't know if we are." She didn't want to talk about this right now. There were enough emotional issues swirling in the air.

Grandpa winked. "Sure you are."

"I don't know, Grandpa. He walked away from me like I meant nothing to him."

"*Ach*, Lilly, he was just not thinkin' right at the time. Thought he was doin' the best thing for the boy. He's come to his senses by now, and I'm bettin' he's missing you up a storm about now. You two have spent a lot of time together these past few months."

"Well, I don't miss him." It was a big fat lie, which Grandpa saw right through.

"Sure you don't," he said, drawing out his words. "Might

take a little more time, but you kids will be seeing eye to eye again soon."

She hoped so, but it had been three days. Of course, she'd made her feelings pretty clear to David when she told him how mad she was. *Wonder if David told his dad?*

She didn't feel any better today than she did on Sunday. However, she was really worried about her grandparents.

Mom, this is so like you to do this.

The screen door slammed, and Grandma joined them on the porch. "Lillian, I've left some supper keepin' warm on the oven. You need to eat yourself something."

"She's waiting to eat with her *mamm*, Irma Rose," Jonas said with a forceful tone.

Grandma glanced at Lillian and then back at her husband. "Jonas, you can't stay out here all night."

When he continued to stare down the driveway and didn't respond, Grandma shrugged. "Suit yourself. I'm going in the den to read for a bit." She turned to head back in the kitchen.

Grandpa moved faster than she'd seen since her arrival. He sprang from the rocker so abruptly you'd have thought his behind was on fire. "There she is!" he yelled. "There's my Sarah Jane!"

Lillian could hardly believe her eyes as a car turned onto the driveway. She reached for her grandpa to steady him. He was so much better lately, but he was sure unsteady on his legs. She strained to see better.

"What?" Grandma asked, turning to rejoin them on the porch. Her voice crackled with disbelief. "Is it true? Is it Sarah Jane?" She put her hands to her mouth and Lillian could see her trembling.

As the car neared the house, Lillian strained even harder to see. She smiled.

"It's Mom," she said, running down the steps. "Thank You, God," she whispered on her way to the tan Ford pulling to a stop. She looked back at her grandparents and waved them to come closer.

The car door opened, and Mom stepped out. Lillian didn't think she had ever looked more beautiful. Her black slacks and conservative blue blouse framed her tall and slender figure. Perfectly groomed, as always, her blonde waves rested at her shoulders, teased for some height.

It warmed Lillian's heart the way her mom's face lit up when she saw her. There was no shock at Lillian's apparel, no snide comments. She just smiled.

"You look beautiful, Lillian," she said.

Lillian fell into her arms. "So do you, Mom. I'm so glad you came."

The embrace lasted a long time. Lillian felt like she could have stayed in her mother's arms forever. Memories of all the good things she experienced over the years came flooding over her. Yes, there had been hard times. But her mother deserved credit for the good times too. This being one of them.

Gently, her mother pulled away and eyed her up and down. "You really do look beautiful, Lillian. The Amish look works for you." She kissed her on the cheek before glancing up at her parents on the porch.

Sensing her nervousness, Lillian said, "It'll be fine, Mom. They are so excited." She grabbed her mother's hand and began pulling her toward them.

Grandpa stretched out his arms wide in front of him. Tears poured down his face. She glanced at her grandma, whose hands were folded over her mouth. The rise and fall of her shoulders indicated she was unable to control her sobs of joy.

"Sarah Jane," Grandpa said, weeping. He took her in his arms and held her tight. It was only seconds before Sarah Jane cried out, "Pop, I'm so sorry. Oh, Pop, I'm so sorry for everything. I'm so sorry . . ."

Grandma ran to them, throwing her arms around them both. "Sarah Jane," she cried.

"*Mamm*, I'm sorry. I'm sorry. I didn't know how to come back. I didn't know what to do. I'm sorry." She turned toward her mother and lovingly embraced her.

Lillian stood frozen, tears streaming down her face. It was a joyous moment. Only one thing would have made it perfect.

No sooner had she processed the thought when she turned to see a buggy pulling up the driveway.

"Samuel?" she whispered.

16

"I'LL BE BACK IN A MINUTE," LILLIAN TOLD HER GRAND-parents and mother over her shoulder. Grandpa acknowledged hearing her, but she wasn't sure what he said. She was focused on the approaching buggy. Disappointment flooded over her when she realized it wasn't Samuel.

It was Samuel's brother, Ivan. Maybe he was here to deliver a message from Samuel.

"Hi, Ivan. What brings you out here?" Lillian watched him step out of the buggy.

"Everything all right?" he asked, approaching her.

She wasn't sure what he meant. Was he talking about Samuel?

"What?" she asked.

"I saw a car I didn't recognize pulling in. I worried maybe Jonas was down again. Just stopping to check on you all."

Not what she was hoping to hear. "Everything is fine," she said, forcing a smile. "Actually, my *mamm* is here, so my grand-parents are very excited to see her."

"*Gut* news," he said, crawling back into the buggy. "Just checking."

"Ivan, I was wondering—" She stopped. She didn't know Ivan well at all. To question him about Samuel seemed inappropriate. "Thank you for checking on us." She waved.

Guiding his horse into motion, he tipped his hat and said, "Anytime," as he pulled back down the driveway.

———

For the next two hours, Lillian listened to her mother confessing to her parents more than was probably necessary. But it seemed to be a cleansing of her soul. She began with her affair with Daniel Foster and subsequent pregnancy and led into how shame and embarrassment kept her from returning to the Old Order district, with the exception of a few visits here and there. Much of what she said Lillian had never heard before or didn't remember. Grandma and Grandpa hung on her every word.

Lillian knew it was difficult for her mother to share her past, and she had never been more proud of her. As Mom released years of pent-up emotion, her face twisted in agony as she recalled certain events. In the dimly lit kitchen, Grandma never let go of Sarah Jane's hand, and Grandpa cried a lot. Lillian sat with her arm around her mother, giving her a gentle squeeze when she struggled to continue.

She concluded with Lillian's confrontation with Daniel.

"Oh, Lillian," Grandma said sadly, shaking her head, "I'm sorry we didn't know what you were goin' through."

"It's all right, Grandma. I have put it behind me. I just needed some answers to be able to move forward."

Not entirely true. It would take a while to recover from the sting of meeting her father.

As everyone attempted to gather themselves after the emotional conversation, her mother asked, "So, Lillian, where is your friend?"

Her heart sank with regrets about Samuel. As she opened her

mouth to try and communicate some sort of response, Grandpa
interjected his own thoughts about it.

"Lillian and Samuel are like peanut butter and jelly. They ain't
nothin' alike, but they're real good when they're together. They're
both mixed-up over some silly nonsense they need to get worked
out. My guess is they'll be workin' it out at the barn raising this
Saturday." He smiled, which was a welcome sight after all the
heartache the past couple of hours. "Nothing like a good barn
raising to lift the spirits. Wish I was a younger man not all eaten
up by the cancer. I'd be out there on Saturday lending a hand."

"I don't know how things will turn out," Lillian said, despair
in her voice. "I miss him a lot, but he's made no attempt to come
see me. I'm pretty sure he meant what he said."

"Hogwash! He'll be back here at suppertime every few days
before you can shake a stick." Grandpa said. "Then the whole
family will be back together again."

Lillian tried to perk up. "I hope so, Grandpa. I really do."

"Pop, maybe you ought to go talk to Lillian," David told his
dad. Samuel dimmed the lantern in his bedroom. "And tell her
you're sorry."

The boy was right. Plus, Samuel knew he'd been a hard man
to live with lately. Hearing David's spirited talk of the *Englisch*
ways had left him fearful about his son's future. But his reaction
to everything Lillian had said to David was from the hip, without thinking about her intentions. He'd been preaching faith to
her, yet his own faith in *her* had temporarily deserted him.

"I'm planning on talkin' to her at the barn raising Saturday.

Ivan stopped by and said he dropped by their place to check on things. Her *mamm* was there. I know they all have lots of catching up to do, so I'm going to let them all be for now."

"Maybe she won't be so mad by Saturday. You hurt her feelings real bad, Pop."

Samuel watched his son's eyebrows jutting inward and his lips scrunching. There was a time when he'd have never allowed David to speak to him in such a manner. But he reckoned he might have made a mistake and it had obviously had great effect on the boy.

"*Ya*, David. I know." He shook his head. "Saturday, I will talk to her."

As Sarah Jane loaded her suitcase into the car, Irma Rose stifled her tears. Jonas had said his good-byes to Sarah Jane upstairs. Irma Rose knew how badly her husband wanted to come downstairs, but he was having one of his bad days. Lillian walked with them to see her mother off, but the child was clearly in another world. Hopefully, she and Samuel would be getting things worked out real soon.

It had been a glorious two days, and Sarah Jane promised to be back for Christmas.

"I'm sorry I can't stay longer." She hugged Lillian first and then Irma Rose. "I would have liked to stick around and go to the barn raising tomorrow. It's been a long time since I've been to one." She looked at Lillian. "I hope that tomorrow you and Samuel will get things worked out. Tell him I'll look forward to meeting him when I'm here for Christmas."

"I don't know if we'll get things worked out or not, Mom."

Irma Rose sure hoped so. Lillian had been a miserable soul the past few days.

"Nothing like the festivities of a good barn raising to set everyone's sights in order," Irma Rose said.

As Sarah Jane gave her a final hug, Irma Rose wished the embrace could last forever. Her daughter's return was a dream come true and a prayer answered. So many issues put to rest. Now it was time to move forward with refreshed spirit and joy. The Lord's blessings were with them.

"I love you, *Mamm*," Sarah Jane whispered in her ear. "I never stopped loving you."

Irma Rose couldn't control her cries of happiness. "Oh, my blessed daughter," she began, "you were our gift from the Good Lord, and you still are. I love you so very much."

As her granddaughter stood watching, Irma Rose struggled to pry herself away from Sarah Jane. It had been so long—and two days just wasn't enough. She would count the days until Christmas when they'd all be together again.

Samuel woke up Saturday with high hopes he would get things fixed with Lillian. It had been a terrible six days since he had seen her. He should've explained his feelings about the situation and not reacted the way he did. She had come a long way since she arrived in Lancaster County, and he should have kept the faith she would never do anything to soil David's upbringing.

"*Guder mariye*, Pop," David said, rubbing his eyes as he walked into the kitchen.

"Good morning to you. I made us some red-beet eggs this morning. We'll need all our energy to help with the barn raising." He shoveled some eggs alongside a piece of toast for his son.

"We'll see Lillian today too."

"*Ya*, we will." And Samuel couldn't wait. He was going to make things right.

"I sure hope things go back to the way they were before you—" The boy clamped his mouth shut, seeming to force back comments that might get him in a heap of trouble.

"I'm sure everything will be *wunderbaar gut*. It'll be a grand day," Samuel said, taking a seat beside his son. "Now, eat your eggs. We need to be there at daybreak and that's sneaking up on us."

There were over fifty buggies parked up near the Zook farm when Samuel and David arrived. John Lapp, an Amish carpenter by profession, was already lining the men out and assigning areas of work. No time to waste. They would need to complete the framing by the noon meal, giving time to eat, and then they'd put on the roof in the afternoon. As long as that much got done, the closing in could be handled by family and friends the following day, if need be.

The last of the buggies pulled in. Samuel reckoned there were over a hundred and fifty people in attendance. The women were gathering in the kitchen to prepare the meal, and the smaller children were scurrying around and playing games. Without a cloud in the sky, it was a fine day for a barn raising. Although it neared the end of August, the summer heat was still upon them. Yes, it was warm. But a slow breeze eased the effects of the sun's brilliant rays.

Samuel watched his son accepting an assignment from John Lapp, then turned and scanned the work area. There was no sign of Lillian. A few of the women were scattered about, but most of them were inside busy with meal preparations. She would have to come outside sooner or later. He hoped it was sooner so he would have a chance to talk to her, explain his harsh reaction.

The men and older boys had been at work about two hours when the first offering of iced tea was made. Several of the women-folk began walking around handing glasses to the workers.

Samuel was ready for a cold glass of tea. More than that, he was ready to see Lillian. He was surprised he hadn't caught a glimpse of her yet. Surely she wouldn't forego the barn raising because of him.

"Why, Samuel, what in the world are you doing here?" Ellen Zook asked, handing him a glass of tea.

Sending her a questioning look, he asked, "Why wouldn't I be here? You know I wouldn't miss a barn raising. I'm mighty pleased to help."

Ellen looked confused. "Well, I guess I was figuring you to be at the Miller place this morning." She paused. "I mean I think the whole district knows you spend a lot of time out there with Irma Rose, Jonas—and their *kinskind*. Word is that you and Lillian might have taken a fancy to each other."

"Isn't Lillian here? I thought she'd be inside helping with the meal?" Maybe she'd decided not to come.

"Uh, Samuel," Ellen began, "I just assumed someone had gotten word to you."

"Word about what?" He didn't like her tone. "Word about what?" he asked again.

"Why, Samuel, I'm sorry to say . . . Irma Rose passed this morning. I just figured you'd be with the family. They said she just went in her sleep and—"

He didn't hear another word she said, as his legs mechanically carried him to the buggy. He yelled at Katie Ann to keep an eye on David while he quickly maneuvered the buggy onto the road. "Let's go, Pete!" he yelled, jolting the horse into a full run.

He and Lillian had talked about death on more than one occasion. One thing Samuel knew for sure: nothing scared her more than death. And as much as Lillian had grown to love Irma Rose and Jonas, he knew she must be over the edge with grief.

"Come on, boy!" he yelled, picking up even more speed.

Lillian was anxious to see Samuel at the barn raising. From the moment she opened her eyes Saturday morning, it was all she could think about. Despite the fact he hadn't come around, maybe, just maybe, he'd had time to reflect on his decision and had a change of heart. Maybe he missed her and realized she'd never, ever do anything to hurt David. She couldn't rewrite her past. Besides, she had changed so much. Didn't that matter?

"You're up earlier than usual," Grandpa commented when she served him some scrapple alongside his eggs. She wrinkled her nose. She had never acquired a taste for this popular Amish meal. She didn't want to eat anything made up of leftover parts of a hog. She was floored the first time she saw Grandma putting parts of hog heads, hearts, liver, and other scraps in the mushy mix of cornmeal and flour. But Grandpa loved it, so she cooked it for him on occasion.

"The barn raising is today," she said. "From what I under-stand, it all gets started at daybreak. So I don't want to be late. *You're* the one who's up early." She smiled.

"Food," he said. "The smell of food gets me movin' in the morning. Your Grandma, on the other hand, is out like a light."

"Well, I'm glad to see you're feeling better this morning." She knew the past two days had exhausted him both physically and mentally. In addition to the heart-wrenching conversations, they'd all stayed up much later than usual while her mother was there. Both her grandparents had looked worn-out the night before.

"Maybe you better go give your *mammi* a nudge. You know how much she likes scrapple, and she'll be all upset if she has to eat it cold." He dove into the soupy mush. "Um, um . . . mighty *gut*," he said.

Thinking how Grandma liked to get her day off to an early start, Lillian headed up the stairs. She knocked on the door twice, but there was no answer. "Grandma?"

Knocking again, she yelled a little louder, "Grandma, I made scrapple. Come get it while it's hot."

Nothing.

She walked down the upstairs hall to the small bathroom. Gently she pushed the door open. "Grandma?" The door swung wide, but no Grandma.

She headed back toward her grandparents' room, pondering whether or not Grandma would have gone outside. No, there wouldn't be any reason to.

An unfamiliar tingling rushed from her head to her toes, caus-ing her to feel light-headed as she turned the doorknob. Something wasn't right. Her heart rate increased, and she was suddenly afraid to enter the room. And yet, unable to turn back, she pushed the door open.

Well, thank the Lord. Grandma was curled up in bed asleep, facing the other way. She hadn't gone missing and wasn't lying in a pool of blood from a bad fall or anything.

"Grandma, wake up. You scared me." She walked toward the bed. "Wake up, sleepyhead. I made scrapple—that nasty mush you and Grandpa like."

As she neared the edge of the bed, the tingling rush shot through her veins again. She stopped. "Grandma?" she said softly. Her feet were rooted to the floor, and she couldn't move. Grandma snored. She always snored. Why was there no snoring?

"Grandma!" Still unable to move, she yelled again, "Grandma, wake up!"

She could hear footsteps coming up the stairs. *Oh God, no. Please, no.* She forced her feet to move and sat down on the edge of the bed. As she reached over and touched her grandma's arm, she knew instantly—Grandma was dead. Her cold, lifeless body was curled into a ball.

Lillian knew Grandpa would be in the room within seconds. Maybe she was wrong. She ran to the other side of the bed so she could see her grandmother's face. The older woman's eyes were closed; she looked peaceful. But clearly she wasn't breathing.

"Grandma." She pushed her gently. Nothing.

"What are ya hollering about up here, Lilly?"

She turned around to see Grandpa standing in the doorway. A tear rolled down her cheek. "Grandpa . . ."

He stood frozen in place. "No, Lilly. She's just sleeping. I'm going first. I got the cancer." Staring at her with a blank look, he asked, "Did you tell her you made scrapple? That'll get her moving."

"Grandpa," she said again, trying to control herself—for once. The man nearing the bed had been married to this woman for almost fifty years. She couldn't even imagine how he must feel. Her own heart was breaking.

His feet edged slowly toward the other side of the bed. "Irma Rose, get on up out of that bed and get you some scrapple."

Lillian couldn't hold it anymore. Crying softly, she attempted to swipe away the tears trailing down her cheeks, in an unsuccessful effort to stay strong for Grandpa. She stood up from the bed and walked to the window to make more room for Grandpa. As she gazed out the window, she heard his sobs from behind her.

"Oh, Irma Rose, not now. It's not time. Sarah Jane will be back for Christmas."

Lillian turned around to see her grandpa lifting the love of his life, limp and lifeless, into his arms. How could this have happened? She wasn't even sick. Grandpa was the one who was sick. Grandpa was the one she'd prayed for, every night, to get well. And he was so much better. Had this happened because she didn't pray enough for Grandma?

She began to go over her nightly prayers, reciting them in her head. Maybe she had given Grandpa more prayer time. But it was because he was sick. This was unfair of God. Had she known her grandma was at risk, she would have prayed harder for her.

First Samuel. Now this. God wasn't listening to her. Otherwise he would have never let this happen.

It was even more heartbreaking to watch Grandpa swaying back and forth, cradling Grandma in his arms.

"Oh, my Irma Rose, my darling beloved," he wept. "Don't leave me on this earth without you. Wake up, Irma Rose."

While her own heart ripped in two, she knew she would need to produce all her strength to see her grandpa through this. She walked to the bed and sat down beside him.

"Grandpa, I think we need to send for someone," she suggested. Tenderly, she stroked his arm.

"Call the Good Lord and tell him to send her back to me, Lilly. Get your cell phone and call heaven. Tell God to send her back to me for a bit longer."

"Grandpa, it was just her time. She's with God now." She wasn't sure where the words were coming from because it *wasn't* Grandma's time.

"*Ach*, no . . . Oh, no." He cried harder, and Lillian didn't think she'd ever seen a more frail creature. Like a lost child, he wept.

"Let her lie in peace," she said softly. "Come on, Grandpa." She tried to pull him away, but he clung tightly. "Grandpa, we are going to have to go into town and let someone know. I think there are, uh, things that we have to do."

She had no idea what they needed to do, and she had no idea where her strength was coming from. Perhaps it was knowing Grandpa's pain was far worse than her own. Seeing him like this was almost as heartbreaking as losing Grandma. She took a deep breath and tried as best she could to gather herself. She hated to leave him alone. Why hadn't she held onto that cell phone? Why hadn't she prayed harder? Why did this have to happen?

She started to cry again.

"Lilly, travel to town to the funeral home. They'll tell you our ways. I want to be alone with my Irma Rose," Grandpa said as he gently laid her back down.

"Okay, Grandpa." She gazed upon the woman who had taught her so much, whom she had grown to love over the past months. Nothing would ever be the same.

Forcing herself to stand up and do as Grandpa asked, she turned to face him when she reached the bedroom door. Still cradling his beloved wife in his arms, his body trembled with grief. He'd cried out to Lillian to do something, to reverse the situation, to beg God for more time. She realized even a man with Grandpa's faith couldn't accept such a loss as merely God's will. It didn't make him any less faithful to God, only human.

As Samuel pulled up at the Miller farm, his heart was heavy. The timing of all this was terrible. *And Irma Rose?* It was shocking. He'd reckoned Jonas would go way before his wife.

He shook his head as he parked the buggy and walked toward the front door. Lillian was going to be a wreck. The girl was as emotional a person as he'd ever known, and he knew she would be falling apart. She should have come to him this morning. He should have been the one to help her with things, to comfort her.

Yet . . . he reckoned if the situation were reversed, he wouldn't have searched her out either. He'd said some pretty strong things to her.

"Hello, Samuel," Lillian said as she opened the screen door and motioned him to come inside. "It's very nice of you to come." Her tone was unusually curt.

"Lillian, you should have sought me out this morning when this happened. I'm so sorry, Lillian." He hugged her—a hug she did not return.

"Grandpa's in the den if you'd like to visit with him. The funeral home has already been here to pick up Grandma. They will be bringing her back on Monday. The funeral will be here on Tuesday. Mr. Jackson said they are familiar with Amish customs and will make sure everything is done accordingly."

She rattled on like a robot, with hardly a hint of expression on her face. But he knew better. Her red, swollen eyes told the tale.

"Lillian," he said softly, reaching for her. "You don't have to be strong for my benefit."

"I'm fine," she said, turning toward the den.

"Grandpa, Samuel is here to pay his respects." She sat down in a chair near her grandpa, and she wouldn't even look at Samuel.

He extended his hand to Jonas, who clasped it with both of his hands. "Thank you for coming, Samuel. The *Englisch* doctor said he thinks Irma Rose's heart just plumb gave out." He squeezed Samuel's hand before letting it go. Hanging his head, he said, "Probably my fault. She'd been working too hard to take care of me. But I reckon it was God's will. I sure will miss my Irma Rose."

Jonas didn't seem to notice, but Samuel caught on to Lillian's attitude right quick at the mention of God's will.

"It's nobody's fault, Jonas. Don't do that to yourself," Samuel said. He glanced at Lillian, trying to make some sort of connection, only to find her keeping a solemn look on her face. She wouldn't even look his way. "I reckon we don't always understand why things happen the way they do."

Jonas' shoulders began to heave up and down, and Samuel could see he was trying to hold back tears. "Sarah Jane was here, Samuel. Irma Rose only had two days with her. She just left last night. She was comin' back for Christmas."

Samuel sat down in a chair on the other side of Jonas, which put him face-to-face with Lillian. "I'm so sorry, Jonas." He reached over and put his hand on his shoulder. "Do you want me to arrange for the coffin carriers?"

"That'd be mighty fine if you'd do that."

"And I'm sure Katie Ann and my sisters will pitch in with the meal, along with a lot of other folks 'round here."

Lillian still wouldn't look his way. "All that's not necessary," she said in an almost hateful tone. "I can arrange the food, and I can—"

"Lillian, let Samuel handle those things," Jonas said.

"Grandpa, we don't need Samuel to handle those things. I can do it," she insisted. She was dead set on hurting him. That was clear. She didn't want him involved in anything to do with her or her family.

"Lilly." Grandpa looked up at her and gave her a look that caused her to sit up straighter. "You know I love you, no?"

"Of course," she answered with questioning eyes.

"I'm gonna say this one time: you get that chip off your shoulder right now. Quit blaming God for this. And get outside and go get things straightened out with Samuel. It's been bad enough, you moping around this house. And now my Irma Rose is gone. I don't have an ounce of tolerance for that attitude of yours."

Before he finished his harsh reprimand, Lillian's eyes were

full of water and she wasted no time jumping up and running toward the kitchen. He heard the screen door slam.

"Don't let her fox you, Samuel. This is killin' her inside, and she's seeing fit to blame the Good Lord. I reckon she's acting the only way she knows how, to be able to help herself cope." He sighed. "And another thing—you know she'd never do a thing to hurt that boy of yours, no?"

Samuel didn't think he could feel any lower. "*Ya*, Jonas. I know that. I made a *baremlich* mistake."

"Then I reckon you need to go out there and tell her that. She's going to need a lot of help getting through this, and I don't have the strength, Samuel. Lilly's come a long way in admonishing her old ways and learning our ways. I don't want to see her fall backward because of this. I know you care about that girl."

"Very much."

"Then get out there and make sure she stays on course with her studies, so she will want to stay with us. Don't let this be settin' her back."

Samuel stood up and headed toward the kitchen. "I'll make things right, Jonas."

Making his way out the back door and onto the porch, Samuel found Lillian sitting in the rocker on the front porch—the same rocker she was curled up in when he left her crushed and heartbroken the previous Sunday. She looked mad as a hatter.

"Leave me alone," Lillian said as Samuel took a seat in the rocker beside her. Grandpa had never talked to her that way, and she didn't need a lecture from Samuel right now either. She would handle this situation as best she could.

"Lillian," he said softly, reaching for her hand. She jerked it away.

"I don't want to talk right now, Samuel." Being angry—at Samuel and at God—was the only thing working for her at the moment.

"We're going to have to talk, Lillian," he said, looking down at the ground. "Because I made a terrible mistake, and I'm here to apologize. I know you love David and that your tellin' him about worldly things was only your way of trying to keep him out of harm's way. I know that, Lillian. And I'm sorry. I should have let you explain . . . should have thought everything through before I said all those things."

It should have been music to her ears, but she couldn't get past everything that had happened. Not right now. Staying mad was all that was keeping her together.

When she didn't respond, he went on. "I know how sad you feel right now, Lillian. We'll get through this together." He reached for her hand again, and again she pulled away. "The pain gets better over time," he added.

A huge part of her wanted to run into his arms and allow him to comfort her. The pain felt like it was eating her from the inside out, nibbling at her heart, a tiny little bit at a time. To be able to function or maintain at all, she would not be able to succumb to his offer. She would handle this on her own.

"Samuel, I can get through this, and I will be just fine." She raised her chin slightly and pulled her lips tight, fearful he might see them quivering. She had never felt more on the edge in her life.

"Lillian, I want to help you. I want to be here for you. I'm so sorry . . . about everything."

In an irrational display of emotion, she bolted from the rocker and put her hands on her hips. "Help me what, Samuel?" She knew she was yelling, and that had not been part of the plan. The plan was to stay void of feeling, to stay angry, so she didn't have to feel the pain ripping at her insides. "Help me to forget that I came from another world? Well, I can't! It is part of my past, and I can't make that go away. Do you want to help me get over Grandma dying? Well, I can't. I loved her. Do you want me to accept this as God's will? Well, I can't do that either."

The tears were falling and she was losing control. Samuel was on his feet, his arms outstretched and waiting to make everything right. Problem was things could never be right again. "I can't accept things as God's will. I just can't." There, she'd said it. Now he wouldn't have a problem walking away from her. Her inability to accept God's will would surely be more than enough for him to not want her around him or his son.

"So, there—you can go now. I will get over this on my own." She took a step backward, only to have him take two steps forward.

"I'm not goin' anywhere, Lillian," he said in a tender but determined tone. He inched closer to her. With no room to continue backward, unless she wanted to fall off the porch, she held her position by trying to stare him down. Although she could feel the tears pouring down her cheeks and suspected she wasn't being very convincing. "I don't need you, Samuel," she cried. "You gave up on our friendship. You gave up on me." She put her hands over her face and wept.

"I made a mistake, Lillian," he said. She felt his hand pull her head to his chest. His other arm molded around her back and drew her closer. "And you can go ahead and be mad at me, mad at God, and mad at the world. I'm not going anywhere."

"But I can't accept this as God's will, Samuel. I can't. I don't know what I'm going to do every day. When I make bread, can fruits and vegetables, wash the clothes, cook, practice my *Pennsylvania Deitsch* . . . All those things Grandma and I did *together*. We spent hours talking." The pain in her heart seemed unbearable, and her stomach was burning. This is what she wanted to avoid. She didn't want to feel this way. It hurt too much. "And what about Grandpa?"

His hand still cradling her head, he held her tightly against him. "It's hard, Lillian, but this is something you have to go through to be able to move on."

"I can't," she cried. "It hurts, Samuel. It hurts too much. I can't."

"*Ya*, you can," he said. "And you will. I'm going to be right here beside you."

"I'm not strong like you are." She shook her head as her nose brushed against his shirt, now wet from her tears.

"You're stronger than you think. And we will get through this together . . . because that's what people who love each other do."

She heard him loud and clear. Her knees buckled.

"I'm tired of fighting it, Lillian." He pulled her closer. Wrapped in the security of his arms, she wept. Then, gently, he eased her away, cupped her cheeks with his hands, and gazed into her eyes. His own eyes were swimming. One blink and he would be shedding tears as well.

"I love you, Lillian."

"Samuel . . ." she whispered.

With slow tenderness, he gently kissed away her tears. The feel of his lips brushing against her cheeks as he continued to cradle her face with his strong hands caused her to cry harder. Samuel loved her. He'd said they would get through this together. Her heart hurt, and nothing was going to change that. But knowing Samuel would be with her softened her feelings about God's will.

When one door closes, another one opens . . . While it was God's will to take Grandma, it was also His will for Samuel to love her. It didn't lessen her grief about Grandma's death, but it gave her hope for the future. Right now, she needed hope to cling to. She needed Samuel.

"Do you love me, Lillian?" he asked, looking hard into her eyes as he tilted her head upward to face him.

"With all my heart, Samuel. I love you with all my heart."

As if knowing her trembling legs struggled to support her, in one swoop he whisked her into his arms. Resting her head in the nook of his shoulder, she'd never known such comfort. She was safe. She was home. And somehow Samuel would help her to make sense of all this.

"We will get through this together," he said again, kissing her on the forehead.

———

Samuel knew from personal experience that in a time of loss, even the most faithful could doubt God's reasoning for things happening the way they did.

"I know you feel real bad right now. But you're not always gonna feel like this." He paused, clutching her tightly within his arms. With watery eyes, he said, "Me and the boy need you every bit as much as I know you need us. I know it's been hard for you to accept God into your heart as openly as you've accepted me and David into your heart. But He is in there, Lillian . . . in your heart. And He will be there to help get you through your grief."

He gently set her down on the porch and coaxed her to sit on the steps beside him. Turning toward her, he reached for her hand. "When Rachel passed, I was angry at the Lord. I never told a soul about it. Just didn't make sense at the time. It seemed awfully unfair to leave me and the boy alone—no *fraa*, no *mamm*."

He paused and looked away from her, staring down the dirt road. "I even had thoughts about leaving here. Taking the boy and just headin' somewhere else. I felt like my faith wasn't strong enough to stay."

He turned to her and smiled. "But I'm glad I did stay. There's nowhere on God's earth I'd rather be than here, in this district, and now with you."

Samuel had envisioned it in his dreams a thousand times, but nothing could prepare him for the reality of when he leaned in and felt the touch of her lips against his. He could feel her love rush through him. Resting one hand behind her neck, he pulled her closer. One kiss turned into two.

"Everything is going to be fine, Lillian," he finally said, as he brushed a loose strand of hair from her face and kissed her gently one more time.

17

THE FUNERAL WAS ALMOST TWO HOURS LONG AND HELD AT the Miller homestead. As tradition dictated, Grandma wore her wedding dress and white apron for her burial. Her wooden coffin was plain and simple—no ornate carving or fine fabrics. The community offered expressions of respect for Grandma, although admonition for the living was plentiful.

Lillian wished there were flowers and a eulogy for her grandma. However, such *Englisch* traditions were not the Amish way. Instead of singing, they spoke the words of the hymn. Following the service, Grandma was laid to rest in the Amish church district cemetery, in a hand-dug grave. The modest tombstone was identical to the others in the cemetery. As was custom, members of the community gathered to share a meal afterward. Sadie Fisher offered her home for the occasion.

"Thank you, Sadie, for organizing the meal," Lillian told her, catching her away from the crowd of women in the kitchen.

Sadie hesitated, then gave her an unexpected but much needed hug. "You're quite welcome. The entire community thought the world of Irma Rose. And it's best if these things are handled by someone not in the immediate family. How is your *mamm* holdin' up?"

Lillian looked toward the den, where her mother was comforting her grandpa. Mom was barely back in Houston when she had to turn around and come back for Grandma's funeral. She was a mess when she arrived, rambling on to Lillian about what a mess she'd made of her life. For Grandma to die the day after Mom's visit was quite a blow, but Lillian wondered how much worse it would have been if they had not been blessed with the time they had together. Bittersweet for sure.

But Mom pulled herself together, for her dad's sake. He needed her, and she needed him. Looking at her mom now, it was clear to Lillian that her mother's utmost priority was taking care of Grandpa. She hadn't left his side since her arrival.

"My mom is tired. She was up with Grandpa most of the night. He was sick. I don't know how much of it is from grief about all this or from his medications. The medicines make him sick sometimes." She paused. "You know, Mom hadn't seen her parents in a long time. She had just seen them for two days, and Grandma died the day after she left, and . . ." She shook her head, finding it hard to go on.

"It was just a real shock about Irma Rose," Sadie comforted, gently rubbing Lillian's arm. "We were all just so sorry to hear."

"You're a nice person, Sadie."

She smiled. "*Ya,* I try."

"I mean, I didn't think you were going to like me—because of Samuel and all."

"*Ach,* I was a tad bitter at first. Samuel's a good catch for marrying. But he was smitten with you from the get-go." She offered her a pat on the shoulder. "Besides, my letter-writing with the Texas man is goin' real good."

Sadie wasn't the only one who had opened her heart during this difficult time. Both of Samuel's sisters and sister-in-law had bent over backward to help with arrangements. Samuel's mother, Esther, was warming up to Lillian as well.

Grandma had worked so hard to make sure Lillian had a clear understanding of the *Ordnung*. Despite her constant questioning of the Amish ways—sometimes defiantly—Grandma never gave up on her. With patience and love, she nurtured Lillian toward a way of life she had been searching for. Lillian would be lying to herself if she accepted where she was now as her final spiritual destination, though. She still had work to do. Her inability to accept everything that happened as God's will would require faith—in God and in herself.

Samuel was proud of Lillian. Those who didn't know her well wouldn't recognize the effort it was taking for her to stay strong. He reckoned the extra effort was due to the state her mother and Jonas were in. Samuel could tell the whole ordeal was taking its toll on Jonas. Sarah Jane was glued to her pop's side and was trying hard to take care of him. But she looked like *she* needed taking care of herself. Lillian was filling the job, even though he knew her own heart was hurting in a big way.

"Lillian sure is being strong today," David said, echoing Samuel's thoughts. He took a seat beside Samuel at a wooden picnic table in the yard.

"She's trying to be strong for her *mamm* and *Daadi Jonas*."

"I remember when you tried to be strong for me when *Mamm* died. I knew you were hurting, like I reckon Lillian is hurting too."

"Sometimes we bury our burdens to tend to the needs of others," Samuel responded, remembering back to Rachel's funeral. At that time, he wasn't sure how he would live his life without her. But time had a way of mending the heart. "God so built us to heal ourselves through our love and faith in Him."

Lillian's fingers entwined with Samuel's as they sat at the overlook. It had been three days since Grandma's funeral and her heart was still leaden, as she expected it would be for a long time to come. But as she and Samuel sat quietly at the edge of the overlook, she reflected on everything that had recently happened. Rickie was out of her life. She'd found her father, however painful. She and her mom were in a new place—a good place. She'd been fortunate enough to get to know her Grandma before she died. She still had her grandpa. And Samuel loved her.

Knowing God didn't keep score, she was trying not to either. But there was a certain balance to it all. Maybe she'd started out looking for proof there was a God—proof that she could reach out and touch. Her search was misdirected in the beginning. But when she asked to have a relationship with Him, to know Him, God showed Himself to her many times over.

Completely accepting Grandma's death as God's will was going to take her a little longer. Just accepting her as gone was a painful conclusion for her right now. But through her faith, she hoped to continue to grow toward a complete acceptance of all things.

"It takes time, Lillian," she recalled Grandma saying during one of their talks—one of the many when Lillian questioned such blind acceptance of certain events as being God's will. "First get to know God, put your trust in Him, and He will work miracles in your life. You will learn to accept His will, even if you can't see the reasoning behind it at the time," Grandma had said.

She'd always wished the *Ordnung* was a book she could memorize and just make herself live by. But so much of the *Ordnung* was unwritten, visible only in the minds of the faithful followers, like Grandma. And Grandma had been a good teacher.

Being at the overlook was the perfect place to tell Samuel her news.

"Samuel," she said softly, squeezing his hand. "I have something to tell you."

He squirmed uncomfortably. "Me first," he sputtered. "I have something to tell you first."

Lillian doubted it was as important as her decision to be baptized into the Amish faith, but her news could wait. Whatever was on Samuel's mind had him extremely nervous. He took off his hat, pushed back his hair, put his hat back on, stroked his beard, twisted around in the grass again. What in the world was wrong with him?

"What is it, Samuel?"

When he didn't answer, she rushed on. "Because my news is pretty important." Playfully, she nudged her shoulder against his.

"Maybe you should go first, then," he said hesitantly.

"No, you go ahead." She was curious to know what news had him so worked up.

Turning toward her, he grabbed both her hands in his. He gazed lovingly into her eyes and said, "I love you, Lillian. When Rachel died, I didn't think I would ever love another woman the way I loved her." Struggling with his words, he forced them out with determination. "I wasn't sure I ever wanted to move on. But you changed all that. I fought it and fought it. You are as challenging an *Englisch* person as I've ever met. But one thing is for sure: I love you. David loves you."

Taking a deep breath, he went on. "It took me a long time before I could give myself permission to move on. But I want to move on with you, Lillian. I've wanted to ask you something since we were on the porch the day Irma Rose passed, but the timing wasn't right."

Lillian felt her heart leap. Quite sure all her feelings were visible to him, she tried to contain herself. Was Samuel about to propose?

"I know you haven't made mention of staying here or getting baptized, but I'm asking you to stay here, with me. I want you to marry me, Lillian. Do you think you could be happy here, in our district, with me and David? I'm real confused because you aren't baptized, and I don't know how you feel about that. It'd be impossible for us to wed if you aren't baptized, but I felt the need to tell you what my hopes were."

Thank You, God. She had struggled with her decision to be baptized, prayed hard that she was doing the right thing and for the right reasons. She still had a lot to learn. But she knew that she wanted to learn it here, around those she loved. With confidence, she had spoken to the bishop about her decision. Although a proposal from Samuel was the last thing she expected so soon after he professed his love for her.

As if reading her mind, he said, "I know it might seem soon, Lillian. But once you know who you want to spend the rest of your life with . . . *Ach*, I just couldn't see wasting time. I know we couldn't marry until after your baptism, if that's what you choose to do, and—"

"How's November sound to you?" she asked, opening her eyes wide and blinking back the salty sting of emotion.

"What?" he asked, confused. "That's only three months away, and your baptism would have to be in October. That's in only a couple of months, and—"

"October 19 to be exact." She threw her arms around him. "Oh, Samuel! That was my news. I talked to the bishop about being baptized. I wanted to make the decision to stay for the right reasons. I had hoped you would want to marry me *someday*, but I was staying either way."

As his lips met with hers, he drew her closer. "Lillian, nothing would make me happier than to watch you receive baptism in October and marry you in November."

"Then that's the plan," she said, leaning in for another kiss.

Lillian was surprised her mother was still around after nearly two weeks. Grandpa had several good days following the funeral, and several bad days. Mom was there for the good and bad. She got up with him at night when he was throwing up, helped him bathe when he needed help, and played chess with him as often as he was able. Seeing them together warmed Lillian's heart. But often she had to walk away to hide her tears. How Grandma would have loved Mom being here.

Something about Mom was different too. While Grandma's death devastated them all, there was something in Mom's demeanor reflective of a significant change. There was a calmness about her Lillian didn't remember seeing—ever. She'd gotten used to having her around too. Surprisingly, she enjoyed having her here. After spending so much time trying to cut the cord from her mother and their turbulent relationship, it was refreshing to be in new territory with her. They were kind and loving to each other. They talked, often late into the night. They shared stories, worries, past mistakes, and hopes for the future. It was the way mothers and daughters should be. In the aftermath of something so sad, something wonderful had happened. And Mom was thrilled about the wedding plans and excited to be involved in the planning.

Samuel and David resumed their places at the supper table almost every night. Much of the food continued to come from Samuel's garden and butchered livestock. Grandpa was able to eat downstairs some of the time, and Mom sat on the bench next to him. Everyone was painfully aware of the empty chair at the end of the table. Mom refused to sit in it, even though Grandpa said he would have more elbow room if she did.

David's summer vacation from school ended, and he wasn't able to help as much with chores around their place. He and Samuel did what they could to help keep both farms manicured, but work was piling up at both farms. Lillian wasn't sure how much earlier they could all get up in the mornings to accomplish all they needed to do. Grandma had certainly made her share of the daily chores look easy. In her absence, Lillian and her mom struggled to match up to Grandma's way of keeping things neat and orderly.

The family talked of Lillian's impending baptism often. Soon she and Samuel would publish their wedding announcement for the first Tuesday in November. Weddings were usually held on Tuesday or Thursday, most commonly the slowest days of the week. November was the wedding month, following the busy fall harvest and before the risk of unfavorable winter weather.

They had avoided the specifics of how all this was going to work since the first time Lillian made mention to Grandpa that perhaps he could live with them at Samuel's place. His gruff response left no doubt he would leave his family farmstead feet first. "I was born here, and I'll die here," he groaned.

But Grandpa's grief was taking a toll on his health. He couldn't take care of himself, and Lillian was not about to leave him alone. She and Samuel had discussed it several times, and each time there was no resolution. As much as they wanted to be together as husband and wife, Grandpa was not capable of taking care of himself.

A few days later, Samuel and Lillian excused themselves from the supper table early. Jonas wasn't sitting as tall as usual, barely touching his ham and potato salad. As they walked hand in hand toward the barn, Samuel knew Lillian had the same thing on her mind that he did.

"Grandpa can't stay alone," she said. "There's no way, Samuel."

"I know." He turned to face her. The sun had yet to give in to the moon, and in the evening light her eyes were full of worry. "I reckon me and David can move here when we're married. I just want us to be a family, Lillian. Jonas is a part of this family."

She sighed. "You love that farm of yours, Samuel."

A lot of heartfelt labor had gone into making his farm a

place to be proud of. The house had been run down and the
fields overgrown when Samuel purchased the old property,
back before he married Rachel. Now it was as nice a place as
any in their district.

But despite his attachment to the farm, his attachment to
Lillian was greater. "I love you, and leaving Jonas is not an
option."

She buried her head in his chest. "What are we going to do?
I love you so much, Samuel. I'll live anywhere, as long as it's with
you. I just hate for you to give up your home, and I hate for
Grandpa to have to give up the only place he's ever lived. But the
only way I see this working is for one of you to let go of your
property. It needs to be Grandpa. He can't take care of this place.
It's hard on you and David tending to both farms."

"Home is where you make it, Lillian. My home is with you,
David, and Jonas."

Kissing her tenderly, he could not imagine his life without
her. Despite their challenges, Lillian filled his heart with love in
a way he didn't think possible again. David loved her too.

But love of the land, tilling of the soil, and producing—it was
the Amish way, and he had done a fine job at it. Letting the land
dissolve into a barren oasis of deeply planted dreams was hard to
swallow.

As darkness neared, they turned their attention to headlights
rounding the turn onto the driveway.

"Are you expecting anyone?"

"No," she said, surprised.

They waited as a large truck slowly made its way down the
dirt driveway. By the time the driver parked the truck, Samuel

noticed Sarah Jane and David making their way down the porch steps. It was a really large truck with a sign on the side that said *Leeway Moving.*

"What's going on?" Lillian asked.

"It's your farm." He joked. "I have no idea."

"Over there!" Samuel heard Sarah Jane yell. "Park over by the barn."

As Sarah Jane and David met up with them, Lillian asked, "Mom, what is this truck doing here?"

Sarah Jane smiled. "It's a few of my things I couldn't live without. You know, my four-poster bed that I finally purchased from that lovely shop at the Trader's Village in Houston, and some other things I really *need.*"

Samuel wondered if an answer to their prayers had just arrived. But he wasn't quite sure.

"Mom, what are you saying?" Lillian's face glistened as the sun faded and the moonlight seemed to focus exclusively on her.

"You should know, Lillian, I will be taking over some of those dresses from upstairs when you leave to be Samuel's wife. So you need to start thinking about sewing yourself some more. Because, if you must know, those dresses you are wearing are *mine.*"

She winked at her daughter and headed toward the truck. "I said, park by the barn!" She threw her hands in the air and pointed toward the barn, continuing to instruct the driver.

Lillian was quickly on her mother's heels. "Mom?"

"I'm staying, Lillian," she confirmed. "We'll figure out what to do with all these things later."

"But, Mom—"

Samuel watched as Sarah Jane faced her daughter. "He's my

pop, Lillian. I'm going to take care of him. You need to start your life with your husband in November. I plan to spend the second half of my life making amends for the mistakes I made during the first half."

"But, Mom . . ." Lillian said again.

"By the barn!" Sarah Jane yelled. "We are putting everything in the barn for now!"

The driver got as close to the barn as he could.

While the moving van distracted her Mom, Lillian latched on to Samuel's hand and gave it a squeeze. "Oh, Samuel," she said, gleaming. "Is my mother answering our prayers?"

It seemed an unlikely source, but one that was upon them. "I think so," he answered.

Once Sarah Jane had the movers unloading her necessary belongings in the correct manner into the barn, she walked toward David, who was standing a few feet from Samuel and Lillian.

"David, your pop and my daughter look speechless," she said, giving the boy a hug.

Samuel noticed David's eyes light up. He had a clear reckoning as to what was happening.

"You're going to stay here and live with Jonas while Lillian comes and lives with me and my *daed*?" he asked, seeming a little unsure.

"*Ya*," Sarah Jane answered. "But I'm hoping I'll still have you to help us in the afternoons after Lillian marries your *daed*."

Lillian's eyes were aglow and she seemed pleasantly surprised at her mother's use of the *Deitsch*.

"You bet," David said. "Jonas will be expecting me to play chess after my chores."

"Well you'll have to beat me first," Sarah Jane said.

"Mom, are you sure about this?" Lillian asked her mother. "What about Paul? What about your job? Are you sure?"

Sarah Jane grew solemn and faced her daughter. "I should have come back here, Lillian. I should have trusted the love of my parents." She paused. "And the love of God. Being here reminds me of what it's like to live a lifestyle void of complications. I want to live out the rest of my years this way."

"Mom," Lillian said, embracing her, "does Grandpa know?"

"I sure do."

Samuel followed the voice to see Jonas hobbling down the porch steps.

"You people are the loudest bunch I've ever known. What does a sick ol' man with cancer have to do to be gettin' some rest around here?" He continued to hobble toward Sarah Jane, a smile stretched across his face.

"Pop," she said lovingly, walking toward him, "and I want to stay together."

He tried to hide it, but Samuel could see Jonas's eyes welling up.

"There's nothin' I'd like more in this *wunderbaar* world the Good Lord created," Jonas said, hugging his daughter. "Irma Rose is smiling from heaven."

Samuel looked at Lillian, whose eyes glazed with emotion. "The Good Lord has a way of takin' care of things," he said.

"*Ya*, He does."

Samuel watched as Sarah Jane gently eased her father away and walked toward him and Lillian. "Will it be all right with the two of you if I boot you out in November, after you're married?

It would be too crowded in this house with Lillian." She kissed her daughter on the cheek.

"Oh, I guess I'll have to take her to my place after we're married," he said jokingly.

"Lillian?" her mother asked. "What about you? Think you can go live with this man in marital bliss while I take care of your grandpa?"

"Mom, *danki*," Lillian said, wrapping her arms around her.

"No, Lillian, thank *you*," her mother said softly, but still in earshot of Samuel. "This is where I belong. It's where I've always belonged. I just didn't know how to find my way home."

Sarah Jane turned to Samuel. "A hug for your future mother-in-law?"

Samuel welcomed the hug. Whatever it took to make his Lillian as happy as she was at this moment.

"Bunch of mushy stuff goin' on, I say." Jonas rejoined the three of them after sharing some time with David.

"Now, I have another surprise for all of you. It's a really big surprise," Sarah Jane announced.

Samuel watched as Lillian's mother lovingly wrapped her arms around her daughter again. "And, Lillian, I'm so sure that everything is going to be *gut!*"

Irma Rose would have been so proud, Samuel thought to himself. *But what in the world was Sarah Jane's surprise?*

18

EVIDENCE OF FALL WAS ABUNDANT. COLORFUL LEAVES swirled around in the crisp air as buggies lined the drive at the Miller farm. It was the perfect day for a baptism. Lillian greeted community members from the den. Most of them she knew, and several she had gotten to know well over the past couple months since Grandma died. Particularly Sadie. They'd become quite close. She took Lillian to a quilting party and introduced her to other women in the community. Lillian even asked her new friend to be a *waiter*—the Amish term for bridesmaid—at her upcoming wedding, along with her mother.

Only two more weeks until she would be Lillian Stoltzfus. She glanced at her husband-to-be across the room, also greeting guests. Being in love with Samuel filled her heart with a joy she didn't know possible. It had been hard to accept God into her heart and to accept His will, but with Samuel and David's help, she had put all doubts to rest. For the first time in her life, peacefulness consumed her. The peacefulness of knowing all things of this earth were in His hands.

She was thankful to Him that Grandpa was having one of his good days. Following a rough couple of weeks, he looked strong and handsome. Glancing upward, she whispered, *"Danki."*

Still, not a day went by that she didn't think about Grandma. She missed her in a terrible way and knew this would have been a proud moment for her.

As everyone took their respective places, as they did in worship service, Lillian prepared to leave all worldly things behind and accept her birthright with newfound faith and confidence. However, once everyone settled in, she turned to her left . . . to see her mother preparing for baptism alongside her. Mom had mentioned she had a surprise, but Lillian couldn't have imagined this. What a blessed moment and a wonderful surprise—to choose baptism after all these years. Mom could have just chosen to stay and take care of her father, without committing her life to the *Ordnung*. It was yet another reflection of God in both their lives.

Despite exhaustion from taking care of Grandpa, Mom spent countless hours making sure Lillian was comfortable with the *Ordnung* and helping her with her *Deitsch*. As she took up where Grandma left off, teaching Lillian the Amish ways, Lillian witnessed an incredible transformation, a profound renewal of faith in her mother. A woman injured by life—and with scars to show for it—she seemed to be exactly where she belonged.

Now she merely smiled and squeezed Lillian's hand before returning to her preparations.

With three females and four males seeking baptism, they each sat with one hand over their faces to represent their submission and humility to the church. The deacon ladled water from a bucket into the bishop's hand, and the bishop sprinkled each of their heads three times, in the name of the Father, Son, and Holy Ghost.

The bishop blessed each new male member with a holy kiss,

and his wife blessed each new female church member with a holy kiss. They were then all welcomed as new church members. And as was the Amish way, a bountiful meal followed.

Samuel took a stroll out to the barn. His Lillian was a church member and now they would be married in a couple of weeks. He wanted some time to be alone, to thank the Lord for all the blessings bestowed upon him and David.

The old newspapers were still scattered on the dirt floor of the barn. He gathered them up and placed them neatly back in the box. What a long way they had come. It was a struggle, but Lillian had put the past behind her and moved forward with hope and determination. He smiled as he recalled her receiving baptism. She had never looked more beautiful.

"I saw you sneaking out here," he heard her say when she entered the barn. "Most of the kitchen is cleaned up, so I snuck out too."

Samuel put the last newspaper in the box and stacked it atop the other boxes. This was a special day, and he hoped seeing the newspapers didn't bring back any painful memories for her. He walked toward her, and she smiled. Pulling her close, he said, "Have I mentioned how beautiful you look?" He kissed her on the cheek.

"Several times," she said, her face nuzzled into his chest. "I feel so good about everything, Samuel."

"Do you feel any different?" He remembered feeling wonderfully different after his baptism.

She gently pulled away and looked up at him, her eyes aglow

with joy. "I do feel different. In some ways, it's all very surreal. I mean, if anyone had told me a year ago that Mom and I would be as close as we are, or that both of us would be baptized into the Amish faith, I never would have believed it." She paused and twisted her mouth into a frown. "Bad things happen sometimes. It was hard for me to accept those things as God's will in the beginning." She smiled again. "But, *gut* things happen too. It's a balance, I suppose. I shouldn't question His will. I miss Grandma every day. But I'm so grateful for Mom, and I never thought I would be able to say that. I'm so thankful, Samuel. To you. To God." He watched as her eyes glazed over with tears of contentment. "I'm just very happy."

"And soon we'll be married." He pulled her close again.

"I am so ready to be your *fraa*, Samuel. I'm going to be a good wife and a good *mamm* to David."

"Not just a *gut mamm* to David, I hope. I reckon there will be a lot of little Stoltzfus *kinner* running around some day."

"There is nothing I want more."

Samuel kissed her tenderly on the mouth. "I guess we need to go back to the others," he said with regret. He wanted to hold her in his arms forever. Only two more weeks—and then they'd be together for the rest of their lives.

Sarah Jane fumbled with the letter that arrived in the mail. With only two days until Lillian's wedding, she tossed the envelope nervously from hand to hand. It was addressed to Lillian and opening it would be wrong. It would be equally as wrong to toss it into the trash bin, but she was tempted just the same. The return address was from Oklahoma, and she cringed as her eyes met with the name above the address. Daniel Foster. Hearing from him was the last thing either of them needed.

"I'm exhausted just thinking of all the things left to do before the wedding," she heard Lillian say while walking into the kitchen. "Maybe we should have waited until the end of November, since we just had the baptism here a couple of weeks ago." She plopped down on the bench at the kitchen table and brushed back a strand of hair dangling in her face.

"I don't think you or Samuel could have waited a couple more weeks." Crossing her arms, Sarah Jane tucked the letter out of sight.

"Mom, I just didn't know I could feel this happy." She smiled. "How's Grandpa this afternoon?"

"Actually, he's having a good day. He's napping right now. Be warned, though—the doctors changed his medicine again, and you know what that means. We just never know how he'll respond to the change."

"*Ya.* I'm glad he's doing so well today. I pray he will be having a good day on Tuesday."

"I'll pray too," Sarah Jane said, smiling, but with the letter still hidden from Lillian's view. She knew she would have to turn it over, but still she hesitated. Despite her exhaustion, her daughter had never looked happier, and she didn't want to ruin that.

"David is going to mow the yard after school," Lillian said. "I'll finish making the bread and apple butter, and then I know we need to—"

"Lillian," she interrupted.

"*Ya?*"

"This came in the mail today." With reluctance, she handed over the letter. As she feared, Lillian's bright eyes lost some of their glow. Her face was solemn and she just held the envelope and stared at it.

"You don't have to open it," Sarah Jane told her, wishing she wouldn't. "We can just throw it away and pretend it never came." She thought about all the letters from her mother she had tossed into the trash. Her heart ached.

Lillian tilted her head to one side and held the letter up toward the window, as if trying to catch the sun's rays to read through the envelope. "No," she said softly. "I have to open it. I'm not going to let whatever is in this letter upset me. I've put all that behind me."

Sarah Jane took a seat on the bench across from Lillian. "I still say we can just throw it away." She cupped her chin in her hands.

"Mom, we can't do that." Lillian's tone was a tad reprimanding, and Sarah Jane knew she was right.

Lillian's heart was racing. Peeling back the flap of the envelope, she slowly removed the two-page letter, handwritten in blue ink on lined white paper.

Dear Lillian,

What is often at the heart of a man's soul is lost or forgotten by the time you reach my age. Bitterness, divorce, and life have a way of doing that. I know it might seem like I'm feeling sorry for myself, but that is not my intention. Rather, I would like for you to know that at my core, I am not the evil person that my actions have certainly dictated. Since you share my genes, I do not want you to fear the passing down of poisonous heritage. It is my hope that by breaking down the iron walls surrounding my heart, you will see a small glimpse as to who your father is——or once was.

Sarah Jane was a beautiful, vibrant woman. She probably still is. I have no excuse for the way I handled her pregnancy. To say I was young, at the height of my career, and afraid seems like a lame excuse. When you arrived at my shop, I assumed you were there to cause trouble for me somehow. Looking back, I know you just wanted to know who your father is. You remind me so much of your mother. Despite her unworldly ways, she had a zest for life she obviously passed on to you. It's unfortunate that as a young man I took advantage of her spirited nature and robbed her of the life she was intended to live. She had no real understanding of life outside of her community. I suppose all that changed when she fled the only life she had ever known to raise a child on her own.

If you sense remorse in this letter, you are right. Not many days went by when I did not wonder about you. When my wife and I married many years later, we were unable to bear children. I often suspected it was my punishment for abandoning you and your mother.

I understand from friends in Paradise that you were baptized into the Amish faith and will be married soon (not to worry——they do not know you are my daughter). There is no wedding gift I can give you to make up for my behavior years ago, or my behavior most recently. I can only hope that, in some small way, this letter will suffice as my gift to you, for it comes with a heartfelt and sincere apology.

May your new life bring you happiness always.

Regards,
Daniel Foster

Lillian handed her mother the letter. "Maybe this will give you some closure too," she said. With no memories of those hard times Daniel referred to, Lillian assumed perhaps her mother had more to gain from the letter than she did. Based on Mom's expression as she was reading, Lillian was right.

"He really wasn't a bad man," Mom muttered, fighting tears. "But I have struggled these past couple of months to forgive him. This helps." She handed the letter back to Lillian.

"I forgave him a while back, but this helps me too." There was comfort in knowing that her father had wondered about her and that he regretted his actions years ago, as well as his more recent ones. The tone of his letter saddened her, though. He sounded like a lonely man. She would say an extra prayer for him tonight. Maybe she would write him back someday.

Tuesday took forever to arrive. As Samuel and David hurried to get ready, Samuel feared he was going to be late for his own wedding. He had heard rumors that over two hundred people would be attending. What a mighty noon feast they would have after the ceremony and another grand meal in the evening. It was going be right crowded in the Miller house.

He couldn't wait to make Lillian his wife. "David, it's time, boy!" he yelled upstairs. "Are you 'bout done?"

Samuel was as nervous as a man could be. From the moment he laid eyes on Lillian, he'd connected with her in a way that made him fearful—fearful they could never be together. Now she had become a church member and today they would marry. And tonight . . . Well, Samuel couldn't help but think about tonight, their wedding night. The passionate kisses they shared were only a prelude to what he knew would be a *wunderbaar* night.

Sharing their love as husband and wife was a vision he couldn't shake. Nor did he want to. The thought of his beautiful Lillian, held close in his arms . . .

He hollered for David to hurry.

It was customary for the bride and groom to stay with her parents on the wedding night, so as to help with the cleanup the next morning. He packed a small duffel bag for him and one for David, since David would be heading to Ivan's place later in the evening.

"We ain't got time to waste, David," he bellowed up the stairs. "Come on with yourself."

"Oh, Lillian," her mom said when she walked downstairs. "You look beautiful."

Dressed in traditional Amish wedding attire, Lillian felt beautiful in her new blue linen dress, black *Kapp*, white kerchief, and apron. She knew this would be the only time she would wear the outfit, until they buried her in it. Sadie had made the dress for her and it fit perfectly.

"*Danki*, Mom." She was nervous, and she didn't think much was going to change that. "Samuel said there are going to be about two hundred people in attendance. That's more than when we held the baptisms here."

"The joining of two hearts for eternity is a blessed event," her mother said. "I'm so proud of you, Lillian. Against so many hardships, you prevailed and turned into a beautiful young woman. And an Amish woman at that." Mom pulled her in for a hug.

"Mom," she said warmly. "I'm proud of you too. I'm proud you're my *mamm*."

Gently her mother eased Lillian away from her. "I have something to give you."

She darted upstairs. When she returned, she handed Lillian an envelope. "It's the money I borrowed from you, Lillian. I had Claire, my friend back in Houston, sell the rest of my things."

"Mom, no," Lillian said, handing the envelope back. "I don't care about this money. I don't need it."

"What am I going to do with it, Lillian? I have everything I have ever wanted or needed." She pushed the envelope back toward Lillian. "Go and buy a wedding present for you and Samuel."

"This would buy a *really* nice wedding present, Mom," she said, counting the money.

"*Ya*, and that's what I want you to do with it."

"Do you miss Paul or your life, Mom?"

"Where did that come from?"

"I don't know. I just wondered." She hesitated. "It's just . . . you've always . . ."

"Had a man in my life?" Mom questioned. "I used to think that completed me, Lillian. I know that's not true. Having God in my life completes me. Besides, I imagine you and Samuel will give me lots of *kinner* to keep me busy. Plus, I have Pop."

"Did I say how proud I am of you, Mom?" She threw her arms around her mother again.

"I think you did. And I am very proud of you. Now, let's get you married. A crowd is gathering outside. Where's the groom?"

It was nearing eight o'clock in the morning when the crowd moved into the house. Lillian glanced around until she finally saw Samuel. Her heart took on a fearful pulse when she realized the time for the ceremony was upon them and Samuel had not appeared. She smiled at him from across the room.

As everyone prepared for the four-hour ceremony, she twisted her hands together. There was no wedding ring and no flowers to carry or flowers in the house. Instead, they placed celery in simple white glasses throughout the house—one of the symbolic foods at Amish weddings. She suddenly had an urge to steal one of the cut stalks and take a nibble. She should have eaten breakfast, but an early-morning bout of nerves had prevented her from indulging in her mother's *dippy eggs* this morning.

Lillian knew the ceremony would be void of the traditional kiss at the end. Of course, there would be no photographers or fancy catering. It was not the wedding she'd dreamed of since she was a child. It was better. The overabundance of love in the room more than made up for any preconceived ideas about what her wedding would be like.

Preparing to take her vows with the man she loved, she looked around the room. As was customary, the women were on one side and the men on the other side. Samuel had never looked more handsome. Grandpa and David stood side by side, each of them with a twinkle in his eye. Mom was beautiful. She had tossed out her makeup and other worldly goods prior to her baptism, and the lines of time and her hardships were evident. However, the radiance in her heart manifested itself across her smiling face, lending her a beauty that makeup could have never matched.

Lillian beamed at several women she had grown fond of over the past couple of months. Struggling to keep her emotions intact, she knew without a doubt that everything was perfect. She was ready to take her place as a daughter of the promise. Her journey of faith, hope, and love guided her to this moment. Now she would begin her life as Samuel's *fraa*.

They sang several songs in German at the beginning of the ceremony. The worship service was in German with a mix of *Pennsylvania Deitsch*. She was surprised how much of the language she now understood. After the preacher presented stories of the Old Testament, he offered marriage advice to her and Samuel.

"The Bible teaches us to treat each other with respect, not to raise our voices at each other, and to always show love," he recited. "Work hard, remember the man is the head of the home, and, Lillian, you are his helpmate."

Fondly, she recalled her learning session with Grandma concerning the preacher's statement. Not so long ago, his words would have caused Lillian to gasp. Instead, she was more than ready to allow Samuel to take his role as head of the home. By his side, she knew their partnership would be one of mutual respect.

Several other pastors spoke to the congregation, and specifically to Samuel and Lillian. It was near eleven o'clock when she and Samuel took their vows in front of their family and friends. With unwavering faith in herself, Samuel, and God, Lillian proclaimed her love to the only man she'd ever loved. "I, Lillian, take you Samuel . . ."

She managed to stifle tears of joy until Samuel professed his love for her. But upon hearing his solemn vow to love her forever, through good times and bad, a tear trickled down her cheek. He gently brushed it away. Had she looked around, she would have noticed there was hardly a dry eye in the house. But all Lillian saw was Samuel.

The wedding dinner was bountiful, consisting of the traditional *roasht*, along with mashed potatoes, gravy, creamed celery, buttered noodles, steamed peas with butter, and homemade bread and jam. There were side dishes of applesauce, chowchow, and pepper cabbage, and more pies, cookies, puddings, and dessert than Lillian had ever seen. Plus she was told no wedding would be complete without Amish *wedding nothings*, a deep-fried traditional wedding pastry. It was an amazing display, and on this day she planned to partake of all of it.

"We sit here, at the *eck*," Samuel whispered in her ear as he guided her to the corner of the wedding table.

They had placed tables together in the den to form a large hollow square with one side open. Samuel and Lillian sat at one of the outer corners, known as the bride's corner, or *eck*. Lillian's waiters sat to her left, along with other young unmarried women. Samuel's waiters sat to his right, along with more unmarried women. Young unmarried men sat on the remaining side of the formation.

Much preparation went into rearranging furniture in an attempt to accommodate the guests during the ceremony. However, they served the meal in shifts. Lillian and Samuel were served first, along with their wedding party.

Lillian realized she had worked up an appetite. A fabulous wedding cake sat before her and Samuel. As she waited for the ladies to serve the meal, the temptation to swipe the white icing with her finger was overwhelming. She felt Samuel's hand inter-twine with hers beneath the table.

"I love you, Lillian Stoltzfus," he whispered, oblivious to the people scurrying around the room.

"I love you too, Samuel Stoltzfus."

It was a glorious day, and Lillian bowed her head in prayer to thank God for the many blessings He had bestowed upon her and her family.

They sang traditional Amish hymns after the noon meal, fol-lowed by folk games in the barn for the children and unmarried young adults. As everyone socialized, mothers put babies down for naps upstairs, men gathered in the barn to smoke cigars and tell jokes. It was an all-day affair filled with fellowship, prayer, and a sense of belonging for Lillian.

"There you are," she said to Samuel, finding him on the porch later that afternoon. "I didn't see you for a while. I missed you."

"Hello, Mrs. Stoltzfus," he said smiling.

"I like the sound of that." She placed her hands on her full stomach. "I can't believe we have to eat again. I'm still full from the noon meal."

"I reckon the ladies are already preparing supper. But before we eat, we get to go play matchmaker for the young people out in the barn."

"Sadie told me about that. We actually get to pick out a boy and a girl and send them in the house holding hands?" She grinned at her husband. It sounded like great fun.

"*Ya*, the matched up boy and girl will go in the house, holding hands, and sit together at suppertime." Samuel arched his eyebrows and whispered, "The married ladies will all be gossiping about who is sitting together, who their parents are, and remarking about what a nice couple they will make."

"What if the kids don't like who we match them up with?"

"Then I guess a wedding won't be in their future," he said, snickering.

"No, I guess not."

She watched as Samuel's face took on a serious expression. "I love you so much, Lillian. I can't wait to show you how much I love you tonight."

<hr />

After matching up the teenagers in the barn for supper, more socializing went on for several more hours. Lillian wasn't sure how she'd managed to eat another meal. It had been a long, exhausting, wonderful day. It was almost nine o'clock when their guests began to leave. Grandpa had a fabulously good day but had been in bed for hours. Mom had been a trooper all day, making sure everything was perfect.

As she sat next to Samuel at the wedding table, Lillian hated for it all to end. But, she reminded herself, it was only the beginning. And she was ready to begin her life as Samuel's wife.

"It's time, Lillian," her mother said as she leaned down and kissed Lillian on the cheek. "Time to start your life as Samuel's *fraa*."

Samuel and Lillian stood up. Hand in hand, they bade farewell to those guests standing nearby. Lillian knew the next morning would start early and members of the district would be on hand to help with the cleanup. The next few weeks would be spent visiting members of the community, as was customary. These post-marriage visits were when she and Samuel would receive a lot of their wedding gifts.

It was to be a busy time after the wedding. But, for tonight, it would just be her and Samuel, his loving arms wrapped around her.

19

THE MID-FEBRUARY TEMPERATURES CAME WITH A BLAST OF arctic air that was keeping most of the community huddled inside with the comfort of woodburning stoves and fireplaces. Luckily, David's trek to school was a short distance from home. After tending to the cows, Samuel had gone to the farmer's market to pick up a few things. Normally, it was a task Lillian handled, but the weather was hardly fit to get out and Samuel insisted on making the trip for her.

Lillian was thrilled to see the delivery truck make it up the drive, and even more excited that her surprise would be in place before Samuel returned. She knew her husband had been goggling over the beautiful handmade table in town since before they were married.

She glanced around her Plain kitchen, void of all the gadgets she was once dependent on. It was amazing how she didn't think about or miss all the modern conveniences she'd grown up with. Everything she needed, she had right here.

With the weather at its worst, Samuel still made a trip to check on Mom and Grandpa daily. His latest report was that Grandpa's medication was continuing to help him tremendously. The two of them were making regular trips to town and playing lots of chess.

Although she had not had an opportunity to talk with Mom, rumor had it that a widower or two in the district were vying for her mother's attention. Sadly, Lillian knew Grandpa wouldn't always be around. Mom said she didn't need a man in her life. But Lillian still hoped that perhaps the right man might come along for her mother, giving her someone to share the second half of her life with.

Lillian was bursting at the seams by the time Samuel's buggy pulled up the drive. He was going to be so surprised—in more ways than one. She pulled a loaf of bread out of the oven and placed it on a cooling rack on the kitchen counter, near a platter of cookies she'd made earlier. She and David feasted on cookies and milk every day when he returned from school. It had become their special time to talk about the day.

Her heart raced as Samuel pushed open the screen door.

"I reckon my toes are never gonna thaw," he said, snow still clinging to his long black coat and speckling his black felt hat. "But it sure smells *gut* in here." He hung his coat and hat on the rack and entered the kitchen.

Lillian clasped her hands together and smiled as she watched her husband's face light up.

"Lillian," he said in awe, his hand skimming the surface of the large table he had been eyeing in town for over a year. He grabbed her in his arms and kissed her tenderly. "But, how—"

"It's a wedding present, from my *mamm*."

He shook his head in disbelief. "I reckon I've been wanting this table for as long as I can remember." His eyes twinkled with boyish appreciation. "This is the best present I've ever received. Someday we will fill it up with little ones."

Lillian smiled. "Samuel," she said softly, with a hint of play-fulness in her tone.

"*Ya?*" He was still enamored with the new table and matching benches.

"Someday has arrived."

All the cold weather in the world couldn't have taken away the warmth in Lillian's heart when she saw the look on her husband's face. "You mean . . . ," he asked, unsure.

She placed his hand on her stomach and smiled. "*Ya.*"

"Oh, Lillian. I love you so much."

"And I love you, Samuel."

Samuel came over to Lillian and held her, then took a seat on one of the benches. Lillian slid in beside him and reached for his hand. "I imagine our family will eat a lot of meals at this table."

Giving her hand a squeeze, Samuel nodded. "*Ya*, our family."

They sat quietly for a while. As the peacefulness and calm she'd so desperately searched for swept over Lillian, she bowed her head and closed her eyes.

Thank You.

Reading Group Guide

1. At the beginning of the story, Samuel had some serious qualms about being "unequally yoked" with Lillian, who was an unbeliever. Do you think that Samuel's worries are justified? Have you ever been in a relationship where you felt unequally yoked? Where did you draw the line between sharing the love and Word of God to unbelievers and being yoked or pulled down by an unbeliever?

2. What are some of the ways the Amish community gathers to help one another in *Plain Perfect*? Have you experienced similar support in your own community? What can we take away from the Amish example of community and fellowship? Are there any disadvantages to this close-knit community?

3. Why do you imagine Samuel feels guilt that thoughts of Lillian intermingle with his thoughts of Rachel? If you were in his place, do you think you could love again?

4. Do you think Sarah Jane made the right decision to leave the Amish community when she became pregnant with Lillian? What do you think the repercussions would have been had she stayed? Why do you think Sarah Jane never told Lillian who her father was?

5. Why does Lillian have such a hard time accepting everything as God's will? Are you able to accept the hard times in your life as God's will? What about the blessings and successes in your life—are you able to credit those to God's will as well?

6. David always believed that his pop and Lillian would end up together. How does that relate to what Christ teaches us about the faith of children? Compare his eager faithfulness to Irma Rose's hesitancy. Why do some adults seem to lose that faith?

7. What do you think Sarah Jane was trying to find in all of the men in her life? Is there someone you know that is guilty of the same misdirection—that is, filling up the emptiness in his or her heart with bad relationships or material things such as nicer cars and homes? Would you ever broach this subject with him or her?

8. Is admitting your past mistakes helpful or harmful in the raising of children? Was Samuel out of line in his reaction to hearing that Lillian told David all about

her worldly past? Should Lillian have denied her past?
What do you think would have happened if she hadn't
told David all about her past and just forbidden him
from those worldly temptations? Is there a benefit to
letting children make their own mistakes?

9. Food is an important theme throughout the novel—
the preparation, the sharing, the eating. Is the Amish
approach to food and meals different than an "outsider" view? Are there similarities?

10. Why do you think Lillian chose to bury her worldly
things in that hole by the lake? Is there anything you
wish you could bury in a hole, eliminating from your
past and present? What's stopping you?

11. Why do you think Sarah Jane decided to come back
to Lancaster County to visit her parents? What made
her stay? Why do you think it took her so long to
return?

12. Are there parts of the Amish life you would like to
incorporate into your own way of life?

Acknowledgments

THANK YOU TO MY FAMILY AND FRIENDS FOR YOUR SUPPORT and encouragement.

To Patrick, for sharing your life with me and believing in me every step of the way. You become more dear to me with each passing day. To my sons, Eric and Cory, you are my most precious gifts from God who inspire me daily. You three are the loves of my life.

Mother, how blessed I am to be your daughter. And what a bonus it is that you are a super, speed-reading, typo-catching queen! And to Daddy, may you rest in peace knowing I write happy endings . . . the way you always thought it should be. Thank you to my Mama, for your unwavering faith in God and me. I know you are smiling from Heaven. To my sister Laurie, who found her true love late in life. May you be blessed with all the happiness you deserve.

To my best friend and lifelong editor, Reneé Bissmeyer. You've read more manuscripts than I care to count, and your unwavering support always keeps me going past chapter six. Thank you for believing in me when I had doubts. We both know there aren't enough pages for me to express what our friendship means to me.

You are my "life editor," as well as my manuscript editor. It is a privilege to dedicate the book to you.

Thank you to Rene Simpson, my dear, dear friend who stepped up to the plate at the very last minute and spent four days at my house editing nonstop until the last revision was complete. And you did it all for "Happy Eggs" and guacamole. You are my hero! Your Samuel awaits. Don't give up.

To my second family at *The Schulenburg Sticker* newspaper, your flexibility with my job during my son's illness, and throughout the publication of this book, far surpasses the employer/ employee relationship. Saying thank you hardly seems enough. A special thank you to my editor at *The Sticker*, Darrell Vyvjala, for teaching me about the wonderful world of editing. You are my mentor and my friend.

Sue and Darrell Buttrey, the miles may seperate us, but you are forever in my heart. Thank you for your dear friendship and support.

Thank you to my good friend and critique partner, Carol Voelkel, for finding time to overhaul the manuscript amidst a challenging job, family, and writing projects of her own. Never stop writing!

Thank you to Mary Sue Seymour for recognizing the potential of the manuscript from the first three chapters. It is a pleasure to work with you and call you my friend. Miracles *do* happen to those who believe.

Many thanks to Barbie Beiler and Anna B. King, who jumped in at the eleventh hour and critiqued the manuscript for accuracy. Your Mennonite and Amish backgrounds provided a wealth of information about the Plain people of Lancaster County.

To the Amish families in Lancaster County who opened their homes and hearts, allowing my endless stream of questions . . . blessings to you all.

A special thank you to Leslie Peterson for her encouragement during the revision process. Your suggestions and edits were delivered with kindness and patience. It was a pleasure to work with you on this project.

A huge thank you to Natalie Hanemann for believing in the book . . . and in me. You alleviated much of my "first-novel fear" by walking me through the process and explaining things as we went along. You, along with the rest of the staff at Thomas Nelson, made this a wonderful experience for me.

And, most of all, to God, for offering me the opportunity to fulfill my dream of writing through words I pray will glorify Him, and for the many other blessings He has bestowed on me.

Amish Recipes

Shoofly Pie

CRUMBS:

- 1½ cups flour
- 1   cup brown sugar
- ⅔   cup lard or shortening

Combine all ingredients. Mix well. Reserve 1½ cups crumbs to mix with liquid mixture.

LIQUID:

- 1   cup molasses
- ½   cup brown sugar
- 2   eggs
- 1   tsp. soda dissolved in 1 cup hot water

Combine molasses, brown sugar, eggs and soda water. Add reserved crumbs and mix well. Pour into 3 unbaked regular sized pie shells or 2 deep dish pie shells. Top with remaining crumbs. Bake at 350° for 60 minutes.

Rhubarb Pie

1   egg
1   tsp. vanilla
2   Tblsp. flour
1   cup sugar
1   cup diced rhubarb

Mix together and pour in regular sized unbaked pie shell. Sprinkle with topping and bake at 425° for 15 min. Then turn oven down to 350° and put pie on middle rack for 10 min. Next, remove pie and cover edges with foil. Bake 20 more minutes at 350°.

TOPPING:
$3/4$ cup flour
$1/2$ cup brown sugar
$1/3$ cup butter

Garden Chow-chow

1	gallon cubed unpeeled zucchini (about 4.5 lbs.)
1	qt. sliced onions (one a half large onions)
3	cups carrots (shredded)
2	head cauliflower (chopped)
4	red peppers (chopped)
¼	cup salt

Mix chopped vegetables in large container with salt and let
stand 2-3 hours. Drain and put in sterilized jars. Cook syrup.

SYRUP:

1½	qt. water
½	qt. vinegar
½	qt. sugar
1	tsp. turmeric
1	tsp. celery seed
¾	tsp. garlic powder

Heat until boiling. Fill jars with syrup, leaving ¼ inch. Then
cold pack* for 10 minutes. Makes 12 pints.

* Cold Pack: Put jars of food in water (up to the neck) and boil for a
  required amount of time. Lids need to be put on tightly before
  putting in water.

Cooked Celery

Always served at Amish wedding dinners with turkey roast.

1½	qt. cubed celery (about 2 bundles)
½	cup water
½	cup brown sugar
1½	tsp. butter
½	tsp. salt

Cook together on stovetop until celery is soft (about 15 min. on high heat). Then mix together the following:

½ tsp. flour

1 ½ tsp. vinegar

1/8 cup brown sugar

¼ cup cream

Pour into hot celery mixture and stir until thick. Do not boil.

The Daughters
of the Promise Series

Visit BethWiseman.com

Also available in e-book formats

Join us for the next
Daughters of the Promise Novel

Plain Pursuit

Now Available.

THOMAS NELSON
Since 1798

About the Author

AWARD-WINNING, BESTSELLING AUTHOR
Beth Wiseman is best known for her
Amish novels, but her most recent
novels, *Need You Now* and *The House
That Love Built*, are contemporaries
set in small Texas towns. Both have
received glowing reviews. Beth's
highly anticipated novel, *The Promise*,
is inspired by a true story.